GREED CAN
KILL

Bob Doerr

Jim West mystery/thriller™

TotalRecall Publications, Inc.
1103 Middlecreek
Friendswood, Texas 77546
281-992-3131   281-482-5390 Fax
www.mousegate.com

Library of Congress Control Number: 2016961932

Printed in the United States of America with simultaneous
printings in Australia, Canada, and United Kingdom.

FIRST EDITION
1   2   3   4   5   6   7   8   9   10

To my family who inspire me to continue in this craft of writing.

Award Winning Author: Bob Doerr

grew up in a military family, graduated from the Air Force Academy, and had a career of his own in the Air Force. Bob specialized in criminal invest-igations and counterintelligence gaining significant insight to the worlds of crime, espionage, and terrorism. His work brought him into close coor-dination with the security agencies of many countries and filled his mind with the fascinating plots and characters found in his books today. His education credits include a Masters in International Relations from Creighton University. A full time author with ten published books and a co-author in another, Bob was selected by the Military Writers Society of America as its Author of the Year for 2013. The Eric Hoffer Awards awarded *No One Else to Kill* its 2013 first runner up to the grand prize for commercial fiction. Two of his other books were finalists for the Eric Hoffer Award in earlier contests. *Loose Ends Kill* won the 2011 Silver medal for Fiction/mystery by the Military Writers Society of America. *Another Colorado Kill* received the same Silver medal in 2012 and the silver medal for general fiction at the Branson Stars and Flags national book contest in 2012. Bob released an international thriller titled *The Attack* in May 2014, and more recently, *Caffeine Can Kill*, his sixth book in the Jim West mystery series. Bob has also written three novellas for middle grade readers in the Enchanted Coin series: *The Enchanted Coin*, *The Rescue of Vincent*, and *The Magic of Vex*. Bob lives in Garden Ridge, Texas, with Leigh, his wife of 43 years, and Cinco, their ornery cat.

The Book

This Jim West mystery/thriller, the seventh in the series, finds Jim traveling to Fabens, TX, in an effort to locate an old acquaintance who had written Jim a cryptic letter asking for his help in finding a briefcase. In Fabens, he discovers that someone has murdered his friend. Jim provides a copy of the letter to the local police explaining that he has no idea where the briefcase is or how to decipher the sets of numbers provided in the letter. Figuring there is nothing more he can do, Jim starts his trek back home. He plans to spend a night or two relaxing at the Lodge in Cloudcroft, NM, on his way only to find that he is being followed. An ominous, unidentified phone caller gives Jim an ultimatum - find the briefcase and turn it over to him within a week.

A violent confrontation in Cloudcroft verifies Jim's worst suspicion; a Mexican drug cartel wants the briefcase. The confrontation also brings the FBI into the picture. They also want Jim to continue his search. The search takes Jim to the New Mexican ghost town of Chloride where the final confrontation takes place and Jim finds out who the bad guys really are.

CHAPTER 1

Eric Stuart Brown hit the ground with a thud. The two men who tossed him out of the trunk of the old Caprice either didn't hear him grunt or care that Brown might still be clinging onto life. Both men watched as gravity slowly overcame inertia, and Brown slid a few feet before he began rolling down into the dark ravine.

"What do you think?" the stockier of the two men asked.

"About what?"

"Think the coyotes or the feral hogs will get to him first?"

"The hogs. There's a ton of them out here, and they eat just about anything."

"Hear that?" They both stood there and listened. The rattle of a rattlesnake broke the silence in the darkness of the ravine below them.

"He must've landed on one. Let's get out of here. It's pitch black out here, and those damn things could be all around us."

The two men climbed back into the old car and drove off.

Forty five miles east of El Paso and a mile north of I-10 was not a good place to be left alone to die. Brown may not have made the effort to save himself had it not been for that snake. He had already lost a lot of blood and hadn't been able to summon the strength to try to resist the two men who had pulled him out the trunk of the car. The sound of a nearby rattlesnake, however, brought a rush of adrenalin and a desire to live that he thought had already abandoned him.

Brown managed to push himself up on his hands and knees and crawled up the side of the ravine before finally collapsing on the dirt road. He saw two headlights coming straight for him. Without the strength to move any further he tried to raise an arm.   Everything turned black, and he slipped into unconsciousness.

CHAPTER 2

I looked at the letter that I had pulled out of my mailbox along with the usual flyers and ads that went directly into the trash. Chubbs sniffed the ground around the mailbox suspiciously. An actual letter and Christmas still six months away.

The handwriting reminded me of my grandmother's. It looked feeble. The return address simply read Stu Brown, and the only Stu Brown I knew would still be under fifty years old. There had been no contact between us since we had worked together in the air force some ten years ago. I had liked Stu, but our relationship had been that of co-workers. Other than the occasional office function, we didn't hang out together off duty.

I wondered why Stu hadn't included a return address. The postmark indicated the letter had originated in Fabens, Texas. I'd never heard of it.

Normally after checking mail, I remain in my front yard to give Chubbs a chance to mark his territory, since he spends most of his time in the house or in the backyard. However, the letter had me intrigued, so I didn't linger. Inside, I gave Chubbs a treat to make up for cutting his time short and tore open the letter.

"Sir," the letter started, no name, nothing further. That sounded like Stu. Even after we've both been retired from the air force for years, it didn't surprise me that he stuck with his military protocol. The letter consisted of one handwritten paragraph on a piece of white paper that looked like it came from a note pad, maybe four inches by seven.

"I need you to help me. To say it's a matter of life or death would not be an exaggeration. I need you to retrieve a brown briefcase from 119833470 and take it to Sue. She doesn't know about it, but I want her to have it. Please, please help me. I know you're doing this kind of stuff, because I've seen a couple of articles on you. The check should cover your expenses. If you hurry, I'll still be here. Thanks, Stu 43227"

The enclosed check turned out to be a money order for three hundred dollars.

I reread the letter, trying to make some sense out of it. Irritation, rather than an explanation, resulted from the effort.

"What do you think, Chubbs? Should I tear up the check and ignore the letter? Why does he think we're for hire? Why didn't he give me some way to contact him? He sends us a check and expects us to go find something. He doesn't even tell us where it is."

None of this sounded like the Stu Brown I knew, yet he referred to Sue. His wife's actual name was Mary Elizabeth, but he used to tell everybody that she looked more like a Sue. If someone else was trying to pretend to be Stu, they would have referred to Mary Elizabeth. Of course, I couldn't think why anyone would want to write to me and pretend to be Stu. None of this made sense.

I tossed the letter and check onto the kitchen counter. Perhaps if I ignored them long enough, they would go away. After a few days, Stu might call me and explain what was up. All I really knew was that I didn't want to get involved.

Sleep didn't come easy that night. Stu's face kept invading my dreams. Never very clear, it kept appearing behind a veil and once partially obscured in fog. I wanted him to say something to me, but he never did. I woke up more frustrated than I had been when I went to bed.

By mid-morning, I stopped trying to ignore the letter and got on the internet. I had found other people on the net and figured finding Stu couldn't be that hard. An hour later, I gave up. I had discovered hundreds of Stuart Browns and almost as many Stewart Browns. Unfortunately, none lived in Fabens, Texas. The internet listed thousands of Mary Browns. After locating my password, I opened my neglected Facebook account and tried to find Stu. The advantage of searching Facebook is that most people post a picture of themselves. I scrolled through the Stuart Browns but didn't find any with a picture remotely similar to how I remembered Stu. I checked the few Mary Elizabeth Browns and several Mary Browns before throwing in the towel.

I figured I could contact someone I knew from the past who also knew Stu and ask for help. However, that would require an explanation that I felt reluctant to get into, and would require me to look for phone numbers that I had never been very good at keeping. My ex would have had everything in an address book. I had let everything slide.

Fabens, Texas, is located about thirty miles southeast of El Paso. On the map it looked like an afterthought. Stu's hometown had been Chicago or another large city in that Illinois, Ohio, and Pennsylvania region. I couldn't remember him saying anything about southwest Texas.

Chubbs and I went out back. He wanted to play one of his favorite games. The one where I threw the tennis ball, and he would chase after it, walk about half way back to me, and drop it. He would stare at me or bark until I went and got the ball and threw it again. He never brought the ball all the way back. I could never figure out why he wouldn't bring it to me, other than the possibility he thought he was making me fetch the ball, too.

"What do you think, Chubbs?" I asked my canine friend. He was no help.

I think I would have totally ignored the letter if I didn't have a certificate for a free night at The Lodge at Cloudcroft. I had purchased it in a silent auction at a charity event I had attended earlier in the year. Even though I knew I would enjoy seeing the hundred year old lodge situated approximately eight thousand feet up the southern edge of the Rockies, I had never been able to overcome my inertia and make the five hour drive to the place.

After I went inside and grabbed a Diet Dr Pepper, I took the certificate out of a drawer in the guest room that I used for coupons and other things that were supposed to save me money. The free night didn't expire for another month. Fabens would only be a couple hour detour. I glanced at the calendar I kept on the kitchen counter half hoping I would find a reason not to go.

"Who am I kidding?"

Chubbs ignored my question.

The calendar, of course, didn't have a single annotation on it for the month. In an effort to prove that I had some kind of a life, I turned to the next month and was pleased to see at least one date flagged. On the seventh, I had a dental appointment to have my teeth cleaned.

"See, Chubbs, who says we don't have a life?"

After ensuring that the neighbor kids could watch my dog

for a couple of days, I threw an extra pair of jeans and a couple of golf shirts in the back of my Mustang. I stuffed the few other things that I might need into my gym bag, found a light hearted mystery by Marilyn Meredith that I had been intending to read, and headed south.

New Mexico is not a state where one can simply jump on the interstate and zoom off to somewhere. Most of my trip would be on two lane roads. On the other hand, the vehicle traffic reflected the population, which is close to nil in the part of the state I had to travel.

I headed southwest to Portales and then pretty much dead south on State Highway 206. I kept my eyes from blinking and got to see the tiny towns of Dora, Pep, and Crossroads, before I started feeling like I needed to watch out for other vehicles more so than antelope outside Tatum. Once past Lovington, I actually found myself on a four lane road for the few miles to Carlsbad, where I thought it prudent to refill my gas tank. I left Carlsbad and civilization again when I headed southwest on Highway 62 and crossed into Texas.

Most people don't think there are mountains in Texas, but that's because most people have never visited this part of the state or seen Guadalupe Peak. Despite it being as tall as many of the mountains in the Appalachians, it tops out at nearly seven thousand feet, some folks dispute its status as a mountain.

The sun had started to disappear below the horizon by the time I pulled into the gas station a mile or so outside Fabens. I couldn't tell much about the town from my vantage point. If it intended to become a suburb of El Paso, it didn't seem to be making much progress. On the other hand, I knew a lot of these old places had very interesting histories. Situated adjacent to the Mexican border, I figured Fabens held a lot of colorful stories for anyone interested in doing a little research. My own research would have little to do with the town.

Despite the small size of the border town, I knew that finding Brown might not be easy. I had no reason to believe he'd be hiding or using an assumed name, but I also knew his name wasn't in the phone book. I thought I'd call all the nearby hotels, check with the police, and the hospitals. I remembered he loved Chinese food, so I'd drop by any Asian restaurants Fabens might have. I'd give myself thirty six hours; then, I'd be on my way to Cloudcroft.

As it was, I didn't need thirty six seconds. That's about how long it took me to walk from the pump to the inside of the station, grab a small coffee, and stroll to the checkout counter. The clerk placed the local newspaper on the counter in front of me when he rung up my coffee. On the page of the newspaper facing me, I saw him.

Despite the years and the grainy, black and white picture, I knew it was Stu's face staring back up at me. I picked up the paper.

"That's mine. You can get your own over there," the old man said.

"I'm sorry," I said. I still read the first few sentences.

"That'll be a dollar twenty nine and my paper back," he stuck out a hand that had three fingers and a thumb.

I gave him his newspaper and the cash.

"How do I get to the police station?"

"You know him?"

I nodded.

"Take the next exit, west. Go straight into town. You can't miss it. It'll be on your right."

I thanked him.

As I reached the door, he said, "I think you're too late."

He may have meant that the investigation had already been solved. After all, that's what the article was about. The paper stated that the police still had few clues in their investigation of a shooting of a man found on a dirt road a few miles outside Fabens. The article went on to encourage anyone with any information that could help in the investigation to contact their local law enforcement authorities. The way the clerk said it, though, gave me a bad feeling.

The local police didn't have the lead on the investigation, because that belonged to the El Paso County Sheriff's Office, but I knew they'd be in the loop. Despite the clerk's comment that one couldn't miss the police station, I drove by the entrance before I saw it and had to make the block.

The lone desk sergeant didn't look too thrilled to see me. His puffy cheeks and squinty eyes made me think he'd worked a desk too long. He had a plate of food in front of him and had taken a bite when I approached him.

"Huh," he grunted and continued chewing. He put on his glasses to see me better.

"Sorry to interrupt your dinner, but is there someone I can talk to about the man who was shot a couple of days ago just outside the city?"

"What? Which one?"

I felt a little stupid. I should have brought the newspaper with me. "The newspaper said you were looking for information on the shooting."

He looked at me for a moment before he picked up the phone and called someone. He asked the person to come talk to me. After hanging up, he pointed with his finger to a chair against the wall and went back to eating his dinner.

I didn't have to wait long before a young police officer in civilian clothes walked in the front door with a carryout bag from a restaurant. The sergeant nodded toward me, and the young cop looked over at me.

"What can we do for you?" he asked.

"I saw a newspaper article that had a picture of a man who had been shot. The article requested that anyone with information about the victim or the shooting contact your office."

Rather than say anything to me, the officer walked over to the desk sergeant, and the two discussed something. The young guy looked sharp. He had on a pressed pair of dark slacks and a light blue short-sleeve shirt. Only the badge, gun, and the usual paraphernalia on his belt identified him as a police officer. His light brown hair had recently been cut. I could see some of the hair clippings on the back of his right shoulder.

He turned to face me. "Would you mind stepping into this office so we can talk?" His hand motioned toward a partially opened door that led into a dark room.

"Sure," I said and followed him into the room. I selected one of the three wooden chairs that sat around a small square table.

"What is this victim's name?"

"Stuart Brown. I got the impression from the article that you all didn't know his identity," I said.

"We didn't at the time." He waited for me to say something.

"Then I guess I'm wasting your time. Do you know where he is? I'd like to talk to him."

"About what?" he asked.

All sorts of things went through my mind, none of them good. "Am I too late?"

"Let's start over," he said. "I'm Detective Kent. May I have your name and address? Better yet, may I see your driver's license?"

I handed him my license.

"What's your relationship to Mr. Brown?"

"I'm a friend. We used to work together in the air force."

"He was in the air force?" he asked.

I nodded.

"When's the last time you saw him?"

"I was trying to remember that on the way down here. I think it had to be eleven years ago."

"What are you doing in Fabens?"

"How about you let me talk to Stu, and then I'll tell you." I had already guessed that Stu had died, but I figured there was a slim possibility he was under arrest for some serious crime.

"Mr. West, I'm afraid your friend has passed on. You won't be able to talk to him. Now, tell me, what brings you to our small town?"

I stared at him for a few seconds before responding. His remark only confirmed what I had felt from the beginning of the conversation, but still it stung. Stu had been a nice guy, a gentleman, and a person I had worked with for a few years.

"He sent me a letter, out of the blue, that asked me to find a briefcase and give it to his wife. The letter didn't tell me where the briefcase was, or what was in it. In fact, to me the letter didn't make much sense. The letter didn't say where he was, or how to get in touch with him."

"Why did you come here?"

"The postmark," I said.

"Do you have a copy of the letter with you?" he asked.

"No, but I can get you a copy." I knew I put the letter in my gym bag, but I wanted a copy before I turned over the original to the police. I should have made copies before I left Clovis.

"Where were you five nights ago?"

"I've been in Clovis, New Mexico, for the last two weeks."

"Do you know who may have wanted your friend dead?"

"No, absolutely not," I said.

"I'd like a copy of that letter as soon as possible, Mr. West."

"Not a problem," I nodded.

"Where will you be staying tonight?"

"I guess at a nearby hotel."

"There's one just down the road. It's not bad. One of the Sheriff's deputies will probably want to talk to you in the morning. Do you have a cell phone?" he asked.

I gave him my number. "Do you know why Stu was in Fabens, Detective?"

"Nope."

That made two of us. I considered getting back out on the interstate and driving on to El Paso. However, the flashing neon sign of a Taqueria Jalisco restaurant reminded me of my stomach, and I turned into the parking lot barely a half mile from the police station. I noticed the Town Hotel a half a block away.

Most of the tables in the restaurant already had customers at them, but I found an empty table for two against the far wall.

As expected, my enchilada and taco dinner tasted great. I've long believed that TexMex dinners get better the closer you get to the border, and Fabens almost touched the border with Mexico.

I looked around for the local paper, but didn't find one at the restaurant. However, a little boy wearing spider man pajamas found me. His family occupied two tables pulled together halfway across the room. His mother would call to him, his name sounded like Baba, and he would return to their table, only to reappear next to mine a few minutes later.

Baba and I carried on a rudimentary conversation in Spanish. I learned that he was four years old and had three brothers and two sisters. His visits took my mind off Stu. When I left the restaurant and drove the short distance to the Town Hotel, I felt a lot better than I had when I left the police station.

The Town Hotel looked old. My ex would've never stayed there, and to be honest, I considered driving elsewhere. One night, I thought. It couldn't be any worse than camping out, and it couldn't cost much. I entered the lobby, and despite the stale smell of cigarette smoke, the place looked clean.

"May I help you?" the young lady behind the counter asked. She had on a sweatshirt with the letters UTEP across the front and wore her black hair in a tight bun behind her head.

"A room for one night."

"A room? I mean, sure we've got a nice king room, no smoking, and it has internet."

"Perfect," I said and couldn't help but smile. My asking for a room almost seemed to have surprised her. I paid by credit card, and the forty nine dollar room charge confirmed my expectations.

"If the room doesn't have any towels, let me know, and I'll get some clean ones for you," she said.

"Okay," I wondered if she thought that I might not ask for the towels, if she didn't encourage me to do so. "By any chance, do you have a copy of the most recent Fabens newspaper?"

"You mean the El Paso paper?"

"No, it looked like a local paper."

"Oh, I know," she said. She turned around and walked to the back corner behind the counter. She rummaged through a couple of magazines before picking up a newspaper. "Is this what you're looking for?"

"I think so. I'm looking for a specific article."

Rather than hand me the paper, she placed the paper on the counter between us and started turning the pages for me.

"That article," I said.

She stopped turning the pages and stared at the article. "Oh, that's terrible."

"Yes. Are you familiar with it?"

"No," she shook her head. "I know him, though."

"Stu?"

She looked at me quizzically. "I mean Doctor Gordon. He operated on my grandmother. He's a nice guy. It says here, he found the guy and brought him into his clinic. Probably saved his life."

I turned the article to face me. She stayed close, perhaps to snatch back the paper, if I tried to abscond with it. I finished reading it before jotting down the doctor's name and the name of his clinic. The article indicated that Dr. Gordon had found Stu on a dirt road and had taken him to his clinic where he had treated him. Stu had been shot twice, but as of the weekly newspaper's publication date, three days earlier, his condition had improved from critical to serious.

"You know him?" she asked.

"Yes. Where's this clinic?"

"Doctor Gordon has a big clinic on the edge of town. Everyone goes there," she picked her cell phone off the countertop. She fiddled with it for a second before turning it toward me. The screen was too small and too far away for me to see any real detail.

"It's on Rio Grande Ave." She turned the phone around, so she could look at the screen. "974 Rio Grande, but it's not open now. It opens at eight tomorrow morning."

"Then, I'll go in the morning." I wrote the address next to the name of the clinic.

I left the office and went directly to my room. I decided to forestall unpacking my car until I checked the room out. Even I had standards. The room turned out okay. The furniture was old and a bit dusty, but the bed had clean sheets. The towels in the bathroom looked clean, and the mousetrap in the corner behind the desk hadn't been tripped.

Chapter 3

The small clinic stood out from the other buildings on the street. Made of brick that had been painted white and with a landscaped front yard, it looked out of place among the rundown establishments that surrounded it. Even the lines in the small parking lot had been recently painted.

The reception area carried on the clean, well maintained theme. I surprised the young woman behind the desk when I walked in.

"We don't open for another ten minutes," she said. She looked distracted and barely looked at me.

"I know I'm early, but I was hoping to talk to Dr. Gordon. I only need a couple minutes."

She looked up at me, and I could tell that she saw me as an interruption for which she didn't have time. "Do you have an appointment?"

"You would know if I did, right?" I said.

"Yes, and we're quite busy today."

"It's rather important –"

"What's so important?" a man behind me asked.

I turned to see a white haired man, pushing sixty, and wearing black rimmed glasses enter the reception area from a side door.

"Dr. Gordon?" I guessed.

"Yes. What do you need?"

"Five minutes of your time. My name is Jim West. A former patient of yours wrote me a letter and asked me to do something for him. I came down here to talk to him, but it appears I'm a couple days too late."

"His name?"

"Brown, Stu Brown."

Dr. Gordon glanced at his receptionist and then back to me. "Come into my office, please."

He turned and walked back through the door. I followed him into a large office.

"I only learned of his name recently. You know, I may not be able to answer your questions."

"I understand. Stu and I go way back in the air force. He sent me a letter less than a week ago and didn't give me any indication that he was injured in any way, much less that he was dying."

"So, what can I tell you that you don't already know?"

"Did he tell you what happened to him?"

"Actually, no. He didn't need to. When I found him on the road, I could see that he had been shot twice in the chest. He had also been tossed down a ravine. I didn't think we'd make it back to the clinic."

"How did you know he had been tossed down a ravine?" I asked.

My question may have caught him off guard, and he paused for a second before answering. "Easy, the blood trail he had left in the dirt and the blood and dirt on his hands and knees he got from crawling."

"Did he tell you who shot him or why?"

"No, but you should talk to the police about those things," he said.

"I have, and I will again. Did he stay here in the clinic?"

"For a couple of days. At first, I didn't think it would be good to move him."

"Was he conscious at all?"

"He was out of it for thirty six hours. His vital signs improved, and despite the odds, I started to think he was going to make it."

"After the thirty six hours that you say he was unconscious, didn't he give you any explanation what happened to him or why?"

"I can tell you that he knew he had been shot, but beyond that you need to talk to the police. They took a statement from him. It was their investigation, and after his death they really clamped down on everything. That's normal, you know," the doctor said.

I nodded my head. "I'm not investigating his death, but I naturally hope they catch the people who shot him. Can you show me on a map where you found him?"

"Yes, but the police have already been out there. I don't think you'll discover much."

"I imagine you're right about that. Did he mention anything to you about a briefcase?"

"No. He didn't talk to me about much," Dr. Gordon said and looked at his watch.

"I'll get out of your hair, Doc. Thanks for the time."

"Do you still want to know where I found him?"

"Sure."

He reached into a drawer of his desk and pulled out a photocopy of a hand drawn map. "Here, it's what I gave to the police. I made this copy. I'm not sure why, but maybe it was meant for you."

I took the map. "What were you doing out there?"

"Returning to town from a house call."

I wondered about that but figured his late night house calls were none of my business. At the door, I turned back to him. "If he was getting better, why did he die?"

"Talk to the police, they might tell you."

I got into the Mustang and studied the map. There wasn't much to it, but then I would have expected a simple description of the location. Something like a few hundred yards past mile marker twelve on this or that road. Gordon had actually drawn out a map and labeled the roads. I didn't have anything better to do, so I drove out to the location. The dirt road on which Gordon found Stu didn't have a sign identifying it, though Gordon had referred to it as the old Dry Creek Road.

A strip of police tape stuck to a dried-up bush on the side of the road helped me locate the crime scene. If it hadn't been there, I never would have found the spot. Even with it, I almost gave up on finding any sign of Stu being there. A flat rock with dried blood covering a good portion of its surface finally gave me another clue I needed. The rock sat on the side of the road next to a fairly steep drop off into what looked like a dry creek bed some fifteen feet below. I followed a few more patches of dried blood on some rocks down the slope.

I didn't see anything of interest. In fact, standing there in the rocky creek bed gave me the creeps. I half expected to see a snake or a Gila monster come slithering out of the rocks around my feet. While I climbed up to the road, I watched a sheriff's vehicle approach and park next to my car.

No one in the car got out, and with the glare of the sun I couldn't see through the windshield. I walked up to the driver's side door with my hands in full view in front of me. When I neared the Sheriff's sedan, the window slid down.

"What brings you out here, Mr. West?"

She looked small in the sedan.

"I wanted to see where my friend was left for dead."

She got out of the vehicle. Her name tag read Luna, and my initial thought about her size turned out correct. If she stretched, she might reach a thin five two. Wiry would be a better description than thin. Her jet black hair was cut short, and her uniform looked clean and pressed. She didn't look like a rookie, and she seemed relaxed despite being in the middle of nowhere alone with me. I put her age close to forty which made her a handful of years younger than my own age. Her sunglasses looked too big for her head.

"You look greyer than in your picture," she said.

"Trying to look more distinguished," I wondered where she got a picture of me.

"I'm Deputy Luna," she offered a hand. "Come on I'll show you."

She walked the few paces to a spot directly adjacent to the small piece of police tape and pointed to the ground. "Here, Doc said he found him here. That night you could still see the blood. It's still there, but the wind dries everything out here and constantly blows everything around. There's maybe an eighth of an inch of fine new sand and dust over the hardpan." Deputy Luna scraped at the ground with the tow of her boot. "Well, you have to find the exact spot."

"That's okay, I believe you. Were you here that night?"

"Very early morning more like it."

"What do you think happened?" I asked.

Deputy Luna didn't answer. Instead she studied me for a few minutes before asking, "What's your interest in all this?"

Since she knew who I was, had apparently already seen a picture of me, and had most likely come out here to find me. I figured she also knew what brought me to the big city of Fabens.

"I knew Stu in the air force, but hadn't had any contact with him for years. Out of the blue I received an odd letter from him asking me to find a briefcase and take it to his wife. The letter didn't say why, what was in the briefcase, or where to look for it. The letter had no return address, but the postmark indicated it had been mailed from Fabens."

"Must have been a pretty good friend for you to make the trip here on nothing else."

I didn't feel like telling her about the three hundred dollars, or the unexplainable fact that I had felt some obligation to take the briefcase to Stu's wife, now his widow. He had no right to count on me to do anything, but he had.

"Maybe he was," I said. "You didn't find a briefcase, did you?"

"No, and if he asked you to find it and take it to his wife, then I imagine he didn't have it with him. Could be why he was killed." She walked over to where I had found the blood on the rock. "This is where he crawled back up to the road. They probably thought he was already dead."

"They?"

"Two men, he said that much. Claimed he didn't know why. He lied about that, and he knew we knew he was lying. I figured at the time he didn't want to give the two guys any more of a reason to return and finish the job. After I heard your story, I think they were after the briefcase, too."

"They killed him, or tried to. They must have gotten the briefcase, if your scenario is correct."

"I don't think so." Rather than say anything more, she walked to her car, reached in, and pulled out a Styrofoam cup. She leaned against the sedan and took a sip.

"Deputy, I have no interest in getting involved in your investigation. However, I've got a lot of questions."

She looked at me through those sunglasses.

"First, what actually killed him?"

"Sepsis. He was tough enough to survive the two rounds he took. Most wouldn't, but when the poison hit, it killed him in twenty four hours. His organs simply shut down. They moved him to El Paso, but it didn't matter, it was too late."

It made me think of the old term lead poisoning, which meant being shot, but was often more accurate of a term than people realized. "Why do you think the people who killed him didn't get the briefcase?"

"He wrote that letter the last day he was in Doc Gordon's clinic. I only learned of that this morning. He wouldn't have written it if the briefcase had been taken from him."

I nodded my head. Her explanation made sense to me. "He had to have help with the letter."

"He did. A nurse got him the paper and envelope, and she mailed the letter for him. She didn't think it had anything to do with our investigation, so she kept that information to herself. She also bought a money order for him. Was that in the letter?"

"Yes."

"What do you think is in the briefcase?"

"My guess would be money, and from what has happened, I

imagine the money wasn't his. I can't believe Stu would have gotten involved with anything illegal, but if he found the briefcase, he might have been tempted to keep it."

"So, not drugs or something else?"

"He wouldn't have asked me to take it to his wife if it was anything but money," I said. "I wondered about it being jewelry or diamonds, but then she'd have to find a way to sell them. My bet is money."

Her turn to nod. Her sunglasses started to annoy me. They hid a good one third of her face and made her harder to read.

"By the way, has anyone contacted his wife?" I asked.

"Until you showed up, we didn't know he had one. He refused to tell anyone much about himself. We still don't know his home address. We hope to have it in the next day or so."

"When you get it, can you let me know it?"

"We'll see. If he didn't tell you where the briefcase was, how are you supposed to find it?"

"Right now, I have no idea."

"Listen, Jim. You don't mind me calling you Jim?"

"Not at all."

"Not James?"

"Never been a James, always a Jim."

"Jim, any chance you'll share this letter with me? I've got the lead on the investigation for the county, and right now I have very little to go on."

"The letter won't help."

She stared at me. I didn't have a good reason not to share it.

"Will you buy me a cup of coffee?" I asked.

She grinned. "A small cup and call me Rose."

"Well, Rose, if you lead me out of here and to a place we can get some coffee, I'll show you the letter."

I followed her to a small restaurant named Carla's Cantina which sat about a quarter mile off I-10. It had a handful of customers, but we managed to find a semi-private area in a back corner. She didn't take off her sunglasses until we sat down.

An old man approached our table. He walked with a slight limp and carried a small notepad in his left hand.

"Rosa, como esta?" he asked. His smile made me wonder if they were related.

"I'm good, Tio. How's Carmen these days?"

"Her back is getting better. Would you like some coffee?"

"Yes, two please," Rose said.

"Bueno," the waiter said and walked away.

"Your uncle?" I asked. I knew enough Spanish to translate "Tio."

"Yes. I grew up here in Fabens and have more uncles, aunts, and cousins than I can count."

"More with law enforcement?"

"No, just me, and I received a lot of resentment when I joined. Our family's history includes more than a few locally famous banditos, and a handful of lesser criminals that ran up against the law. For some, it's still a source of misguided pride."

"I hope they're all coming around to accepting you as a deputy."

"For the most part they have," she said, and I sensed a bit of pride in her voice. "After all, I've been doing this for a while now."

Her uncle returned with two mugs of coffee. "Would you like something to eat?"

"I'm fine," Rose said. "You want anything, Jim?"

I did, but decided to wait. "I'm good."

"Now, how about that letter," Rose said.

"You can make yourself a copy, but I'd like to keep the original."

"Not a problem," she said.

I handed her the envelope. She studied it before taking the letter out. It only took her a few seconds to read it. She turned the letter over and looked at the blank side of the paper. She held it up over her head and studied it with the light behind it.

"Is this some kind of military code?" she asked.

"Not one I know."

"How are you supposed to find this briefcase?"

"I haven't figured that out," I said.

"And you said that you don't know where his wife is?" she asked.

"That's right, although she'll be easier to find than that briefcase. The numbers in that letter must mean something, but just what I haven't figured out yet."

"Map coordinates?"

"Could be, but what map? Plus each set of numbers is different. I thought about GPS coordinates, but they aren't," I said.

"A code where numbers equate to letters?" Rose jotted some letters on a napkin. "No, that doesn't make sense."

"I'll spend a couple days trying to figure it out, and then I'll call Stu's widow to pass on my condolences. She might have some idea about this whole mess."

"My bet is he came across a briefcase full of cash. He may have thought it had been abandoned, or he may have outright stolen it, but I agree with you, it's cash. You hear stories about people turning in large amounts of money that they have found, but most people try to hang onto it."

"Guess you can't blame them," I said.

"I can, it's not theirs. They know it, but they want it."

"Some might really need the money."

"We all need the money. It's not theirs. It's theft by opportunity. There's a process to turn it in, and if no one claims it, they can keep it or at least a good portion of it. Often, there's a reward. It's greed that makes them take it for themselves, and greed can kill."

"You've thought about this," I said, trying to suppress a grin.

"Oh, I don't mean to lecture you, but I've debated about everything that has to do with right and wrong."

I took a sip of coffee and waited for her to continue. She had pretty brown eyes that didn't need to be hidden behind sunglasses, and seeing the rest of her face only made her prettier. I didn't see a wedding band.

"Too many in my family and too many of my friends still want to play the oppressed Mexican card. It's like the United States stole south Texas from Mexico last year. Both my dad's and my mom's families have lived in Texas, not Mexico, for a hundred years. I understand being proud of your roots, but sometimes I think they carry it too far. They get mad at me when I refuse to talk to them in Spanish." Her face took on a mischievous look. "I do that on purpose to get under their skin. Not everyone, but some."

"I wonder why Stu didn't give the doctor or the police his address or his home phone number?" Before Rose answered, I answered my own question. "I guess he didn't want anyone to know it, so the people who shot him wouldn't be looking for the briefcase in her direction."

"He could've been trying to protect her, but dying alone? Not telling your wife? Doesn't make sense," Rose said.

"I agree. Maybe the drugs were affecting his thinking."

Her uncle walked up to the table. "Are you sure I can't get you something to eat? We just had some cinnamon rolls come out of the oven."

I broke down and ordered one.

CHAPTER 4

I wanted to talk to the nurse who had mailed the letter for Stu. He might have given her some idea of what he wanted me to do. Rose had given me the name of Liz Graham, but had asked me not to tell Liz or anyone who might ask that she had done so. She didn't have a very high opinion of Graham, since she had interviewed her twice, and Graham had never mentioned the letter before being confronted early this morning.

The receptionist at the clinic didn't appear to be any happier to see me this time than she had before.

"Dr. Gordon is with a patient. He has another patient waiting. If you give me your number, I'll have him call you."

"You want my phone number, don't you?"

"Don't flatter yourself," she said without any hint of a smile.

"Actually, I'd like to talk to a nurse who works here. Liz Graham."

"She's off today."

"If I give you my number, would you pass it onto her and ask her to call me?"

"Of course," she said.

I wrote down my name and number on the back of one of the doctor's business cards that were on the desk. She glared at me like I violated some rule, but she did take the card.

"Thank you," I said and left the clinic. I had no expectation of ever hearing from Nurse Graham, but to my surprise my phone rang in less than five minutes.

"Mr. West?" a voice that sounded feeble and frightened

came through the phone.

"Yes, that's me," I said.

"I'm Liz Graham. I understand you want to talk to me."

"Yes, that's right. Is there any place we could meet, so I could ask you a few questions about Stu Brown? I believe he was a patient of yours."

"Can't we talk on the phone?" she asked.

"I'd rather we do it in person."

She didn't say anything for about ten seconds. She almost outlasted me, but before I said anything, she continued talking. "I don't know."

"I could come to your place," I paused for effect, "but it would be better if we met some place public." As frightened as she sounded, I figured that she didn't want me showing up at her home.

"Okay."

"There's a restaurant named Carla's Café's or Cantina, something like that, near I-10—"

"I know it," she said. "When do you want to meet?"

"Now?"

"Now?" she asked.

"Would that be a problem?"

"No. I guess not. I can be there in fifteen minutes."

When I drove the Mustang into the restaurant parking lot, I noticed a Sheriff's sedan parked in the lot. While Rose had not left the restaurant when I had, she had indicated she needed to get a few things done. I didn't think she would still be at the restaurant, and this sedan was parked in a different spot. It therefore surprised me when I almost bumped into her when I entered the restaurant.

"Looking for me?" she asked.

"Not really," I said. "I didn't know you would still be here."

"I left and came back. My uncle asked me to get a couple of gallons of milk for them. What brings you back?"

"I'm meeting Nurse Graham here in a few minutes."

"That was fast."

"She sounded a little nervous, but she agreed to meet me here," I said.

"I'll get out of here. My presence might spook her. Here," she handed me her card. "Call me after you're done. I'd like to know what she has to say."

"Will do."

She hurried over to her car and drove out of the parking lot. I entered the restaurant. A few more customers sat at the tables than before, but I didn't see a single woman at any of them. I took the closest empty table and sat down to wait. A teenager came over and took my order for a Diet Coke.

After twenty minutes, I decided I was being stood up. I waved at the waiter to get the bill, when a short, square woman with short, straight brown hair walked into the restaurant and looked around. I stood up and gave her a slight nod. She looked at me and paused, as though she was trying to convince herself it was alright to approach me.

"Mr. West?" she asked.

"Yes, and you must be Nurse Graham." I offered her my hand and she shook it. "Please sit down."

She perched on the chair opposite of me like she wanted to be able to dash off at any second.

"I appreciate your coming here. This has been a very frustrating trip. I understand you're the person who helped Stu get a letter to me."

She nodded, but didn't speak.

"Did he tell you why he sent the letter to me?"

For a second, I thought she wasn't going to answer me. She looked around again.

"Yes. He said you were a friend and were the only person he knew who could help him. He seemed like a nice guy and was a good patient. Dr. Gordon didn't think he would survive that first night, but he did. I came in at four that morning. The doc called me in early to stay with him. I sat with him and monitored all the equipment."

"By him, you mean Stu?"

"Yes. We're equipped for patients to stay overnight, but they only do every now and then. When we have someone overnight, Linda and I usually share the shift."

"Was Linda there with you that night?" I asked.

"Only at first, she came in to help in the surgery. She left shortly after Dr. Gordon went home. Stu didn't wake up until the next night. Not that night, the next night. Of course, a lot of that was because of the drugs we had him on. We were all surprised how well he seemed to be recovering."

I didn't care to clarify which night things happened, but I did care what he said to anyone.

"So you were there when he regained consciousness?"

"Yes. Like I told the police, it was about seven in the evening. The last of the staff had left about a half hour earlier. Dr. Gordon wanted me to call him right away when he came to, but Stu only asked for some water and wanted to know where he was. We talked for about three or four minutes, before he fell back asleep. I texted the doctor and told him I'd call him the next time he was awake."

The waiter showed up and Nurse Graham ordered a coffee and some apple pie.

"Did he wake up again that night?" I asked.

"Yes, about ten o'clock. This time he was hungry. I called Dr. Gordon and he came in. Linda came in about a half hour after that."

"What did he tell you about being shot?"

"Nothing, other than he knew he had been. None of us asked him about it. We didn't want to agitate him. Even though the cops wanted to talk to him as soon as he came to, we waited until the next morning to call them. I went home around four in the morning, so I wasn't there when they came."

"When did he ask you for help in mailing the letter?" I asked.

"The next day, or I mean night. Despite his improvement from the gunshot wounds, his vitals started giving us signs something else was wrong. I can't really go into that, you know, but Dr. Gordon told him what was going on and that he would be sent to a better equipped hospital in El Paso in the morning."

"What reason did he give you for asking help with the letter?" I asked again trying to keep her focused.

"He only said that he needed to get in touch with you so you could do something for him. He said it was important, and that it had nothing to do with his being shot. It was a little weird, too. He had little chance of surviving at that point, but he was in a good mood. Maybe it was the drugs he was on, but he called me an angel that night."

I could see her eyes get a little moist as she remembered that night. Before I could prompt her with another question, she continued.

"He asked me to get him a piece of paper and an envelope. That was easy since we had them right there in the office."

"Did he say what he wanted me to do?"

"No. Like I already said, he wanted you to do something for him. He never told me what or why."

"Did you also purchase the money order for me?"

"Yes,"

"I'm surprised that he had that much money on him," I said. I already knew that whoever shot him had taken his wallet.

"That was by sheer luck. Per normal procedure, we bagged his clothes and shoes for the police, but he had a fancy belt. Linda kept that separate, like we would do with glasses, hearing aids, or other items. In his case, it was the belt. He asked for it, and I got it and gave it to him."

"Money belt?"

"Yes, the best one I've ever seen. There was no zipper or flap or anything. He removed the belt buckle and pulled the belt apart. A thin layer of Velcro kept it together at one end. He pulled out three one hundred dollar bills and a twenty. He asked me to buy a money order and stick it in the envelope before I mailed it."

"That was nice of you to do that. A lot of people would've just kept the money."

"I don't need money that bad," she said. "I considered this his dying wish. If you could do something to help his family, then I wanted you to do it, too."

Since I hadn't mentioned anything about the contents of the letter and she insisted he didn't tell her what he wanted me to do, I assumed she had read the letter before mailing it.

"I bought the money order that morning and mailed it."

"And I got it the next day. I'd like to follow up on Stu's wishes, but the letter didn't tell me much. Did you share the letter with the police?"

"No. It had nothing to do with them," she said.

I disagreed, but kept my thoughts to myself. I had little doubt that whatever he wanted me to find was what his killers were after, too.

"How did he have my address?" I asked.

She looked at me like I had asked a dumb question, which I guess I had.

"How would I know? I thought you two were friends. He had it memorized."

"Yeah, silly question," I admitted.

"They took him by ambulance that morning, and he died that night. You know, nothing that we did at the clinic caused him to die."

"What do you mean?"

"Dr. Gordon is worried that we may get sued, and he has cautioned all of us not to talk about this."

"I'm only interested in trying to do what I can for Stu. Nothing else," I said.

"I know. That's why I'm talking to you. He counted on me to get the letter to you, and he counted on you to help him. I felt like I owed you and him this much. That's why I'm here," she said.

"Well, I thank you."

"I was hoping no one would ever know about my helping him with the letter," she said.

"Why?"

"Someone tried to kill him. Well, I guess they did kill him for something they wanted. It seems obvious that that something may be what he asked you to find. I felt it would be safe to talk to you, but I wouldn't want to talk to the people who shot him. They might not be so accepting of my telling them I really don't know anything. I don't like the police knowing that I mailed you that letter."

"You think the police are a threat?"

"No, but they talk too much," she said.

We continued talking for another five minutes, but it became obvious that she could add nothing more. She left first, and I left a few minutes later after paying the bill. I had already considered that I might not be the only person looking for the briefcase, but the danger involved had been something I hadn't dwelled on. From my perspective, like Nurse Graham, I had no idea where the briefcase was or even what was in it.

However, she had made a good point. If others looking for the briefcase discovered I had been asked to find the briefcase, they might think I knew more than I did. Even I felt it was stupid for Stu to ask me to find it and take it to his wife without telling me where it was or giving me a better hint. I decided to watch and see if anyone left the restaurant after I did.

Sitting in my Mustang, I called Deputy Luna while I watched the front door of the restaurant.

"How'd it go?" she asked right away.

"Fine, but she didn't know anything more about the missing briefcase or the shooting."

"What was her excuse for not telling us sooner about the letter?"

"She's very concerned the people who shot Stu might find out she mailed a letter for him, and that they'll come after her, thinking she knows more than she does."

"And she doesn't trust us?"

"Not so much that she doesn't trust you all, she simply thinks the police talk too much. Those are her words," I said.

"Any thoughts?"

"A couple of things struck me. Stu had memorized my address. We hadn't corresponded at all since I last saw him a decade ago. He must have known he might need help and had already decided to contact me some time before he was shot. I think he was running from these guys for a while before they caught up with him."

"Makes sense. I can also appreciate her concerns, but I wish these people would understand that they put themselves at more risk by not talking to us."

"You're right, but a lot of people don't see it that way," I said.

"I know. You're talking about fifty percent of my relatives. So, what do you plan to do next?"

"I'm not sure. I've got a free night up at the lodge in Cloudcroft. If they have a room for tonight, I may head up there."

"Sounds nice, I've been to Cloudcroft, but I've never spent the night up there."

"Yeah, me neither. Do you know if anyone interviewed the ambulance staff and the people at the hospital in El Paso to see if Stu said anything to them?"

"They were all interviewed, but he didn't say a thing about the shooting."

"Do you know where he stayed while he was in Fabens?" I asked.

"He didn't stay here. There's no record of him staying anywhere around here or in El Paso. At least, none that we've discovered."

"How about his car?"

"Same. We've got nothing. He gave us the description of his car, but he claimed he couldn't remember the tag number."

"Do you think he was shot out there on that dirt road or someplace else and taken out there?"

"He said he was forced off the east bound access road to I-10 this side of El Paso. He stopped to get gas and when he tried to get back on the highway someone cut in front of him. His memory allegedly went fuzzy after that." She sounded skeptical.

"You think he was holding back?" I asked.

"Yes. He said his next real memory was coming to out there next to the road. We didn't find any shell casings out near where the doc found him, so the theory is that he was shot elsewhere and taken there."

"He sure didn't help out much, did he?"

"No, and because of that, there's not much of a push from the top to get this resolved."

"I'm not surprised. My only guess is that whatever is in the briefcase must have really had an effect on him."

"Well, he certainly considered it more important than helping us bring the men who shot him to justice," she said.

"Rose, I appreciate your sharing all this with me."

"This is my area of the county. Even if my boss isn't that interested in catching the shooters, I am."

"I wish you luck," I said.

"If you find the briefcase, will you let me know?"

I thought about this for a second before I answered. "Yes."

"Then I wish you luck. Be careful, Jim."

After my conversation with Rose, I drove out of the parking lot barely missing a stray dog that ran across the lot in front of me. I headed west on I-10 leaving Fabens and not really sure of my next step. My obligation, if any, was to Stu, but there were too many reasons why the briefcase should be turned over to the police rather than to Stu's widow. If I gave it to her, I would be putting her into the same dangerous situation Stu had found himself. What would I say to her? Here's your money, now start running.

Chapter 5

I hadn't driven ten miles west on the interstate before I got an antsy feeling someone was following me. No one had followed me out of the restaurant or out of its parking lot, but I didn't watch to see if someone might have been waiting out on the street that ran in front of the restaurant. Traffic on the highway had picked up as I neared El Paso, and too many vehicles appeared in my rear view mirror to get a good picture in my mind of all the cars behind me. I knew once I got through El Paso, and especially after I left I-10 and started driving on the state roads that would take me to Cloudcroft, anyone following me would become obvious. Rather than continue to worry about someone on my tail, I thought about the money in the briefcase.

I had once heard that if stacked right, you could cram a half million dollars in a briefcase. That would be fifty packs of one hundred dollar bills with each pack consisting of one hundred individual bills. I imagined they would have to be new, crisp bills, too. It seemed plausible. Of course, the size of the briefcase would make a big difference.

Thinking about it that way, I could almost empathize with Stu. That amount of cash would make anyone's eyes water. All one would have to do is throw it in their trunk and drive far away. It would be so very easy. It probably seemed that way to Stu, too.

Temptation is the devil's tool, and like Rose had said, greed can kill. Most of my male friends in the past who had fallen for temptation had found it in the form of a pretty face and a tight skirt. I couldn't remember anyone running across a half million dollars before and having to decide between right and wrong. Maybe some had and had gotten away with it. I didn't know.

If it happened to me, I thought I would do the right thing and turn it over to the authorities. Of course I didn't have a family to take care of, kids to send to college, or medical bills piling up. Besides, who would be the right authorities to whom to give the briefcase? Could I trust anyone? Maybe the decision would be tougher than I thought. I had once found an old, soiled dollar bill in a parking lot and had kept it. I didn't think a dollar would be missed, and it wasn't worth the effort to try to find its owner. What would I have done if it had been a twenty dollar bill or a hundred? It didn't seem rational at the time to try to track down the owner of the dollar bill, and it wouldn't have been any more rational if the bill was a hundred dollar bill. Yet, as the value of my imaginary discovery went up, I could feel more guilt in my desire to abscond with it.

Traffic slowed for a broken down truck on the side of the interstate as the highway passed through the middle of the city. I could see Juarez, Mexico off to my left. If the briefcase belonged to a Mexican cartel, then I really did need to be careful.

El Paso has more hills than one might expect. When it gets a little rain and plants turn green, it can be a pretty city. A sign mentioned Franklin Mountain which I figured had to be the tallest of the hills that El Paso now sprawled up against. On the other side, the Rio Grande River sliced through the city and separated it from Juarez, Mexico.

I had never spent the night in El Paso, but years back I had spent a weekend in Juarez. The hotels, restaurants, and shopping were cheaper on the Mexican side of the border. It might still be cheaper there, but it had become a dangerous place to spend any time.

I turned off I-10 onto Highway 54 a few miles after leaving El Paso and headed north towards Alamogordo, New Mexico. A brown pickup truck made the same turn about a half mile behind me. I watched in my rear view mirror but didn't see another vehicle follow us. I drove a few miles before I stopped at a gas station. The brown pickup slowed but drove by the station. The darkened windows in the truck made it impossible to see if anyone inside was looking at me as they drove past. The already large pickup had been jacked up, making the body of the vehicle an extra foot above the ground.

The Mustang didn't need much gas, but I topped off my tank before continuing north. Barely a mile up the road, I passed the brown pickup. It had pulled off the side of the road and parked in front of a dilapidated, abandoned building that may have once been someone's home. I watched as the pickup drove back onto the road and continued following me. The driver of the pickup seemed content to keep a steady distance behind me.

I drove by a highway sign that claimed the city of Orogrande, New Mexico, was a dozen miles ahead of me. A thought occurred to me that I could stop at the police station in Orogrande and mention the pickup. It didn't take long for me to discard the idea as lame, and as I drove through the small town, I wondered if it even had a police force.

A better idea had come to me, anyway. Alamogordo, New Mexico, was another twenty miles ahead of me, and Holloman

Air Force Base sat right outside the city. I accelerated the Mustang up to eighty miles per hour after leaving Orogrande. The time it took the pickup to get away from Orogrande, and for the driver to realize I was no longer driving at the speed limit, allowed me to stretch the distance between us to almost a mile. The southern edge of the Sacramento Mountains broke the horizon far ahead of me.

The pickup had kept its distance behind me, but I thought it might be smart to keep it a little further away. The additional distance would allow me to reach Holloman AFB, before my pursuers could stop me at the last minute, if they were so inclined. I didn't think they could follow me into the air base.

In no time my plan fell apart, as the pickup slowly gained on me while we both darted through the empty desert-like surrounding. I pushed the Mustang to eighty five, but the pickup continued to cut into the gap between us. The driver of the pickup had to realize that I now knew he was following me. A handful of cars drove by us going south, and I had to pass a couple going north, but for the most part the remote highway seemed to belong to the two of us. About five miles out of Alamogordo, the pickup had closed to within a hundred yards and didn't seem to have any desire to slow down. At this speed, if he rammed the back of my car, I didn't know if I would be able to maintain control of the Mustang. I had to keep him behind me. If he pulled the pickup along side of my Mustang and hit me from the side, it would be all over.

I did the obvious and floored the accelerator. I eased off a little at ninety five miles per hour and watched the space between us start to slowly lengthen. I sensed that the driver of the pickup wanted to stay up with me, but there were enough bends in the otherwise straight highway to discourage him. We remained at that crazy pace until we approached the city and the speed limit dropped.

Up ahead, I saw a police sedan with its lights flashing had pulled over a white van. Both were parked on the side of the road. I slowed more as I passed it and noticed the pickup backing off a little. Traffic increased, and a few cars pulled in between us. When I saw the turn to the air base, I took it without using my blinkers. It didn't fool the driver of the pickup, and I saw it follow me toward the base. A few minutes later when I turned off the road and drove into Holloman, I couldn't help but smile when the pickup slowed but drove by the entrance to the air base.

If I had known how to get to a back or side gate to the base, I would have driven straight out the other side and on up to Cloudcroft. Since I didn't, I drove to the Base Exchange to stretch my legs and find someone who could give me the directions. The Exchange is the military version of a department store. I didn't go there to buy anything, but I knew it would be a place where I could find plenty of people.

Entering the store, I noticed a number of food vendors set up off to the side. A young airman with two stripes on his sleeve sat at a table by himself sipping a soft drink. His uniform identified him as a member of the base's security forces, formerly known as the air police and later the security police.

"Can I ask you question?"

He looked up at me. With my hair trying to turn grey and my presence on the base, he reacted as though I might be an officer or a senior non-commissioned officer. He stood up. "Sure, sir."

"Please sit down. I'm down here from Clovis, and I'm not really familiar with your base."

"I've only been here a few months."

"Where are you from?" I asked.

"Cincinnati," he said.

"Go Bengals."

He grinned. "What do you want to know?"

"Is there a side gate to the base that's open during the day?'

"Yes."

"I thought there would be. I know Cannon has a back gate for people coming in from Portales, and I thought Holloman would have something similar."

He explained how to get the side gate and suggested the route to take from the gate to avoid a stretch of street lights in Alamogordo. I thanked him for the information and for his service, and decided to take a stroll through the store before leaving.

Without any prior intent, I started looking at handguns in a small section in the back of the store. The selling of guns in the military exchanges has come and gone over the years. For whatever reason, the stores had started selling them again. Throughout my military career, I had been assigned a variety of handguns and had to stay proficient with each of them. Since my departure from the service, I had not purchased one. I wanted to think I didn't need a weapon. Despite several situations in the past few years where I could have used a handgun, I rationalized that in each of those cases, I hadn't gone out looking for danger. Rather, those situations found me.

A number of the law enforcement friends I had made throughout the southwest in the past several years had suggested I wise up and buy a handgun. I always resisted the temptation. I had no desire to become a licensed investigator and certainly didn't advertise my services. My goal when I retired from the military and moved back to Clovis, New Mexico, consisted of one main objective: get over a divorce that I never saw coming and had hurt me a lot more than I would have thought. I wanted the world to leave me alone. Along with adding ten pounds to my six foot frame, I thought I had finally made it back to a somewhat normal emotional state.

What nagged in my mind, while I stood at the counter looking at a shiny black Sig Sauer 9mm pistol, was that if I decided to go after the missing briefcase, I would be doing what I always claimed I didn't do. I wouldn't be looking for a missing teenager or stuck in some mountain lodge where a murder occurred. I would be making a conscious decision to stick my nose into a situation where it didn't belong, and that would be stupid. I started walking away from the counter.

My phone rang. The caller ID identified the number as "Private."

"Hello," I said.

"Mr. Jim, you don't know me, but I've been watching you. Don't think you've gone somewhere where we can't reach out and touch you. I have many, many friends at Hollowman." The man's speech gave me the definite impression that English wasn't his primary language. I pegged the caller as someone who hailed from Mexico or one of the countries south of it. His pronunciation of Holloman also indicated he might not be as familiar with the air base as he wanted me to believe.

"What's your interest in watching me? I don't lead a very interesting life."

"You are trying to find something that belongs to me."

"Not any more. I don't have the slightest idea where it is."

"I think you do. I give you one week to find it and give it to me. If you do, everything will be fine. I might even pay you for your trouble. If you don't find it in a week, you and me may have to talk. You don't want that to happen."

"What am I supposed to be looking for?" I asked. No answer came, and I realized that he had already broken the connection.

"Great," I said to no one and returned to the counter. I looked at the Sig Sauer through the glass.

"You've stared at it long enough," a young salesman with a thin mustache and greased back short hair said to me. He looked like a throwback to the 1950's. I hoped the style wasn't making a comeback. "Now you have to buy it. Don't blame me; it's store policy."

I guess he thought he was a comedian.

He unlocked the cabinet and removed the pistol. He looked at it a second or two before placing it on the counter in front of me. I picked it up and wondered if this was how an alcoholic felt with his first drink in his hand after years of abstinence.

I left the Base Exchange with the pistol and a box of ammunition. I felt what I knew was a false sense of security. I also had a little buyer's remorse. Before driving out of the parking lot, I called Deputy Rose Luna.

"Rose, this is Jim. Something's come up."

"Is everything okay?"

"Yes, but I'm being followed by a large brown pickup, maybe a Dodge Ram. It's been jacked up to be a little taller than a standard one, and it has Texas tags. I think the first letter is a

"T", but the tags have dirt or mud smeared on them."

"That's not much for me to go on. Where are you?" she asked.

"I'm in New Mexico. I received a telephone call a few minutes ago from someone who had their phone number blocked on my caller ID. The man had a south of the border accent and said he was having me watched."

"How did he get your number?"

"I only gave it to you and the cops in Fabens." I stopped talking to let her think about what I said.

"Sorry, Jim. Your name and number are in our shared system. Every deputy and Fabens police officer has access to the information. It's an open homicide case. It also has a description of your car," Rose said.

"So, maybe Nurse Graham's paranoia was justified."

It was Rose's turn to remain silent.

"I'm heading up to Cloudcroft. That doesn't need to be in your report, does it?"

"No, but I'll double check to make sure that it's not in our files. Jim, I promise you I'm not passing any information about you to anyone."

"I didn't think you were. I've already told you where I was going, and that I'd get in touch with you if I found the briefcase."

"Why don't you go home and forget about all this?"

"I keep asking myself that same question. Ten minutes ago, I had all but decided to do that, but the phone call gave me a week to find the briefcase or the caller was going to pay me a visit," I said.

She muttered a few choice words in Spanish that even I

understood. "This is not good, Jim."

"Kind of what I was thinking."

"I'm going to do a few things at my end. Be careful, and promise me that you'll call me tonight once you're checked in."

I said I would. After the call I sat in the car a full five minutes and tried to determine if I should trust Deputy Rose Luna. It didn't seem logical that anyone would follow me in the manner they had or call and threaten me if they already had someone in close contact with me. Their surveillance could be considerably more discreet. Then again, why should I expect any logic from a group of thugs?

CHAPTER 6

I drove out a side gate to the base and didn't see any sign of the brown pickup or anyone else who might have an interest in me. The large, beautiful White Sands Desert bordered Holloman, and I resisted a temptation to drive out into it. Under different circumstances, I'd enjoy exploring the desert. Today, however, wasn't a good day to be out there alone.

After about three miles of circuitous driving, I made it back to the main road that took me north out of Alamogordo and to the steep climb up into the southern reaches of the Sacramento Mountains. Tall Aspens and pines lined the winding road. Signs cautioned me about the deer that might be silly enough to cross the road in front of me. I didn't see any wildlife, but I knew many different species called the forests in these mountains home. Smokey the Bear came from somewhere around here, and yes, unlike Yogi and Boo Boo, Smokey was a real bear.

The short trip up the mountain took a while. With all the bends and the steep incline, my speed sometimes dipped below twenty miles an hour. Once in the small town of Cloudcroft, I followed a sign to my destination. The Lodge at Cloudcroft sat a few hundred yards off the main road that ran through the small town. I found it without difficulty and parked the Mustang in one of the lodge's small parking lots.

After focusing so hard on the road during the drive up the mountain, I took a moment to stretch once I got out of the car. I looked around to get a feel for the area and felt a slight dizziness. I knew the altitude here reached a little over eight thousand feet above sea level, but the terrain affected me the most. The lodge appeared to have been cut into the side of the mountain and might have been the only level thing around me. The undulations of the ground combined with the surrounding peaks, steep slopes, low clouds that streamed across the sky, and trees swaying in the wind contributed to the uncomfortable sensation. The fact that the parking lot sloped a bit didn't help.

I left everything in the car and walked up the stairs that led into the old lodge. The reception desk stood immediately to my left as I entered. A short, thin man who looked to be around eighty years old fiddled with some papers on the desk.

"Good afternoon, may I help you?" His voice had a raspy sound, but his eyes looked sharp.

"Yes. I called yesterday." I couldn't believe it was only yesterday. "The person I talked to said he was sure there would be a few rooms available all week."

The man smiled. "So, do you want to know if that's still true, or by chance do you want a room for tonight?"

My turn to smile, I had stepped into that one. "Yes, do you have a room I could have for tonight? In fact, can I have the room for two nights?"

"Absolutely. You by yourself?" he asked.

"Absolutely," I answered.

He gave me the keys to a room on the second floor.

"The bar is open and the restaurant will start serving dinner in a few minutes. It is without a doubt the best place to eat in Cloudcroft."

"Thanks," I said and left to find my room. I liked the lodge immediately.   The floors creaked and were uneven.   Old photographs with small placards that described the contents of the pictures and the dates when the pictures were taken hung from the wall. In an odd way, the lodge reminded me of the old Miramont Castle in Manitou Springs, Colorado.

The room they gave me would have almost fit into the walk-in closet at my old house in D.C.. The double bed took up all the space but a two foot wide area around it. A tiny dresser and a nightstand made up the remaining furniture. The bathroom had a sliding door, a small pedestal sink, a tiny shower, and a toilet with walls so close that many of my larger framed friends would find it a challenge simply to use it. One hundred years ago, this same room would have been considered luxury living, especially anywhere around this remote area of the country.

I went out to bring in what little luggage I had. The man at the front desk had his back to me when I left.

"How's the room?" he asked when I re-entered.

"I like it. I do," I said.

"It may be too cloudy today, but if you go up to the top of the tower, you can see the sunset and nearly a hundred miles to the west." He pointed to a set of stairs across the foyer.

"I'll check it out." I doubted if anyone could see for a hundred miles, but I took his comment as an acceptable exaggeration. After all, how many times had I heard "you can see forever"?

The idea of climbing to the tower intrigued me, but I knew that heavy clouds had already settled in over the area. Besides, in the thin air, walking up the steps to the lodge had winded me. The tower would be a challenge.

A young woman entered the lodge. She had on a grey sweatshirt, black hiking shorts with white polka dots, thick grey socks, hiking boots, and a grey headband. She carried a backpack. The black shorts reminded me of some boxer style underpants I used to have. Her face had a pink glow to it, and her hair looked like she had been out in the wind for a while.

"Hey Fred, how's the back today?" she asked.

"About the same," the man behind the counter asked. "See him again today?"

"No. It's been three days now. I hope he's okay."

"I'm sure he is. There's not much that can hurt him out there."

"I know," she said. She turned toward me, "Hi."

I nodded, and she walked down the hall. She wasn't particularly attractive and could stand to lose twenty to thirty pounds. Of course, she probably was thinking the same thing about me.

"Good kid," Fred said.

"Related?"

"No. She's a graduate student up here studying the bears."

"The bears?"

"Yep, the bears."

After dropping off the few things I brought from my car on the bed in the room, I decided to check out the bar. Two couples shared a table, but no one occupied the stools along the bar, so I decided to grab one in the middle. A lot of wood and old furniture gave the bar its ambience.

"What can I get you?" the bartender asked.

"A Bud Light is fine," I said.

He reached into a cooler and brought out a bottle. He looked like a younger version of a Morgan Freeman, except he had a shiny gold front tooth that looked out of place. I didn't think people got gold teeth anymore.

"Here you go," he said, before moving off to a stool he had in the corner.

I pulled Stu's letter from my pocket and reread it for the umpteenth time. It didn't make any more sense to me now than it had before. The numbers had to be the clue, but they didn't mean anything to me. I sat there sipping my beer and waiting for the solution to jump out of the letter.

"A Dear John letter?"

I turned and saw the young lady bear watcher walk up to the bar next to me.

"Just kidding," she said.

"Hey, Kay, same again tonight?" the bartender asked her.

"Of course, Will."

The bartender already had a bottle of white wine in his hands, and he poured an oversized portion into a wine glass.

"You're spoiling me," she said as she accepted the glass from him.

"Did you see him today?" Will asked.

"No, not today. Hopefully tomorrow."

"I hope you're not a bounty hunter," I said. It came out without much thought.

They both looked at me like I had said something dumb, which I had. Then, she smiled. "Good one. I'm Kay." She extended her hand, and I shook it.

"I'm actually tracking this guy," she fiddled with her cell phone before extending it out for me to see a picture of a young bear cub.

"Cool. How old do you think he is?"

"A year old, he's too big to have been born this spring.

Here's a picture of his mom," she clicked to another picture of a much bigger bear.

"I wouldn't want to run into her out there," I said.

"I've had a couple close calls. Luckily, each time her cub was on the other side of her. I would not want to accidently get too close to her cub when she was around."

"Are there a lot of bears up here?"

"No, not any more. There used to be a lot of cougars and bears, but we've all but wiped them out. It's getting better thankfully."

"We?"

"Man. It's only been thirty years or so that the government has made any real effort to protect them," she said.

I always wondered when people said the government did something, if they thought government was a living thing with a mind of its own, rather than a bunch of men and women making decisions based on whatever constituency or supporter they were trying to please at the moment.

"It's the same old story. We've encroached on their habitat, and then we want to get rid of them when they appear on our property."

"I understand you're working on your doctorate," I asked.

"Yes. I hope to be done next summer. My grant money will run out in December. I should have all my research done by then. If not, I might have to take a part time job here at the lodge, so I can stay here until I've finished."

"Have you spent all your time tracking this cub?" I asked.

"Oh, no," she said with enough emphasis to make me realize I should know better. "This is my third trip here."

I didn't think that clarified much, but I didn't ask any more questions.

"Although I could be wrong, there are two mother bears that have dens within a ten mile radius of Cloudcroft. One of the mothers has two young bears that should be leaving home soon. The other only has the one cub."

"No daddy bears?" I asked.

"Of course, but they're more nomadic. I've only seen one."

"Sounds like you've put a lot into it."

"It's the fun part," she said.

She moved down to the end of the counter and talked to the bartender for a while. I finished my beer and got Will's attention to pay my tab. Kay drifted in my direction, shadowing Will more than approaching me.

I left the bar and found a menu at the entrance to the restaurant. I studied it and glanced around inside. A couple of large windows faced west and might provide fantastic views when the weather was better. A young couple sat at a table next to one of the windows. I looked up and saw Kay leaving the bar.

"Say, don't take this wrong, but if you're going to have dinner alone in the restaurant, can I join you? I eat a lot of meals here alone," she said.

"Sure," I said and hoped she didn't hear the lack of enthusiasm in my voice.

"And I'll pay for my own meal."

"Okay."

"Hi, Kay," a young hostess said from halfway across the room. The hostess had her black hair cut as short as mine.

"Abby, how's your day been?" Kay asked.

"Don't ask," Abby said. She looked at me, "Are you two together?"

"Yes," I answered.

"Follow me," she said, but grabbed Kay by the hand and pulled her next to her. The two led me to the table.

They talked in low whispers and giggled all the way. I thought I heard Abby say, "At least he's a little younger than the last one."

The dinner turned out more pleasant than I expected. Kay did most the talking, so for the most part, I only had to listen. Being there early allowed us to have quick service, and I thoroughly enjoyed my steak.

While the conversation touched on a variety of topics, and most of which were easily forgettable, I enjoyed her telling me about the history of the lodge.

"Do you know much about this hotel?" she asked.

"A little," I admitted. "I glanced at the brochure."

"Do you know it's supposed to be haunted?"

"No, but I imagine most of these old hotels are," I said.

"The ghost's name is Rebecca. She worked here as a chambermaid about a hundred years ago. She disappeared one night after her fiancé found her in bed with another man."

"That was her picture in the lounge, right?" I asked.

Kay nodded. "It's also who the restaurant was named after. Beautiful, wasn't she?"

"Sure was. I'd rather have her haunting me than some scary looking thing."

"You and ninety percent of the male guests who stay here," Kay said. "This lodge was originally constructed in 1899. You know New Mexico wasn't even a state then. It burned down a few years after it was built, but it was almost immediately rebuilt. Since then it has been remodeled and improved, but its general appearance has remained the same. You could've rented a room for twelve dollars a week back then."

"Wish we still could," I said. She impressed me how she could rattle off the facts.

"Conrad Hilton owned the lodge for a while, and Judy Garland and Clark Gable have stayed here. There are miles of hiking trails. I love it here," she said.

"So, did you choose to come here because of the bears or because of the lodge?"

"I didn't know this place existed until my advisor suggested I do my research in these mountains. The Sacramento Mountains are somewhat cut off from the rest of the Rockies, so the animals that live in these mountains have evolved in partial isolation."

By the time we parted ways after dinner, I could see why the staff seemed fond of Kay. I liked her, too, and if I ever saw her returning from a trek in the woods, I'd probably be like the others and ask her if she saw the cub again.

CHAPTER 7

The next morning, I awoke with a slight headache. I only had a little wine with dinner, so I attributed the headache to the thin atmosphere. The air in the room felt fresh and cool, and I looked forward to a day of exploring the small town and the forest around it. After grabbing a cup of coffee in the lodge, I set out on foot to find a coffee shop or a café. It didn't take me long to find a small place with a neon light that flashed "donuts".

The server gave me some advice on a good hiking trail that was nearby. She explained, and I later verified, that one could walk around the entire city of Cloudcroft in an hour. Not that I walked around it, but from the donut shop I could see the west end of Cloudcroft, and I walked the main road to the east edge of the city in fifteen minutes.

I found the trail out of Cloudcroft that the server in the donut shop had recommended. It immediately took me up a steep hill and into the trees. After about a half mile, I came to a spot that provided a good view of Cloudcroft and the surrounding area.

The trail had been cut through the forest over the years to such an extent that I had no trouble following it. I had the thought that it might have been widened in recent years to accommodate snowmobiles and cross country skiers. I hiked for another half hour before stopping to rest. The up and down terrain tired me out quicker than I thought it would.

As I sat there, I heard some rustling in the woods. I couldn't see anything, but some creature was definitely out there crunching through underbrush. My conversation with Kay came to mind, and I decided I had walked far enough. I got up and as quietly as I could, started walking back toward town. I never saw an animal, and if it never saw me, that was okay. More than likely, I had heard a deer or a fox, but the idea that a large bear might come charging out of the bushes toward me was enough to motivate me to retreat.

My hike back to the overlook seemed shorter than my trek into the forest. It's possible I walked a little faster. I stopped at the small clearing and once again studied the small town below me. My concerns about encountering a bear vanished when I saw a large brown pickup driving slowly down the main street in Cloudcroft. I knew it was the same pickup before it came to a stop and retraced its path back into town.

I'd be lying if I claimed that the sight of the pickup didn't send a small twinge of fear down my spine, but more than anything else, it made me mad. I began to rehash the question to who had tipped them off on my being in Fabens? It had to be someone in law enforcement. While I had only talked to Detective Kent and Deputy Luna, the desk sergeant knew about me, and my presence had been documented in the case files. Anyone with an interest in the case and access to the files would have been able to find out about me. The doctor came to mind, too. Was it possible he tried to keep Brown alive so he could be further questioned?

I also wondered for whom the people in the brown pickup worked.

At some point in the next week to ten days, I knew I would be involved in some sort of a confrontation. Knowing that, I decided to make initial contact on my terms if possible. I started down the hill into town while watching the pickup turn off the main road onto the street that would take it to the lodge. I didn't think I would reach the intersection before the pickup truck drove away, but somehow I made it to only about twenty steps shy of the corner when the pickup came to a stop in front of me.

I waved and motioned them to follow me into the same donut shop I'd been in an hour or so before. Not knowing what they would do, I turned and went inside.

"Back for more?" the young woman behind the counter asked. She had served me earlier, and while the place had a handful of customers then, only two young men, possibly twins, occupied the place now. The two guys leaned against the counter and displayed more interest in the young woman than in me or the donuts.

"Sure. How about another cinnamon cake donut and a coffee?"

I took my order and sat at a table for four. My chair faced the front window. I didn't know if anyone in the truck would come in, but I wanted to get some pictures of whoever did. The photos might take away some of the advantage these guys had. I didn't expect any serious trouble here in the open, and besides, I've been given a week.

The brown pickup pulled up right in front of the window. All four doors to the pickup opened, and four very unpleasant looking characters climbed out. I took a couple of pictures through the window and put away my cell phone before they entered. When they entered, they ignored the counter and came straight at me.

As calmly as I could, I motioned for them to join me at my table. Two of them sat down at my table, and the other two sat at an adjacent table. All four looked-liked they had never learned to smile. While I knew it wasn't nice to profile, the fact that these four looked like they might have driven straight in from a Mexican drug cartel anniversary party didn't escape me. My confidence in a peaceful discussion started to shrink.

"You need to come with us," the one sitting next to me said. His nose had been broken at least one time before and now pointed a little to his left. I tried not to stare at it. "Hey! You hear me!"

I imagine everyone in the building heard him. "Of course. You know your boss said that I had a week."

"He thinks maybe we should help motivate you."

"You already have. You can tell him I got the message." Even though the odds for anyone going up against four opponents are dismal at best, I started to assess the situation. I had a size advantage on each, and I had my new friend loaded and in a holster under my jacket. On the other hand, size advantage may help against one or possibly two at a time, but not four. I also doubted that these four came unarmed. "Why don't you call him right now? I'll talk to him."

"You're not talking to no one but us. Let's go," the same guy did the talking.

I shook my head, and despite the usual suggested behavior when you're surrounded by man eating predators, I maintained eye contact with him.

In a flash, he yanked a knife out of some pocket or his belt and tried to press it close to my neck. I slid my chair backwards out of reach and stood up. The man to my left took that for a signal to pounce. He almost managed to grab me, but I moved to where the chair was between us.

All three of the others were now at their feet and maneuvered to surround me. That's when they made their first mistake. One of the men, who might have been nicknamed "Scarface" since he had a three inch scar that ran up the side of his face, positioned himself between me and the donut counter. He pulled a revolver out from his belt and started to aim it at me about the same time one of the young men standing at the counter smashed his wrist with a baseball bat.

The man screamed as the bones in his wrist snapped, and the revolver dropped to the floor. I turned back to watch the other three men in time to see all three now pulling out their own hand guns.

"Hey! Don't do this!" I shouted. I felt instant dread for the poor guy who had tried to help me. The three men had their eyes fixed at the targets behind me and didn't show any sign that they had heard me shout.

I started to reach for my pistol. One of the three fired, and the room exploded in a series of loud blasts. All three of the men appeared to jump backwards as parts of their bodies disintegrated in front of me as they fell. Two fell quietly, while one screamed in agony and squirmed on the floor.

I left my pistol in the holster and held my hands out away from my body to make sure anyone left standing in the room could see my hands. Someone whimpered behind me, but the loud gunshots had muffled my hearing. I turned around and saw the young woman comforting the man who had swung the baseball bat. He had taken a bullet to the right shoulder. I saw a shotgun on the counter next to the two of them. The other man still held onto his shotgun. His eyes bounced wildly around the room.

"Are you okay?" I asked the man with the shotgun.

"Yes," his voice squeaked, or maybe it was my hearing. I thought he might be about to hyperventilate or pass out.

"Here, sit down," I shoved a chair over next to him.

He sat down. I thought about asking him for the shotgun, but didn't press it. Instead, I walked over to the four men on the floor. Only one showed any sign of life, but I didn't think he'd last long. The man whose wrist had been broken by the baseball bat had also been shot. I didn't know if he had made a move to get his revolver, or if he had been shot in the brief chaos despite being unarmed. I didn't really care, it was simply my curiosity.

I looked back at my three rescuers. "Have you called the police?"

None of them responded, but they didn't need to. I turned and saw the flashing lights of a patrol car as it stopped in front. One or more of the shotgun blasts had shattered the front window. Two policemen climbed out of the car. They paused to study the area around them and to look at us through what was left of the window. When they came in, they moved with caution and had their weapons drawn.

"Put the shotgun on the floor, Fitz. We've got the situation now," one of the policemen said.

I heard the gun as it hit the floor behind me.

The two policemen did their best not to disturb anything while they walked around the room.

"This one's still alive," one of the cops said. "I think."

"Is an ambulance coming?" the young woman asked.

"Gerry's hurt."

"It's coming. It'll be here soon," the one who had asked Fitz to drop the shotgun said. "How bad is it, Gerry?"

"I'll live," he said. His voice didn't carry much confidence.

"Those assholes started it. They attacked this guy with a knife, and then when we tried to stop it, they shot Gerry," Fitz said.

"Fitz, you okay?"

"I think so."

"And you, Suzi?" the policeman asked.

"I'm okay."

She sounded better than the two men. I figured the guys were in their early twenties, and she was right around twenty. It dawned on me that she had been the one who used the shotgun on the counter.

An ambulance came to a stop out front, and I could see people start to crowd around on the edge of the street trying to see what had happened in the donut shop.

"We just stopped this guy from getting killed," Suzi said. "Those guys started everything." She looked at me to say something.

The police turned their attention to me, too. "Are you okay?" The one cop who had been doing all the talking asked.

"Yes, thanks to them," I said and motioned toward the counter.

"What caused all this?"

"Long story, but bottom line is that they think I can help them find something."

"Can't help them now," he said. "After the medics check you out, you'll have to come with me."

"I'm fine."

"You're bleeding," he said and touched his left ear.

I touched mine and didn't feel anything. He shook his head and indicated my other ear. I felt it, and my fingers came away with blood.

"Maybe your shoulder, too."

I felt my shoulder and found a spot next to my neck where I was oozing a little blood.

"It doesn't look serious," the policeman said.

Within five minutes, more first responders than could fit into the place had arrived. By then, someone had collected all our driver's licenses, and three of the four of us we were sitting in chairs against a wall. Gerry had been taken out to an ambulance that I saw drive away.

"Sorry about your ear," Suzi said. "I think I did that."

I couldn't help but smile. "So you and Fitz had the shotguns?"

"Yes. We keep them behind the counter. Cloudcroft is a peaceful place, but for some reason twice in the past year, we've been robbed and once a couple guys got into a fight and broke up the place. We got the shotguns after that, but never used them before. We've always had the baseball bat."

"I'm surprised you all jumped in to help, but I'm glad you did."

"Gerry asked for the bat when we realized you were in trouble," she said.

"Guess it was obvious."

"I think he struck the guy's arm without thinking. It was a reaction to seeing the pistol. Once he did that, I saw the others go ballistic. Luckily, Fitz saw the same thing. I tossed him one of the shotguns, and I grabbed the other. When they drew their weapons and one of them shot Gerry, I reacted without thinking. I imagine Fitz did the same."

I looked past Suzi at Fitz, but his head was against the wall, and his eyes were shut. I couldn't imagine that he was asleep, but he didn't give any indication that he heard us.

"I nicked you on my last shot. I thought I might hit you, but that guy was about to shoot someone. You were so close. I hoped the spread would be small. Luckily, it was."

The more I thought about my ear, the more it started to sting. With my typical male bias, I had a hard time imagining Suzi picking up and tossing a shotgun to anyone, much less keeping cool enough to take out two armed men with a second shotgun. Even now, she appeared to be handling the situation well. Fitz showed a lot more of the effects of the adrenalin rush all of us had experienced.

One more moment of excitement came when they asked one of the younger deputies who arrived late to take me to the substation to get my statement. As we approached his vehicle, I mentioned to him that I had a pistol on me. In the chaos of the crime scene and intermittent arrivals of law enforcement and medical personnel, no one had checked me or inquired if I had a weapon.

The poor deputy froze in place, but only for a brief moment. "Hands out!" he shouted a little louder than necessary.

"It hasn't been used," I said, while I extended my hands away from my body. "I doubt if it's ever been fired. I bought it new yesterday."

The deputy drew his own weapon, but thankfully didn't aim it at me. "Slowly hand it to me. Barrel toward the ground." He extended his free hand, and I handed him the Sig.

"Damn," he said.

"Thought you should know before I climbed into your car."

The next four hours turned tedious. My statement turned into a full discussion of everything that had happened in the last forty eight hours. They made a copy of the letter Stu had sent me, and after my repeated request, they contacted Deputy Rose Luna with the El Paso County Sheriff' office.

By the time they dropped me off at the lodge, it was already late afternoon. I had missed lunch and couldn't decide if I needed a beer or a nap.

Kay saw me enter the building and hurried toward me waving her hand to get my attention. She didn't need to, as we were the only two people in the open foyer. Her face, flushed with excitement, contrasted with her black jeans and black sweater.

"Jim, I heard you were involved in that terrible incident this morning. Are you okay?" Her eyes focused on my bandaged ear.

"Yeah, I'm okay."

"I think they might have been the same men who damaged your car."

"What?"

"No one told you?" she asked.

"No."

"Come on, I'll show you." She started walking, and I followed her out of the lodge and toward the Mustang. "I saw them do it. It was just by chance."

I figured her seeing it was by chance, not their doing the damage. "What did they do?"

"Here, you'll see," she said and pointed to the Mustang.

I couldn't see the damage until I got closer. One of the men had used something, perhaps a crowbar, to break my driver's side tail light. I didn't see any other damage. I leaned in close to inspect the damage. A small dent scarred the car's body above the tail light. I could live with that, but I would have to get the tail light fixed.

"I was way over there," Kay pointed to a hill top that looked like it could be a mile away. "I was searching for any sign of my bears. I was using my binoculars. By chance, I looked at the hotel and saw this brown pickup truck parked behind your car. I didn't know it was your car at the time. What got my attention was this guy standing next to your car with what looked like a stick. All of a sudden, he struck the car twice. I could see the glass spray from the brake light."

"It was the same guys, unless there were two brown pickup trucks carrying thugs around Cloudcroft today."

"I couldn't believe it when I saw it," she said.

"Well, they got what was coming to them."

"They should never have messed with Suzi."

"What do you mean?" I asked.

"She's like a state shooting champion. Someone said she almost got into the Olympics or something. I've seen the two boys, but I know Suzi better. I think they also shot in the same gun clubs with her. Didn't you see all her trophies?"

"No."

"It's her mom's place."

"The donut shop?"

"Yes," she said.

"I guess it won't do much good to report this to the police."

"Oh, we already did. That's how I found out it was your car. I came straight back and told Fred, and he called the police. I think they got the call about all the shooting while they were still here."

It irritated me that they had done this to my car, but due to the circumstances I didn't feel any need for revenge. No way I'd be pressing charges. The last of the four had passed away sometime during my interview at the substation. Although the police didn't tell me anything, I got the impression that the guy didn't say anything of value before he died.

I wondered if any of the four phoned in that they had found me and reported where I was staying. I didn't want to have to start looking for a different place to spend the night.

"Are you okay?" Kay asked.

"Yeah, why?"

"You looked like you zoned out for a minute."

"Oh, I was just thinking."

"It must have been terribly frightening."

"It happened so fast I didn't have much time to feel anything until it was over," I said.

"I would have had a heart attack," she said.

The vision of the man's face being ripped apart as dozens of pellets tried to remove the man's head from his neck raced across my mind.

"It'll trouble me for a while," I said.

I wondered how much she knew about the shootout. The initial police statements usually only included the basics. Of course, I had left the donut shop hours ago. Since then, I imagine half the town had gone by to see whatever carnage they could. The mayor may have given a speech by now.

"I guess you didn't need to see the damage to your car right now. I'm sorry. It seemed important at the time."

"Don't be sorry. This is something I would've wanted to know about sooner rather than later."

CHAPTER 8

After thanking Kay for telling me about the damage to my car, I went inside and showered. The injury to my ear consisted of a small tear to the edge of the lobe which the medics fixed with butterfly bandages and then with a larger bandage that covered most of my ear for added protection. My shoulder needed less attention and simply sported a large flat bandage.

I knew they said something about keeping the area dry for a while, and I gave a half-hearted effort at following their instructions, but I needed the shower. Afterwards, I crawled under the covers, and despite the day's excitement, fell right to sleep.

Someone laughing loudly in the hallway woke me about an hour later. I crawled out of the cocoon I had made with the blanket. If I didn't, I knew I'd end up sleeping until morning. I couldn't remember having lunch and recalled that I didn't get to eat that last donut. For some reason, that now made me angry.

I dressed, first making sure that I hadn't bled through any of my bandages, and left the room. Checking my phone as I walked down the hall, I realized I had not turned it on after my time with the police. After doing so, I saw that I missed a call from a number I didn't recognize. A slight rush of adrenalin occurred before I rationalized that if the person who had me followed had called, a number wouldn't be showing on the phone. Still, since the caller did not leave a message on the phone, I didn't return the call.

Unlike my first evening, a noisy crowd occupied the bar. I considered going somewhere else, but I didn't know of another nearby option. As I approached the counter, the room grew quiet. I glanced around and saw that most eyes were aimed back at me. Too stubborn to turn around and leave, I leaned against the bar and glanced down to make sure I hadn't forgotten my shoes, pants, or shirt. Nothing was unzipped, so I came to the obvious conclusion these were mostly locals who had heard about all the excitement and had come to see one of the strangers involved in the shootout.

I ordered a beer and watched the people behind me in the large mirror behind the bar. I saw one older woman in a blue and red striped sweater take a picture of me with her phone. I saw a young man at a table for four crowded with six people stand up and start walking in my direction.

"How's your ear?" he asked when he got close.

"You're the guy who fixed it for me, right?" I said and extended my hand.

"Yep, that was me," he said. He shook my hand and did a half turn with his head to ensure his friends were watching.

"Well, thanks again for everything."

"Just doing my job," he said with that half turn of his head. "Let me know if it starts bleeding or anything."

"Sure," I said, even though I didn't know his name.

"I better get back to my friends." He left, and while I couldn't see his face, I could see all his friends smiling at him. I'm sure someone was giving him a thumbs-up gesture.

Kay walked into the bar wearing grey leggings and a black jacket zipped up to her neck. She strolled over to a couple sipping wine in the back of the room. I watched as the couple at the table pointed up at me. Kay saw me and talked another minute or two before she left them and headed in my direction.

"Will, I hope you aren't charging this man for his drinks," Kay said.

Will smiled back at her, but didn't respond.

"You do know that you're the reason for the crowd here tonight?"

"I figured that out, but it doesn't make any sense. I didn't do anything," I said.

"If Suzi, Fitz, or Gerry were out at a local restaurant tonight and people knew it, I imagine most of this crowd would be there, but best guess is that those three are at home."

"Lucky them," I said. "Care for a drink?"

Before she could answer, Will placed a glass of white wine in front of her.

"Would I be correct in guessing that you didn't check Facebook today?" she asked.

"I'd say it was a safe bet. Why?"

"The incident has been on the national news. Not much has been released about it yet, but enough that my parents, my advisor, and a bunch of my friends have contacted me via Facebook to make sure I was okay. Not my parents, they called. I've friended a couple people from here, and I can tell you the locals have talked about nothing else today on their pages. They're even debating whether the guys were from a Colombian Drug Cartel or some Mexican group. Someone's even claiming that you have something that they claim is theirs."

"What? How would..." I stopped talking. Earlier that day, I had told the half dozen different law enforcement people who had interviewed me that the men who attacked us at the donut shop and whoever was behind them believed something similar to that. One of the investigators may have mentioned that information to someone they shouldn't have, and now the news was being bounced around on Facebook.

"Is that what you're doing, looking for something?"

"Believe me, the less you know about all this, the better it is for you. These guys are dangerous and not very rational."

"Why are you still here? I'd be hiding somewhere."

"I'm fairly sure they know where I live. Besides, once they find or someone else finds what they want, they'll lose interest in me."

"I don't understand," she said.

"I'm not sure I understand it either. How smart are you?"

She laughed. "Oh, I don't know. How smart do you want me to be?"

"Well, you're finishing your PhD, so you're probably a lot smarter than me."

"No, I -"

"Don't downplay your intelligence, and despite what I said a minute ago about your being in danger, I guess by tomorrow most everyone in town will know about as much as I do."

"I don't understand," she said.

"How about I buy you dinner tonight, and you can use that big brain of yours to help me resolve my dilemma?"

"If all I have to do is use my brain, then I'm in," she said with an arched eyebrow.

"You don't think this crowd will follow us, do you?"

"Some may. Most are too cheap." She took a big gulp of her wine.

"Don't rush," I said.

"Will you still be leaving tomorrow?"

"I'll need to touch base with the police and whoever is in charge of this whole thing tomorrow. If they say I can go, then I probably will. I live in state, so they can always find me." I realized when I said it my mind thought more of the people who were following me than the police.

"There's not much of a police presence up here," she said.

"I know. By tomorrow, the state or even the feds may have taken charge. That's one of the reasons they wanted me to stick around."

We finished our drinks and left the bar. Most of the eyes in the room watched us leave.

"I think your being with me might hurt your reputation," I said.

She laughed. "I imagine there are a more than a few people up here who believe the worst about me. I've shared dinners, lunches, drinks with most of the people in that room. If I stuck to myself every day I've spent in Cloudcroft, I would have gone mad. More than once, the same married men have shown up at the lodge offering to buy me dinner."

"That's not good," I said.

"It was a learning experience. The staff has been amazingly protective, and I've learned from whom I need to stay away. Nothing bad has happened, but I imagine a few of the residents think I'm really here to steal someone's husband or pay for my education the old fashioned way."

I liked Kay. I found her easy to talk to and even kind of fun to be with, but I also wondered if she enjoyed the notoriety.

During dinner, I filled in the few blanks that Kay hadn't

already learned from Facebook. I showed her the letter, and she wrote down the numbers. If she was working for the cartel, so be it. Maybe they'd find the briefcase and leave me alone.

We parted ways after dinner, and while I hadn't done much besides the walk in the woods, I returned to my room and after reading for a while, I fell asleep. Shortly after dawn, I woke from a deep sleep with a start. Someone had jiggled the room's door handle or had bumped against it. I stood up, still trying to get the last of sleep's cobwebs out of my mind. It might have been a dream, but I approached the door to listen. The glass in the door's peep hole had been chipped at some point in the past, and enough moisture had worked its way into it that I felt I was looking through a prism into the fog.

I stood there listening. I started to think that it might have been a dream when someone tapped on the door. I glanced at the radio clock on the small dresser. Seven thirty in the morning was early for a visitor.

"Jim," a woman's voice came from the hall too softly for me to recognize who she might be.

I had only met a few women in Cloudcroft, and the only one well enough to call me Jim would be Kay. It didn't make any sense for her to be coming around this early.

"Yes," I answered.

"It's me, Rose. Can we talk?"

"One second," I grabbed my jeans off the floor and slipped them on before I opened the door. "Good morning, I didn't expect to see you here. Come in."

She did, and I closed the door behind her.

"How are you?" she asked.

"I'm okay, and you?"

She looked at the bandage on my ear and set a small backpack on the bed before answering. "I'm good, but I'm concerned."

"I hope not about me."

"Of course about you, but it's bigger than that. Someone assaulted Liz Graham in her home last night."

"Damn, that's not good. How is she?" I asked.

"She's going to live, but they smacked her around. Broke her jaw and threatened to do a lot more to her."

"How did they-"

"That's why I'm here. Obviously, someone is leaking information. Call me naïve, but this is the first time I've been around anything like this, and it's got me a little pissed."

"It doesn't have to be someone who works with you."

"I know. There are a lot of possibilities. I've seen deputies and the city cops warn family members or friends about things now and then, but it's usually over small things. That's to be expected, but this is going too far. Whoever is doing this is going to get someone killed, and they know it."

"This could be leaking at the fed level," I said.

She nodded. "I didn't get the call, the city guys responded to Graham. I went by the hospital to see her. She looked bad. I had already heard about what happened up here. I was too agitated to sleep. About three in the morning, I gave up trying, sent a text to my boss reminding him that today and tomorrow were my off days and I decided to take a day of vacation to make it three days straight."

"Besides buying me breakfast, what do you plan on doing up here?"

"I want to see the four men who were following you. I want

to make sure ballistics share what they get with us."

"Think one of these guys shot Stu?"

"I doubt it, but it would be a lucky coincidence. I also want to make sure you get home in one piece," she said.

"I don't think they'll leave me alone, but I imagine they'll be more discreet next time." My comment made me wonder about Rose's presence.

"By the way, your gun is in the pack."

"How'd you get it?"

"I stopped by the Sheriff's office to make contact and one of the deputies had it. He said he had been instructed to return it to you when he got off shift. I told him I'd save him the trip. I thought you said you weren't carrying."

"I wasn't until two days ago. When I called you and told you about the pickup following me out of Texas, I decided it might be a good idea."

"It is," she said. "Where can we get this breakfast you talked about?"

"Downstairs."

"Can I leave my stuff in your room?"

"Sure," I said, even though I hadn't see anything but the backpack for her to leave.

I washed my face and put on a sweatshirt before we departed the room.

"This is an interesting place," she said while we walked down the hall.

"I imagine it has a lot of stories it could tell."

She paused at a couple pictures before we reached the dining room. As we walked in, I saw Kay at a table not far from the entrance. She saw Rose with me and her eyebrows immediately got a little higher.

Rose noticed Kay's reaction and when we sat down at a table, she leaned in close to me. "I hope my presence isn't going to cause you any trouble with the young lady."

I couldn't help but smile. "Do you mind if she joins us?"

Rose looked at me a little confused. I thought I might have seen a slight flare of anger or maybe jealousy.

"No."

"You'll find her interesting, and by the way, she's just a friend." I turned my head toward Kay and called to her. She looked up.

"Kay, come join us."

Kay stood up and walked the few paces to our table.

"I'd hate to disturb you," Kay said.

"You won't be," Rose said a little less sincere than necessary.

"Please sit down. If you're still hungry, Rose is buying."

Both women looked at me, and I figured my continued teasing of Rose might be a bad idea.

"Okay, no more of me trying to be funny. Rose, this is Kay. She is a grad student here in Cloudcroft studying the bears. She also knows a lot of what goes on around here. Kay, this is Deputy Rose Luna. Rose is working a murder down in Texas that may be related to yesterday's incident."

"Is all that related to the briefcase you're trying to find?" Kay asked.

Rose looked at me curiously.

"Yes, at least I think so. The whole town knows about it, Rose."

"You should check out Facebook," Kay said.

A waiter interrupted our conversation.

"I just arrived a few minutes ago," Rose said.

"I know," Kay said. "I only gave Jim my raised eyebrow look to tease him. After all, walking in for breakfast with a pretty lady on your arm could mean a lot of things, Jim."

Rose honed in on the "I know" part of Kay's remark. "How did you know?" she asked.

"I stop by the registration desk each morning to say hi to the clerk. It's something I like to do, and it's usually Fred. He just about lives there. He mentioned you were here."

"One big family here," I said. "Kay, show Rose the pictures of the cubs."

For the next fifteen minutes, the two looked at the photos on Kay's phone and talked about bears. Rose's stiffness toward Kay dissipated. Our breakfast arrived, and I decided to change the subject.

"Anything more on Facebook this morning, Kay?"

"Oh yeah, the event yesterday is still all the people here in Cloudcroft are talking about. Everyone claims to know somebody who knows about it. One person even started an online place to donate money to get the donut shop fixed up."

"What would we do without Facebook?" Rose said.

"I know, it's crazy," Kay said. "It's even stirred up the gun control debate. Some argue that having guns is what saved everyone there, while others argue that no one should have had a gun to start with."

"How do you feel about that?" Rose asked looking straight at me.

"Mixed feelings," I said.

"Cop out," Rose said.

"I'd rather have a bear eat me than shoot one," Kay said.

I felt like saying that I've heard that before, but kept silent. Rose looked like she wanted to say something, too, but didn't.

"I'd better get going," Kay said. "I didn't get anything done yesterday. Be careful today, Jim."

"Now there goes a very independent young woman," Rose said as Kay left the dining room.

"Amen. She's smart, too."

"She's getting her PhD. When I was her age, I was still working on my Bachelor Degree," Rose said.

"You seem pretty smart to me."

"Street smart, maybe, but I couldn't tell a brown bear from a black bear."

That made me smile, until I wondered if I could. "I guess I need to see if I could stay one more night here."

"Don't you think you should head home?"

"I'd like to, Rose, but I have a feeling I'm going to be asked a bunch more questions today, and I need to get my car fixed."

"What happened to your car?"

"The same people that followed me to the café busted my tail light for good measure. I think they can fix it here in town."

"Seems petty that they would bust up your car," she said.

I shrugged, and ate the last of my eggs. Rose had her coffee refilled.

"You've got to be beat," I said.

"I'm tired, but I'll be okay. It's too early for check-in, when we get done here can I use your room to freshen up?"

"Of course. Like I said, I need to get my car fixed anyway. I may have to drive into Alamogordo. I also expect to get called in for some more questioning. The room is all yours this morning."

I left Rose in the room with the key and stopped by the front desk on the way out.

"Fred, where can I get my tail light repaired in Cloudcroft?"

"What kind of car you got again?" he asked.

"Mustang."

He picked up his phone, and after looking at a sheet of paper full of names and numbers, he dialed a number.

"Jay, is that you?" he said and paused for a minute. "I've got a guest here at the lodge who needs a tail light replaced." After another pause, "A Mustang... What?... One minute." Fred offered me the phone.

I took the phone, and after passing on the year and other information he needed about my car, I discovered my good luck. Jay utilized a van service that ran everyday out of Alamogordo and brought a variety of items to merchants in Cloudcroft. He thought he could still catch the driver before the van left Alamogordo, and said he would have the part in a half hour.

"It's not far from here," Fred said when I asked him how to get to Jay's Auto Repair. "But then nothing is," he laughed at his own comment.

Jay's was situated down a side street that peeled off the main road as it entered Cloudcroft from the west. I knew that even with Jay's optimistic thirty minute arrival time, I had beaten the part by twenty minutes, but I figured the earlier I got in line for service the quicker I would get out. As it turned out, I was the line.

Jay squatted in the garage tinkering with a jack. When I got out of my car, he stood up and limped toward me. His grey hair was cut close to his head and the brown skin on his face had more wrinkles than a good mystery. He wore a typical, denim mechanic's work shirt that had an embroidered "Jay" above his pocket.

"You the guy I just talked to on the phone?" he asked.

"Yes. Any luck getting that part?"

"Oh yeah, caught him in the nick of time."

"Will you be able to fix it this morning?"

"Oh, I can most likely work it into my schedule," he grinned. "Come on in, and I'll write up the work order."

Jay's didn't have a waiting room or a public coffee pot, so I left the Mustang and walked back to the main road. A phone call summoning me to the local law enforcement substation resolved my dilemma with how to kill the next hour or two. I turned down the offer for someone to come and get me. The ten minute walk would do me good.

At the substation, an FBI agent by the name of Roger Stillman greeted me like an old friend. I couldn't remember him, so I took his friendly enthusiasm as his way of showing we were on the same team. He asked about my ear, if I was able to sleep last night, and how I liked the lodge. He was good, and while none of this foreplay was necessary, I actually did start liking the guy.

"Agent Stillman," I said.

"Please, please call me Roger," he said. His smooth voice and casual smile indicated to me that he had been doing this kind of thing for a while. He looked to be in his late thirties, looked fit, and had the clothing and haircut of someone who took his job with the FBI seriously.

"Roger, what can I do for you? I've already told my story a dozen times."

"Do you know who these guys were? The four that followed you from Fabens?"

"No."

"No, no, I don't mean their names. I mean who they work for?"

"Still no," I said.

"They're muscle for a Mexican drug cartel. The cartel is second rate, always being pushed around by the big boys, and always vying for support from the big boys. However, they are far from insignificant, and are extremely dangerous."

"You don't have to convince me."

"I know. We know who you are, and that's one of the reasons we want you to help us."

"Help you?" I asked. "How?"

"We want you to find the briefcase."

Resisting the urge to scream that I had no clue as to how to do that, I asked, "How?"

"I know, I know, the letter doesn't offer up much help, but we've got a lot of people studying the letter. We're back tracking Mr. Brown's movements, his phone records, etc. It's only a matter of time before we know where the briefcase is."

"Then why do you need me?"

"You're already on the inside. They expect you to find it," Agent Stillman said like it should have been obvious to me.

"If your people figure it out, why not go get the briefcase without anyone knowing?"

"Believe me, we've discussed that, but the decision was made that there was much more to gain by having you do it. Besides, you are already on the hot seat. Our involvement will make it safer for you."

I wasn't too sure about that, but I knew that with or without their involvement, I was indeed on the hot seat.

"What do you know about this Deputy Rose Luna?" he asked.

His question surprised me. "What do you mean?"

"She came up here asking about you."

"I know. She's at the lodge right now. Why?"

"Are you two an item?" he asked with his face forming a sly smile.

"No, why?"

"We were just wondering."

"Do you suspect her of anything?" I asked.

"No, I wouldn't say that. We do find her following you up here interesting, especially after the other people who were following you were killed."

"Have you checked into her?" I asked.

"Yes, she has a stellar record, top notch, but still, we find it interesting."

I had my own theories, but didn't share them. "How is our cooperation supposed to work?"

My question brought a big grin to his face. I began to see myself as a big, fat catfish that swallowed the hook and was now destined for the fire pan. Over the next thirty minutes I discovered how involved the feds wanted to be. I signed a number of forms authorizing them to monitor my movements, my phone calls, my credit card purchases, and put a tracker on my car.

"Do you have any idea how the guys who followed you out of Fabens knew about you?" he asked after all the paperwork had been completed.

"No."

"Although I would have to get this approved, I would like to have Deputy Luna remain with you throughout the next week. How would you feel about this?"

"I think it's more important how she would feel about it," I said.

He nodded. "It would be all right by you?"

"Yes."

"Okay. I think it might make things safer for you."

"And you could more easily keep tabs on her," I added.

He grinned and nodded. "It's just a thought. Like I said, I would need to get it approved."

When I left the substation and started my walk back to Jay's, I had to keep telling myself that for twenty years I had sat on the other side of that table and had asked others for help. I hadn't made a big mistake agreeing to cooperate. I had increased my chances of surviving a very dangerous situation. By the time I reached the garage, I still hadn't convinced myself.

My Mustang sat out front of the garage looking as good as new. Jay beamed with pride while I inspected his work. He had the invoice for the repairs in his hand, and it was only after I studied it, that I realized his smile most likely had more to do with the outrageous charges than the work he had done.

Of course, I could smile, too. One of the forms I signed was an agreement that said the FBI would cover all my expenses relating to my lodging, transportation, and meals for the next week.

CHAPTER 9

I stopped at the front desk and asked Fred for a second key to my room. With a barely perceptible smile, he handed me another key. I imagined Kay would get an earful now.

My motivation wasn't as romantic as Fred might have wanted it to be. I had been gone longer than expected and figured Rose could be gone or asleep. If she had left the key with Fred, he would have said something.

I entered the room trying not to disturb her. As I had guessed, she was all but hidden under the covers and breathing heavily. I picked up the small backpack and opened it. The Sig I had bought a couple days earlier along with an empty clip and a zip lock bag containing a number of bullets were the backpacks only contents.

With the backpack in hand, I left the room and went back down to the hotel lobby. The lodge had a couple of rooms that were set aside for meetings. I selected one and after reloading the pistol, I took the letter out to study it for the umpteenth time. Nothing made sense to me. I sat there for twenty minutes not making any progress before my phone rang.

"Were you just in the room?" Rose asked.

"Yes. You were sleeping, so I didn't want to bother you."

"I'm sorry, but I was more exhausted than I thought. I meant to sleep for an hour or so. I'm up now if you want to get your room back."

"Okay, see you in a little bit," I said.

She must not have realized how close I was, because even

though I knocked before opening the door, I still caught her darting into the bathroom carrying most of her clothes.

"Sorry about that," I said.

She didn't respond right away. "How'd your car turn out?" she finally asked.

"Just like new."

"Have you heard from anyone yet?"

"Yes," I said. "Met with an Agent Roger Stillman today."

"DEA or FBI?"

"FBI."

"Can you believe they want me to keep looking for the briefcase?"

The bathroom door opened and Rose walked out in a pair of jeans and a dark gray sweatshirt. I glanced around the room and saw a small suitcase in the corner that I hadn't noticed earlier.

"I'm not really moving in," she said, noticing my discovery of the suitcase.

I didn't comment. I didn't know how I wanted to respond.

"It doesn't surprise me that they want you to keep looking."

"Guess it didn't surprise me much either," I said.

"You know, it's easy to think the briefcase is full of money and nothing more. What if there's a ledger in the briefcase with names or other information that is important for the original owners to keep from getting compromised."

She was right. Now that she said it, it seemed obvious to me. I should have considered it before, but my mind had focused more on what could be of value to Stu and more importantly his wife. That would only be the money. However, a list of names could be even more important to the cartel.

"You mean names of people getting payoffs?" I asked.

"Could be, or it could be names of the middlemen, or others in their organization. The money would be important, but what if there are names of some important people in that briefcase?"

"Excellent point."

"See? And no PhD for me. What are they going to do to keep you safe or help you find it?"

"They have their experts trying to figure out what we're missing in the letter Stu sent us."

"I hope they figure it out," Rose said. "I'd love to know what we're missing."

"Me, too."

"Maybe invisible ink?" she said and smiled.

"Could be anything as far as I'm concerned. I'll just be happy to get this over with."

"You only answered how they might help you find the briefcase, what are they going to do to keep you safe?"

"Besides monitor my every movement? Not much. I have a number to call."

"I should extend my time off a few days. It doesn't make any sense that they want you to risk your life to help them find this briefcase," she said.

"I doubt if your boss would want you to babysit me."

"I'll just tell him I need the time off."

"I'd enjoy your company, but I don't think you should risk your job over this," I said. I felt a little guilty knowing that right now the FBI could be in contact with her boss asking for her to do what she had offered on her own. I forced back my desire to say something.

She seemed to focus on only the first part of my remark.

"My company would include separate rooms. Don't get your hopes up."

"Of course, but I warn you, hanging around me and my charming personality for more than a couple of days can be quite risky."

"That's why I'm always armed," she grinned.

"Why don't we do lunch first, while you decide what you want to do, and I try to figure out what I'm supposed to do."

She agreed, and we walked out to my car discussing which of the few restaurants in Cloudcroft would make a good pick for lunch. We finally settled on the Texas Pit BBQ. An hour later, we left the restaurant without deciding anything more about our immediate future than when we arrived. I treated and saved the receipt for the FBI.

"This is ridiculous," she said and shook her head. "I don't see how we can ever figure out the location of the briefcase."

"You're right. That's why I've been so frustrated from the beginning. Why in the hell did Stu send me a letter asking me for help, but not include something in the letter that could help me do what he wanted?"

"I guess what we really need to do is make a plan to keep you safe once your week is up. That's what the FBI needs to be doing. Everyone has to stop worrying about finding the briefcase and start worrying about how they can keep you safe once your time is up."

"If you're suggesting the witness protection program, forget it," I said.

"Over the long term, it may be the only way."

"Not an option."

As I turned into the parking lot to the lodge, I noticed a man standing off in the distance who appeared more interested in my car than I thought was normal. Rose noticed my interest in the man and studied him as I parked.

"What do you think?' she asked.

"About him?"

"Yes."

"Don't know," I said. "I don't recognize him."

Without any hesitation, as we walked toward the lodge steps, the man moved in a line to cut us off.

"Stay here," she said. I saw her hand move down to her side.

The man was close enough to see my hesitation and Rose's reaction to his presence.

"It's okay! I'm with the press. Mr. West, you are Mr. West, right?" he spoke loud enough for us to hear him. With some fifteen yards separating us, he stood with his hands opened toward us and in plain view.

"That's me, but I'm not interested in talking to the press today. Sorry."

"How about if I just give you my card today? I'd like to get the chance to interview you when you're ready. You can't imagine how much the people in this state are interested in what happened yesterday."

"I can imagine," I said and followed Rose as we both approached the man.

"I've already talked to the police and to one of the young men who were in the café with you. They filled me in with a lot of what happened, but it seems you're the key to everything."

"A lot of people may think that, but I'm not. I'm afraid you're wasting your time."

"Well, I'll be around Mr. West, and ma'am did I catch your name?"

"No you didn't," I said.

The man held out his card, and I took it.

Rose glanced at me. I couldn't tell if I had annoyed her or not by my answering for her. The man stayed for a few seconds, but when neither of us said anything, he nodded, turned, and walked away. Rose and I continued up the steps into the lodge.

"Think he was for real?" she asked when we entered the lodge.

"Probably. It would be easy enough to check him out."

"No, that's not what I mean. I'm sure he has some relationship with the press. I wonder if he's here for his paper or for someone else."

"I think he's just an aggressive journalist." I did think that, too, but her remark made me wonder if the cartel could have moved fast enough to have been behind his appearance here.

Rose walked over to the unmanned reception counter. "Hello," she called out. No one responded. She looked back at me, "Trying to get a room."

"Good, we will need a bigger bed."

"In your dreams."

"He'll be back in a few minutes," I said.

Rose's phone rang interrupting us. She walked off a few paces and answered it. The more she talked the further away from me she walked. It could have been an angry boyfriend, but my gut told me this call came from her boss and was in response to a call they had received from the FBI.

Even with the dim lighting and the distance that separated

us, I could see Rose's face flush. Despite her predicament, I started worrying about mine. How was I going to answer her when she asked me if I knew this was going to happen? The call ended, and she looked at me. I had not yet come up with a good answer.

"Guess who that was?" she asked.

"I have no idea," I said.

"Oh, good," she said looking past me.

I turned and saw a lady I hadn't seen before now standing behind the reception counter. Rose brushed past me, not too gently. After she got her room key, rather than go and check out the room, she grabbed my arm. "Let's go for a walk."

She led me outside and we started walking down a path that led away from the lodge and downtown. "Why didn't you tell me?"

"What?"

She smacked my arm with the back of her hand.

"Okay, okay. I simply thought I should let things unfold on their own. Roger wasn't -"

"Roger?"

"Special Agent Stillman. He brought it up as a thought, not as a fait accompli. He did ask me if I would mind having you help keep me safe. I told him you were sharp and that I'd have no problems with you."

"Oh, wow, thanks. No one thought of discussing it with me first. Besides having to put up with you, no one asked me about how it might affect my career, how my boss might respond to this."

"How did he respond?" I asked.

"Not well. He's not the best when it comes to dealing with

women in the department. He thinks I worked this behind his back."

"So, what did he say? Do you have to go back, or can you stay?"

"The only benefit in this for you is that you may survive the week. Nothing else, forget it."

I fought the urge to make another stupid, joking comment. "Hey, I promise, no more teasing. I'll leave your personal space alone. I didn't mean for any of this to happen, but I'm glad you're staying."

"I'm going back to my room now. Don't go anywhere without telling me. If you get your ass killed, everyone will put the blame on me. And if anyone is going to shoot you this week, it'll be me, no one else. Got it?"

We walked back to the lodge in relative silence. I made a couple of comments about the lodge but they didn't generate any conversation. Once inside, she took a left heading to her room, and I turned right to go to the bar. The bar looked closed, but as I entered, I saw Will stand up and motion for me to join him at the bar.

"You open this early?"

"We're flexible," he said. "I came in early to start working on the inventory. Since I'm here, we're open."

"How about a Corona with a lime?"

"Sure. How's your day going?"

"Not so good, but a lot better than yesterday," I said.

"How's your ear?" he asked when he placed the beer in front of me.

"Fine," I had forgotten about my ear. I touched it.

"Well, shout out if you want anything else. I may be in the

back." He walked back over to his stool and picked up a tablet, the old paper kind, and jotted down something with a pencil.

I decided to take my thoughts over to a corner of the room. It wasn't that I was feeling depressed, but it was close. I felt for the Sig under my lightweight jacket and wondered if New Mexico allowed me to carry a concealed weapon into a bar. New Mexico's gun laws are some of the least restrictive in the country, and I knew that being a retired military law enforcement officer also gave me some status, but I had little doubt that somewhere along the line I needed to get a state license.

Kay peeked around the corner of the door that led out into the lobby.

"Hey, I was looking for you. I've got an idea," she said.

"Come on in, the bar is open."

"You've got that letter with you?"

"Never go anywhere without it." I pulled it out of my back pocket.

"It's a long shot, but I was thinking." She looked at the letter and pulled a piece of paper out of her own pocket. "It could be."

"Could be what?"

"Do you have some magazine or journal that the two of you would share?"

"What are you getting at?"

"Journals and magazines use numbers to identify a specific issue or copy. I was thinking if you two had a journal in common, maybe a military one, the numbers might refer to a certain issue."

"How in the world did you come up with that?" I asked, but I already knew of at least a half dozen possibilities that Stu could have referenced.

"Long story, but it's worth a try, don't you think?"

"Of course."

"There's a problem, though. There are two sets of numbers. The first is too long and the second is too short," she said.

"Now you're confusing me again. If they're not the right size, what made you think of it?"

"Let's don't go there right now. Let's experiment."

"Okay."

"Name one."

"The Air Force Times," I said. It seemed the most obvious. Each branch of military service had its own "Times", a weekly newspaper that focused on news of interest to that particular branch of the military.

"Okay good," Kay said and started playing with her laptop. "This may take a while, so if you'll jot down all the periodicals you can think of that the two of you have in common, I'll do the research."

"Most of these have an online version. Would they have the same identifying numbers as the paper copy?"

"I have no idea," she said.

CHAPTER 10

"None of these work, but I think we're on the right track. You see how these numbers seem to work out. If we go with the ISSN first, and then the volume or copy number along with the page number for the second set of numbers, it could take you to a certain page of a magazine or newspaper."

"I'll have to call someone to get you that data for our retired agents' quarterly magazine," I said. Despite her optimism, I didn't think we had a chance. It was a nice effort on her part, but we still had to consider the zero at the end of the first group of numbers as meaningless, and we had to find a matching set of numbers that belonged to some periodical. We'd gone through all but one of my ideas.

"Don't you get them?" she asked.

"Yes, but I don't have a copy here."

"At your house?"

"Yes."

"Don't you have someone that has a key to your house? A girlfriend?"

"Better than that," I said and called my neighbors. Any one of the kids could get into my house. Whenever I'm gone, they spend a lot of time there playing with Chubbs and raiding my refrigerator. In fact, after several complaints by them not me, I learned to stock my refrigerator before leaving on my trips with items they liked.

Ten minutes later, I relayed the numbers being read to me over the phone to Kay. I could see from her expression that we had hit pay dirt.

"Don't let him go," she said, and held out her hand for the phone. I gave it to her. "Hi, I'm Kay, I'm Jim's friend.... No, not his girlfriend, at least not yet." She winked at me. "On the same page where you found this last number is there a copy number or a volume number?.... No? How about on the cover page?.... What is it?.... That's okay, read me the numbers.... Great, thank you."

Kay passed the phone back to me. After I asked about Chubbs, I added my thanks and said goodbye.

"Did we really get a match?" I asked.

"Not with the volume number, but we did with the ISSN, and the volume numbers are small enough to work. It's just the one he had didn't match."

"We need to find the one that does, and the page number should be the last two numbers at the end of the second set of numbers, right?" I asked.

"Yes, I think so. It looks right," she said. "I wonder what we're going to find on the page?"

"I don't have the slightest. I know the guy in charge of the quarterly. I'll have to find his phone number, but I'll give him a call. Volume 43, copy 2, page 27, right?"

"Yes. If he can describe to you what's on that page, you ought to be able to recognize something that makes sense."

Before I could do anything more, my phone rang.

"We've got the approval for Deputy Luna, that means moon in English, I think, to stay with you," Roger Stillman said.

"Good," I said. "I hope we aren't getting her in trouble with her boss."

"Don't worry about that. Let's hope our experts can find a

clue in that note you received."

I could've have told him what we had discovered with the ISSN, but I didn't. I could've also told him that I already knew Rose was staying. I had the bruise on my arm to prove it. Holding back gave me some type of childish satisfaction, but it felt good.

"The three of us need to meet. The sooner the better," he said.

"Do you have her phone number?" I asked.

"Yes. I'll give her a call. Maybe it would be better to have her pick a time."

During the call, Kay had grabbed a second beer for me and a glass of wine for herself.

"I don't know what you're looking for, but if there's a reward, I get a piece of it."

"Agreed, but I'm almost certain there's no reward. However, it may help keep me alive, so I'll owe you a lot."

Her eyebrows shot up at my comment. "Are you serious?"

"Yeah," I nodded. "I don't intend to let anything happen to me and finding this damn briefcase should work in my favor."

"That's what that was all about yesterday" she whispered.

"We talked about it already."

"Yes, but I, you're right. We did, but I guess it didn't sink in."

I had to smile. As smart as she was, the obvious had eluded her until now. I imagined in her innocence the search for a clue was the challenge, a puzzle that needed to be solved. Rather than seeing the shootings yesterday and my presence there as part of an ongoing scenario, she saw it as an anomaly.

"I don't mean to scare you," I said.

"No, no, you didn't. I knew it. They will send more men after you, won't they?"

"At some point. They want the briefcase, or whatever is in it."

"Will you give it to them?" she asked.

"I don't want it, so I guess if I find it, I'll give it to someone. If it happens, I imagine I won't have much choice who I give it to."

She looked at me like she wanted to ask another question.

"I already have a couple of different groups watching me. Before this is over, I may have more. When I find the briefcase, if I do, a handful of people are going to pop up wanting it. None of them will give me a choice."

"Even the police?"

"Right. They'll want it, too. No one will let me walk away with it."

"I don't think I'd want to look for it, if I were you," she said.

"That's just it. I don't, but both sides want me to find it. One side isn't giving me much of an option."

"And that's why Rose is here?"

"Kind of. It's a long story, better told by her if she wants to."

"Sounds like I'm safer with my bears," she said. Kay waved at someone behind me.

I turned and saw Rose wearing a dark running suit and drying her face with a small towel.

"Guess what?" Kay called to her.

Rose looked at me, and I sensed she wanted to say something sarcastic.

"You'll want to hear this," I said.

"What's up?" she said as she approached us.

"We may have solved the letter," Kay said.

"Not we, her," I said. "If there's any reward, she gets one third."

"What reward? There's no reward," Rose said.

"I know. Sit down, and let me buy you a drink." I wanted to tell her to lighten up.

"I don't need a drink, I need a shower."

"The numbers in the letter Jim got belong to a quarterly magazine he gets," Kay said.

"What?" Rose said.

Five minutes later, Rose bought a round for the table. Nothing like a little success to bring up one's spirits, but I knew I wasn't out of Rose's dog house yet.

"How in the world did you even think about comparing these numbers to what was it, ISSN's?"

"I made a list of everything that could be identified by a number. You know zip codes, phone numbers, addresses, and then I thought of books. From there, magazines and other periodicals fell in place. There's an extra zero at the end, but I had already experimented discounting some of the numbers earlier."

Rose shook her head. "I'm really impressed."

Kay beamed.

"You know, Kay, knowing this puts you in danger. We need to keep your name out of everything." Rose said and looked at me. "This means we can't tell Roger that Kay is involved with us in any way."

"I agree, one hundred percent. We can simply say that we came up with the link." I wondered why I sensed bitterness in Rose's voice when she said Roger. I hoped it was because he was now pulling her strings, rather than her still thinking that Roger and I were partners in setting her up.

"I won't say a thing to anybody," Kay said.

"Good," Rose said. "I don't mean to be rude, but Jim and I need to take off and figure out what our next step will be."

"I can leave, and you two can stay here," Kay offered.

"Thanks, but I think we need to get some fresh air."

The two of us walked outside. The wind had come up and it felt a lot colder than it had been in the morning.

"We need to get a few things straight," she said.

"Okay."

"No more secrets from me. No back channel to the FBI without talking to me. Understand?"

"Yes," I said, and for the moment, I meant it.

"While the FBI may have the lead and will want to make all the decisions for us, we aren't going to let them get us killed."

I nodded. "Have you talked to Stillman?" I decided not to refer to him as Roger anymore around Rose.

She shook her head.

"He called me and told me you were in. He wants to meet us. I told him he needed to discuss that with you," I said.

She looked at me. For a second, I thought she might snap at me, but then she said, "Thanks."

"You know that no secrets thing goes both ways. Don't be planning any surprises with Stillman without telling me, too."

"It's a deal," she said.

We walked in silence for a minute or two. "You still have that business card form the reporter?"

"Yes." I reached into my pocket and handed it to her.

"Victor Spann," she read from the card. "Freelance

reporting, no company name, that's interesting. What was he, about six feet tall?"

"Yeah, he was my height. Had less hair though," I grinned.

"A lot less and his was darker. What do you think, about your age?"

"Maybe a few years younger, say around forty."

She nodded. "We have a phone number and an email. No address or birth date, but we should still be able to check him out."

"He may check out to be exactly who he says he is, but that won't tell us if he is or isn't working with the cartel?"

"I know. What did Stillman tell you about this cartel?"

"Only that it wasn't one of the big two or three. In his mind, I guess that matters," I said.

"Anything about where they're based or their history?"

"No, but in his defense, I didn't ask."

"When we get back, I want you to call your friend about the magazine. The sooner we can figure out where to look for the briefcase the better. I'd like for us to stay ahead of everyone."

"The FBI?" I asked.

"No, not in the sense of not telling them. I'd like for us to make our own decisions on what to do next because we have the answers before they do. I don't want to sit around on our thumbs while the FBI is trying to figure out what they should tell us."

It made sense, but her desire to get out ahead of the FBI also fed that small kernel of suspicion about her that wouldn't go away.

"Okay. I hope whatever we find isn't as vague as his first clue."

"That would not be nice," she said. "We may have to put Kay on retainer."

I knew her remark about Kay was a joke, but I wondered if it wouldn't be a good idea. We didn't need Kay to travel with us anywhere, but we could certainly use her brains.

"Unless there is something very specific on the page we're looking for, I'm afraid it may still be difficult to find the briefcase."

"You mean like if he simply references a city?"

"Not even that," I said. "What if it references a hotel, a river, a campground? Unless he tells us to look under this rock or behind that tree, it will still be tough to find the briefcase."

"Perhaps, but it'll be a lot easier than the proposition we were facing a few hours ago."

"Yeah, and I'm ready to do something."

CHAPTER 11

The page proved Kay's theory. It contained a short article submitted by Stu about exploring the old mines in the ghost town of Chloride, New Mexico.

"A ghost town, how about that?" Rose said when I told her what I had learned. "You say he was exploring an old mine?"

"Yeah."

"He wasn't crawling around deep inside it, was he? I don't think I could do that," she said.

"I don't think so. I got the impression he was more interested in their history and checking out what's left of them. Nothing in the article indicated he crawled around inside them. The caption in the picture was of him in front of what's left of the Wall Street Mine."

"Are they still active mines?"

"I don't think so," I said. "After all, Chloride is a ghost town."

She whipped out her phone and started typing. At first, I thought she might be texting someone, but then she started reading to me.

"The Wall Street Mine was one of several mines that opened around Chloride, New Mexico, in the 1880's. Chloride, in its heyday, had nine saloons, a brothel, a general store, a dry goods store, a millinery shop, a restaurant, a butcher shop, a candy store, a pharmacy, a Chinese laundry, a photography studio, a school, and two hotels. The Black Range newspaper was printed in Chloride from 1882 to 1896. Then it looks like there was a silver glut and the whole place shut down." She paused for a few seconds as she continued reading. "Looks like frequent Apache Indian attacks had something to do with the town's demise, too."

"A neat history, it almost sounds like it would've been a fascinating place to live."

"Not for me," Rose said. "I think you missed the part about the Apache attacks and focused solely on the nine saloons and one brothel."

"The article didn't mention if anyone still lives in Chloride."

"Doesn't matter. I think we still have to go there. Should we assume he's telling us that the briefcase is there now and not that he found the briefcase there?"

"Yes, definitely. The essence of the letter is a request for me to go and retrieve the briefcase. There's nothing in the letter mentioning Stu's discovery of it. I'm sure that the briefcase is somewhere close to where he is in the picture."

"I hope you're having a copy of the article your friend wrote, to include the picture, emailed or faxed to you today," Rose said.

"It is. He said it would take a few minutes, but we should get it today."

"Did you tell him why we're interested?"

"No. He was curious, but I asked him to give me a day or two before I told him what was going on."

"Was he okay with that?" Rose asked

"For now, but when word gets spread around about Stu's death, which I'm surprised hasn't happened already, he'll get real impatient. I'm counting on him calling me back when that happens." I knew the fraternity of retired OSI special agents was pretty close and very efficient at getting word out of someone's passing. The only reason news of Stu's death hadn't already hit the street was that Stu had not been forthcoming with his own background information. The authorities had only started piecing together who he was a day or so before my arrival.

"I think we should leave early tomorrow," Rose said.

"What should we tell the FBI?" I said. I didn't want to hold anything back, but I also knew it irritated Rose that Stillman had not yet called her.

"Everything, but not until we have seen the article."

Rose went back to her room to follow up on Spann, and I walked out to the Mustang to study the road atlas. I doubted many people carried paper maps anymore, but I still liked to have them around. I found Chloride and plotted a course to it. The fact that Chloride made the map gave me hope that despite its status as a ghost town, enough people lived there that someone might remember Stu's visit.

I returned to my room and showered, only to find out afterwards that I had missed two phone calls during the few minutes I was in the shower. The first voicemail told me that the email with a copy of the article had been sent to me. The second came from Rose who asked me to call her.

"Stillman wants to meet tonight at eight at the LE substation. I couldn't put it off. Do you think you'll have a copy of the article by then?" Rose asked.

"I think it's here already. I'm going to head down to one of the business offices to print it out."

"Good, I'll join you, and then we can grab a quick dinner before heading over there."

We printed out two copies of the article: one for us and the other for Stillman. The article didn't contain any hints that we could see other than the picture. Of course, we didn't expect any since he had written the article years before he discovered the briefcase.

Stillman sat across the desk from us with a scowl on his face. "West, you should know we don't like being played with. You sat across this desk earlier today and claimed you had no idea where the briefcase was. Now you suddenly have this?"

"I didn't know anything then, and the correlation of the numbers to the quarterly was a lucky guess we made just this afternoon. Believe me I was as surprised as you when it panned out," I said.

"I've been on the phone all day working out the scenarios and telling people that we didn't have any leads on the briefcase and now I've got to call them all back. If I find out," he didn't finish his sentence, but he did continue staring at me shaking his head.

"He's telling you the truth," Rose said. "I was surprised as you an hour or so ago when he tried to match the numbers. It was a lucky guess."

Stillman stared at Rose. His veins on his temples shrunk back out of sight.

"I want us to leave early tomorrow," Rose said. "We need to put some distance between us and those following Jim."

"We can get to Chloride by noon tomorrow if we leave before eight. That means there is a chance we can find the briefcase tomorrow," I said.

"Where is Chloride?" Stillman asked.

"A little northwest of Truth or Consequences?" I said.

He nodded. "Just off I-25?"

"Yeah, maybe thirty miles," I guessed.

"Leave at eight?" he asked.

"Yes," Rose said.

"Okay, unless you hear otherwise from me. I'll be about a mile behind you all the way. You shouldn't see me. We'll have someone there before you, too, but they won't make contact."

The conversation returned to ground rules wherein Stillman once again reminded me and now Rose that he called the shots. He didn't come out and tell us to behave like brainless robots, but we got the message.

When we left, Rose surprised me by saying, "That wasn't that bad."

"I thought he kind of overdid it."

"Maybe, but he's following the same script we all use."

"Are you going to mind leaving your car at the lodge?" I asked. Since my car had the FBI tracker on it, Stillman wanted us to take it. I'd rather drive, and it didn't seem to bother Rose.

"My car has enough mileage. I don't mind at all, except I'll leave it at the substation."

We had decided to keep Kay's name out of everything for now, as we weren't sure how far her involvement would drag her into the official investigation. We knew there were leaks and didn't want to take a chance with Kay's safety. While we kept her name from Stillman, in our defense, Kay didn't see the page from the quarterly and therefore had no knowledge of the connection to Chloride.

"Are you going to call your boss and update him?" I asked.

"No. Stillman said they would keep him informed, so unless he calls me, I don't plan on passing any information to him."

When we got back to the lodge, we went our separate ways. Exhausted, I fell asleep within minutes of getting under the covers.

I felt a little cheated when checking out of the lodge. My stay was definitely not the relaxing vacation I had in mind when months ago I had made my bid for the night in the lodge.

"Has Ms. Luna checked out yet, Fred?"

"Haven't seen her yet."

"Okay. If she shows up, tell her I'll be in having breakfast. That is after I put this in the car." I held up my gym bag.

A beautiful blue sky welcomed me as I left the lodge. The cool air would warm up fast once the sun moved high enough in the sky for its rays to reach the lodge. I noticed a lone man in a heavy jacket sitting on the hood of a small Kia in the parking lot. He smiled at me and even raised a hand for a slight wave. The reporter, I thought, and wondered if he planned on following us all the way to Chloride.

Perhaps because my mind remained focused on the reporter and ways to get away from him, I never saw the second man. Well, never may be an exaggeration, but the first I saw of him was in a reflection in my car's window when I went to open the driver's door.

"Damn," I muttered and spun around.

His hand had already come out of a coat pocket gripping a small handgun.

"Freeze!" Rose screamed from too far away to be a real threat.

The man hesitated.

"Drop it! Now!" a man ordered from close behind me.

My would-be assassin looked past me at the man. He

dropped the pistol and raised both hands.

"Stay still!" the man behind me said.

Rose ran toward me. I turned and saw two men approaching my car.

"FBI," one of the men said.

"I wasn't going to shoot him," my would-be assassin said. "I only wanted to talk to him. I thought he might be dangerous."

"Sure you were," one of the FBI men said. "Turn around and lean against that car." He began the process of checking the man for other weapons.

"Special Agent Bob Thomas, Mr. West. We've been here the last hour. Saw him pull up about twenty minutes ago. He seemed interested in your car, so we've had an eye on him."

"Thanks. I'm impressed and also grateful. Something tells me, if you and Deputy Luna hadn't shown up, he would have shot me."

Rose arrived by my side as I spoke.

"You okay?" she asked.

"Yes."

"Excuse me, I have to make a couple calls," Agent Thomas said and took a few steps away from us.

"Thanks, Rose."

"I wouldn't have been much help from that far away. Must be forty yards."

"Your shout is what did it. I think that stopped him altogether. My guess is he didn't want any witnesses." My comment made me think of the reporter. I looked around for him but didn't see him. The spot where I had seen him was partially hidden from view by other cars in the lot. I wondered if the man with the gun had seen him and was still willing to come after me. That could only mean one thing, but did he see him?

"Did you know they would be here?" Rose asked, nodding at the agents.

"No, but it makes sense."

She nodded.

A state police car rolled into the parking lot and parked next to us. Two troopers got out and were met by Agent Thomas. He escorted them over to the man who now would become their prisoner. He then returned to us.

"Did you recognize the man?"

"No," I said.

Thomas looked at Rose. She also said she didn't.

"Did you see the weapon?"

We both answered yes.

"Does the name Jim Jamison mean anything to either of you?"

"No," we both said in unison.

"We need you both to stick around here for another hour or so while we figure a few things out. Agent Stillman said he still wants you both to head out this morning, but we need to up channel this and see if we can't get a few things answered."

"We haven't had breakfast yet. We'll eat here," I said.

"Okay, do that," Thomas said.

"Agent Thomas, let me show you something," Rose said and walked him to a small Nissan parked a couple slots away.

I finished putting my gym bag into my car before watching the state troopers drive off with Jamison. The FBI car followed them.

"I wonder why that guy, Jamison, didn't see the FBI agents and abort his run at me altogether," I said while we walked back into the lodge.

"I don't think they saw him until he was almost on top of you. He came out of his passenger side door and stayed low as he came around his car so you wouldn't notice him. It blocked the agents' view, too. Unfortunately for him, it made him look awful suspicious to me."

That meant the FBI agents hadn't gotten out of their car until Rose shouted.

"Thanks," I said again.

"You can buy me breakfast."

I did. We never saw Kay that morning, so we weren't able to tell her goodbye or thank her once more. I did leave a note for her with Fred telling her I'd call her when everything was over. We owed her that much.

"I wonder how long they'll hold onto Jamison?" I said. "I mean, we know what he planned to do with that gun, but he could claim anything, even that he thought he saw a rattlesnake by my feet and that he was going to shoot the snake."

"I'm sure they'll hold him as long as they can. He may have an outstanding warrant or something else that may let them keep him longer."

"He didn't look like someone a Mexican cartel might use."

"You never know, but I did wonder," Rose said.

We loaded Rose's bags into the trunk and sat on the front hood while we waited word from Stillman. Our conversation focused on the view that went on "forever" to the west. If you haven't been to the mountains, you can't appreciate an open mountain view. Unfortunately, from our position in the parking lot trees blocked a lot of our view.

"You know they have a tower you can go up and get a clear view," I said.

"Let's go up and see it," she said.

I hadn't intended when I made the comment to indicate that I had any interest to climb all those stairs, and now I regretted saying it, but there was no manly way out.

"It may be up a lot of stairs," I said.

"Who cares? Come on, show me."

We returned to the lodge, and I led her up the stairs to the tower's observation room.

"This is awesome!"

I didn't sense any of the effects of the climb in her voice. I nodded instead of saying anything so she wouldn't notice my gasping.

"I wonder if we can see all the way to Chloride from here?"

"If we could, it would be over there by those mountains," I pointed out to the horizon.

We stood close together in the small room enjoying the view. I couldn't help but think of her and had an urge to reach out and touch her. She must have felt something, too.

"Let's go back down," she said and started down the stairs ahead of me.

When we reached the front porch of the lodge, Rose's phone chirped. She walked a few steps away from me and took the call.

"We've got the green light, let's go," she said after the call ended.

The drive took us back through Alamogordo, but then I took US-70 rather than the road to El Paso. We stopped in Las Cruces for gas and a coffee break. Stillman joined us in the coffee shop.

"It shouldn't be a surprise that Jamison denies having had any interest in shooting you or anyone," Stillman said.

"That's what we expected," Rose said.

"The address on his driver's license and what he wrote down on his rental car agreement is in Dallas. The address in Dallas is legit, except initial checks with neighbors indicate they've never seen anyone living there. He's giving us no other information and insists on talking to his lawyer."

"That was quick. It sounds like he's not new to this," I said.

"The lawyer is a big shot from Dallas. One who our office in Dallas claims has some very shady clients," Stillman said.

"Any Mexican connections?" Rose asked.

"Not that we've found."

"Well, I'm fairly certain he wasn't in Cloudcroft for a friendly chat. He knew where I was staying, and didn't seem to want to waste any time getting to me," I said.

"Oh, we're in agreement there. We're thinking some American connection is also worried about the briefcase's discovery," Stillman said.

Rose looked at me and nodded. We had thought of that, too.

"Hopefully our departure this morning will shake any other tails," I said.

"Only a handful of people know where we're going. I did inform your Sheriff," Stillman said to Rose.

"I haven't mentioned it to anyone," she said, and I nodded.

I mentioned Spann's presence at the scene that morning, and Stillman's pleasant mood evaporated.

"Why didn't you tell me back there? We could have grabbed him on the spot."

"To be honest, I didn't think of him. After everyone left, I realized he was gone, too. This is the first time we've talked since."

He looked at Rose.

"I didn't mention it to her either," I lied. "Have you learned anything about him?"

"Only that he is what he says he is," Stillman said. His composure returned a little. "He's a freelance guy. Drifts around the country staying at cheap hotels. He has had a couple good exclusives that have given him some credibility, but for the most part is continually looking for his next paycheck."

"Nothing bad on him?" Rose asked.

"No."

"I haven't seen anyone following us," I said.

"I haven't seen any tails on you either," Stillman said. "We're okay. Let's stop again in Truth or Consequences. Get our act together before heading into Chloride."

When I drove away from our meeting, I watched Stillman pull out into the road about thirty seconds behind us. Seconds later, I glanced in my rear view mirror and saw a small, light green car pull out onto the road behind Stillman. Nothing out of the ordinary, I thought, but I couldn't help but make a mental note of the car. I'd watch for it at our next stop.

The drive from Las Cruces to Truth or Consequences on I-25 takes about an hour. Rose slept for the first thirty minutes.

"I should have brought a cup of that coffee with me. Didn't mean to fall asleep on you," she said while she rubbed her eyes and looked at her hair in the visor mirror. "This is no better than west Texas. Miles and miles of nothing."

"Beautiful isn't it," I said.

About ten miles out, her phone rang.   I thought it was Stillman suggesting a place, but after hearing her side of the conversation, I realized it wasn't.

"That was interesting," she said after the call.   "One of the rounds they got from the shootout in the donut shop came from the same weapon that was used to shoot Brown."

"Well, how about that," I said.   "That's an unexpected good break."

"That it is. We knew they had to be connected, but knowing something and having the evidence to prove it is totally different."

"I know that doesn't prove that one of the men there actually pulled the trigger on Stu, but we all know these guys don't share their weapons. It's good enough for me," I said.

"For me, too."

"I still find it hard to believe they shot him before they actually had the briefcase in hand," I said.

"Did those guys seem overly brilliant to you?"

"No, not at all."

"Your friend probably gave them a fictitious location and they shot him without double checking," Rose said.

"And not only did they not find the briefcase, look at all the trouble they caused us by doing so," I said.

She nodded.   We passed a sign that said Truth or Consequences was ten miles ahead. "Was this city named after the television show with the same name?" she asked.

"Yes. I think it was some type of publicity stunt."

"What road are we looking for? The one that will take us to Chloride."

"Fifty two, highway fifty two, but I doubt it will mention Chloride. It should mention Winston or Wilson, whatever the name is to the town not far from Chloride. I think it's north of the city," I said.

Rather than respond to my comment, Rose called someone on her phone.

"Hey, Steve, how did you know I was on a trip?" She listened for a few seconds. "No, that's okay. Do me a favor and keep the fact that I'm out of the area to yourself..... What? Oh, ok, thanks." She ended the call and looked at me. "So much for secrecy. They may not know that we're on the way to Chloride, but apparently everyone in El Paso County knows that I was in Cloudcroft and am now working on a joint task force in route to somewhere in New Mexico."

"What?"

"The last comment Steve made on the first call was 'be safe on your trip.' It didn't register until after that call ended. Apparently, after your statements to everyone about the shootings in the donut shop, a series of calls went back and forth between the investigators in Cloudcroft and both the sheriff's office and the Fabens Police Department. That's normal, but what happened after I arrived, that fact got interspersed with the follow up calls."

"How did that evolve into your participation in a joint operation?"

"This morning, someone mentioned to someone else that they would have told me about the match with the weapons except that I had left with the FBI, or something to that effect. Anyway, gossip in our department spreads faster than a fire in a paper mill."

"Should we mention it to Stillman?" I asked.

"I don't know."

"Since they don't know exactly where we are, I don't know how significant it can be. What would we tell Stillman? That your office knows you're somewhere in New Mexico working with the FBI. This is a big state."

"Yeah, you're right," she said.

Stillman called and suggested a Denny's for our stop.

"That's cutting it close," I said as we arrived at the Denny's less than thirty seconds after his call.

CHAPTER 12

Stillman grunted a "good," when we mentioned one of the weapons matched the one used to shoot Brown, but the information seemed more of a distraction than something that mattered to him.

"Most likely we won't simply walk out there and find the briefcase and walk away," he said.

"Agreed," Rose said.

I nodded.

"We don't need much of a cover. No mention of our law enforcement connection, of course. You two need to pose as a couple, not married or anything like that, just at some early point of a relationship. We'll use our own names, of course, and I'll be a friend."

"Do you think anyone is going to care who we are? It's a ghost town," Rose said.

"There are a dozen or so people still living in the area and the occasional tourist. We don't expect anything, but we just want to keep everything simple and consistent," Stillman said.

"What are the plans if we don't find the briefcase this afternoon?" Rose asked.

I had thought of that, too. I didn't want to be sleeping in the car or on the ground somewhere.

"We have already thought of that. The two agents coming down from Albuquerque will be bringing a trailer and a couple of tents."

"What?" Rose asked with a little anger seeping into her voice.

"Don't sweat it. You two get the trailer."

"So it's like the five of us are gathering there for a little adventure?" I said before Rose could say anything more.

"Absolutely. Our understanding is that such excursions by people to Chloride are common."

The way Stillman said it made it sound like we were going to some remote part of the planet. I guess his New England accent should have told me something.

"Then we may run into other groups?" Rose asked.

"Possible, but we called the small general store in Chloride, and the proprietor said we'd have the camping area pretty much to ourselves."

I knew Stillman's "we" referred to the FBI.

"I hope you're a good cook," Rose said to me.

"Best hot dogs in the county."

"Good," Stillman said, "because they're only bringing the basics."

"How long do you anticipate we'll stay out here, if we don't find anything?" I asked.

"Our target is three days."

"Shouldn't we have brought shovels or something," Rose asked.

"Way ahead of you, Deputy," Stillman said.

"I hope so. I feel like I'm just tagging along," Rose said.

"You and me both," I said.

"We've got your basic tools, like shovels and pick axes, and we have some higher tech equipment," Stillman said.

"At least I'll get a workout and get a chance to work on my tan," Rose said.

"I need to get some different clothing," I said.

"Now that you mention it, we'll have to stop in the nearest Target or Walmart," Rose said.

I didn't think to look for the small light green car when we left Denny's, but when we left Walmart, I saw what I thought was the same car follow Stillman out of the parking lot.

"Rose, it may be nothing but when we left Las Cruces, and just now again, I've noticed what appears to be the same light green car following Stillman."

"Another FBI guy?" She turned her head around and looked out the rear window.

"Could be FBI, could be someone following him to stay with us," I said.

"I don't see anything, but Stillman is so far back I can't get a good look at who might be behind him."

"I know. It won't matter until we turn off up here anyway. Once we leave I-25 it may become more obvious."

We turned northwest off of I-25 onto state highway 52. I watched for Stillman to take the same exit, but we wound around a hill, and I lost sight of the intersection before he made the turn.

Rose had turned her head to watch. "Can't see him," she said.

"I suggest you call him."

"And tell him what? That he might have a tail on him. He's an FBI agent. He should be able to figure out that someone might be following him."

"You think he might say he's well ahead of us again?" I said and grinned.

"More than likely. Looks like we're heading out into the middle of nowhere. Once we pass through Winston, we can pull off the road somewhere and simply wait to see if anyone is behind Stillman."

"That last stretch of road only goes to Chloride. I suggest we stop in Winston."

"Okay, but that still doesn't do much to hide our final destination," Rose said. "I'll wait to call Stillman when we stop."

The stretch of road to Winston only had a few spots of highway long enough and straight enough for us to see Stillman in the distance behind us. We couldn't tell if anyone was following him. In Winston, I parked the Mustang in an empty parking lot in front of an out of business shop. Rose called Stillman and told him our plan.

"He didn't sound happy," she said.

Two minutes later he turned into the lot and parked next to us. He shook his head at us but refrained from saying anything. After a minute, he rolled down his window and Rose rolled down her window.

"How long do you want to give him?" he asked.

"Just one more minute," I said. I had to give him credit for not saying anything. Of course, it only made sense to make sure we were wrong before giving us a hard time.

A small, light green Kia drove by us a few seconds later.

"That's it," I said. "Been with us for a while."

Once it was out of sight, Stillman barked, "Let's go. Follow me." He backed out and took a side street a block to the county road that would lead us out to Chloride. At that point, he accelerated to a speed I didn't think was safe for the small winding road.

"What's his hurry?" Rose said.

"Who knows? Did you get the license number?"

"No. Looked like a male driver by himself. I didn't get a good enough look at the guy to say much about his appearance."

"Me neither," I said, but I had a gut feeling the driver was Victor Spann.

When we reached Chloride, Stillman parked in front of the General Store, and I pulled the Mustang alongside of him. The store was one of a handful of old buildings still standing in the old town. Only two others looked like they might still be used. A new pickup truck sat off to the side by the general store and a new Subaru had been parked by an old, unmarked building a short distance down the street. I didn't see any people. We got out and went inside.

Rose and I walked around the inside of the store while Stillman talked to the proprietor. I figured we had beaten the two FBI agents from Albuquerque, but discovered I was wrong when Stillman told us we needed to head out to join the others.

The drive to the camp ground only took a couple minutes. Sunlight reflected off the silver trailer. It looked small, and I didn't think it would provide much privacy for Rose. I saw two people putting up a tent next to a second tent that had already been erected. About ten yards separated the tents from the trailer. A large pickup sat in the shade of a large tree off to our left. After pausing for a second, Stillman drove over to the pickup and parked next to it. I did the same.

"Home sweet home," Rose groaned.

"Better than the tents," I said.

"If you're a munchkin."

We walked over to the two agents staying about ten paces

behind Stillman. He had made no effort to wait for us and was already shaking hands with them when we got there.

"Deputy Luna and Jim West meet Special Agents Charles White and Kaiden Small," he said.

I did my best to keep any emotion from my face. The two were not what I expected. Agent Small was a very young looking blonde who didn't look twenty one. Agent White on the other hand looked like he had to be near the mandatory retirement age.

"We're posing as father and daughter," White said with a laugh.

I thought they could, except it might be a stretch since Agent White was definitely black and Small looked pure Scandinavian.

"Adopted daughter, that is," White added.

"Charles, seen anything out of the ordinary?" Stillman asked.

"This whole place looks out of the ordinary for me. Good thing Small here was a Girl Scout. I've never put a tent up before, much less slept in one. Until you three showed up, we hadn't seen anyone."

"Piece of cake," Agent Small said. "Deputy Luna, how'd you get roped into this?"

"Please call me Rose, and you can blame Agent Stillman for that."

Small stood a good six inches taller than Rose. Like Rose, Small looked like she was in very good physical shape.

"And I'm Kaiden."

I looked around the campground. Not much more than a small clearing, it didn't look like it had ever experienced much use. Quiet and peaceful, I hoped it would stay that way.

"Jim, let me give you a tour of your living arrangements for the next night or two," Agent White said.

"Sure," I said and followed him into the trailer. "How about if Agent Small stays in here with Deputy Luna, and I'll stay in one of the tents."

"Sorry, no way. Not only is it FBI policy to give you two the trailer, Small would never go for it. It would be easier to talk me into swapping with you."

"I think she and Deputy Luna will get along very well," I said.

The inside of the trailer looked clean and new, but the entire interior could best be described with one word: small. Its advertisers might claim it came with all the amenities, but the entire truth would require a modifier like miniature.

"Not very big, is it," White said.

"No, it really isn't."

"If you don't mind me asking, are you and the Deputy an item?"

"No."

He chuckled. "How is she going to handle this?"

"I don't know. I guess she'll put up with it. I could sleep on the couch, and she does have a gun."

This time, he laughed so hard he had to lean against the small kitchen counter. "Stillman just said you two were together. We didn't know what he meant."

"That's okay. I was married for twenty years, so I know what the word no means."

"Hell, I've been married and divorced twice."

We left the trailer to find Rose and Agent Small waiting outside.

"Our turn," Rose said.

While the women were inside the trailer, White showed Stillman and me the various tools they had brought with them to assist us in the search of the area around the mine.

"Hopefully we won't have to do a lot of digging," I said. "I can't imagine it's buried in some unmarked location."

"If it's there at all," White said.

"I think it's there. Nothing else makes sense. There was nothing in the article that referenced a different location."

"The article?" White asked.

"Long story," I said.

"It's how we found this place. I have a copy of the letter Jim received from the man we believe hid the briefcase out here along with an article that he wrote. Once we get settled, you can read them. Maybe you can see something in either of them that we didn't," Stillman said.

It only took a couple minutes to transfer what little we had in the Mustang to the trailer. Rose threw her luggage on the small couch.

"You can have the bedroom," I said.

"You'll never fit on this couch."

"I'd feel stupid taking the bed, --"

"Hey, I'm here to keep you alive. That means someone trying to break in has to get through me to get to you. That's how it works."

"I offered to swap locations with Agent Small," I said.

"So did I," Rose said.

We both laughed.

"I never meant to drag you into this," I said.

"You didn't. I did that all by my little self."

I opened the small refrigerator to see if it contained anything and was surprised to see that it was packed full of cokes, diet cokes, and water. A pack of bacon and a container of eggs made up the only food items.

"The essentials," I said.

"Kaiden said that Agent White loves his breakfast. She offered to do the cooking."

"What did she say when you offered her the trailer?" I asked.

"You mean did she jump at the chance to spend a night in a trailer with a rugged man like you?"

"No," I said, although I couldn't help but wonder. "White cautioned me from asking her if she wanted to swap places with me."

"She wants to stay in the tent. That's where the other FBI agents are, so that's where she wants to be. It's that simple."

Stillman knocked on the door and shouted, "Meeting time, come on out."

"We need to go over some basic ground rules," Stillman said, while we followed him to a spot next to the tents where the other two were already seated on small portable chairs. He pointed to a third empty chair for one of us to use.

Rose looked at me.

"I've got the bed. You should at least get the chair," I said.

She sat down, and I stood a little behind her.

"Okay. This will be short and sweet. From now on, while we're out here, we go by first names. No more Agent so-and-so or Deputy Luna. We're supposed to be a bunch of friends, so first names only: Charles, Kaiden, Jim, Rose, and me, Roger. We may not see another soul, but let's get into the habit in case we do. Next, we'll go back and forth to the mine in the pickup. We can all fit into it and supplies can be tossed in the back. Jim, hope you don't mind leaving your car parked here. I doubt if they have much vandalism out here."

"Not a problem," I said.

"Conceal your badges and weapons in something that you can keep on you while you're searching. We've brought along small back packs and hip packs. If you have something else you like, that's okay. We've got a first aid kit that we'll take with us, and we'll take water. As you can see there aren't any facilities around here. We've got the trailer here, but I doubt if there's anything by the mine, so be prepared."

Kaiden smiled and jabbed a finger into Charles shoulder.

"So I need to cut back on the chili cheeseburgers," he said. He took off the navy blue ball cap he had been wearing and scratched what was left of his salt and pepper hair.

"I don't expect any trouble while we're here, but the people who want this briefcase have already given us enough of a reason to be vigilant. We have a small backup team that should be arriving in T or C by tonight," Stillman said.

I didn't know what value a back-up team would be forty five minutes away in Truth or Consequences.

"If we find the briefcase, I'll up channel it. No one else will do so. Understood?"

"If you're trying to tell me something Roger, you don't need to. I won't be telling anyone anything," Rose said. She impressed me by keeping her voice neutral.

"I didn't mean anyone specific," Stillman said. "As you know, we're more interested in any documents that might be in the briefcase, than any money or drugs."

Kaiden nodded in agreement. She had certainly dressed for the mission. She had on hiking boots with thick socks rolled up above the top of the boots, camo shorts, and a loose fitting olive green tee shirt. She had put on wrap-around sunglasses and a white sun visor to shade her face.

The rest of us dressed casual enough, but not as appropriately for the task ahead of us. We all wore jeans, but our shirts were more fitting for a golf course than digging around a mine, and none of our shoes looked like they would survive a couple days of hard labor. I noticed Rose studying Kaiden and wondered if she was thinking the same thing.

"If we find the briefcase, the first thing we do is take plenty of photos. You all know how everyone loves pictures. We handle it as evidence and we don't open it until we make sure it isn't booby trapped."

"It won't be," I said. "It would make no sense for Stu to booby trap something he asked me to get for his wife."

"We agree. Our concern is that the cartel may have gotten to it first and have left a surprise for us. They know we're looking for it," Stillman said.

That still didn't make sense to me. If they had it, why would the cartel give me a week to find it for them? I wanted to ask Stillman how they were going to be able to determine if it was booby-trapped, but decided I might as well wait and see.

"From what the old man in the shop told me, the mine is only a few minutes from here, so if anyone needs to use the trailer, do so now. We'll be heading out in five minutes."

No one moved toward the trailer, but since Stillman had given us five minutes, I walked over to double check that the Mustang was locked and that nothing could be seen through the windows that might entice someone to break into it. Rose came with me.

"I'm tempted to call him Sarge. What do you think?" Rose said.

"Stillman? I think he loves being in charge, but I've seen worse."

"Yeah, me too. I thought that comment about making calls was directed at me, but I wonder if he thinks you might call your cartel buddies."

"I didn't think of that," I said. "I hope not."

The five of us piled into the pickup, and Charles drove us out of the clearing. We drove about a mile over a bumpy dirt road before we had to stop. A rough looking walking trail veered off to the south. Someone had written "Wall St Mine" on a small, makeshift sign in black paint. The sign looked like it was about to fall over on its side.

Charles leaned over and tried to straighten the sign; however, the hole had widened over time, so no matter what he did, the sign wouldn't stand straight up.

"A little concrete in that hole would do the trick," he said.

No one responded, and Stillman led our little gaggle down the winding path.

"How about our equipment," Kaiden asked.

"Let's take a look first," Stillman said.

We walked a few hundred yards before we came to the mine.

"A bit of a letdown," Rose said.

"This is either going to be real easy or real hard," Charles said.

I agreed with both comments.

CHAPTER 13

The entrance to the mine had four, long two-by-fours nailed to a wooden frame. Crisscrossed into two large X's, the two-by-fours did little to actually block a determined person's access to the mine's interior.

"Danger, keep out," Kaiden read the sign that hung from the frame. "What do you think?"

Stillman peered through the barrier. "I might crawl around just inside there, if we can't find anything out here, but I don't want any of you to go in there."

"No argument from me," I said. "I can't believe Stu would've gone very far in there if he went in at all."

"It looks safe for the first five or ten yards, so he might have," Stillman said. He turned and studied the terrain around us. "There's a lot of places, especially on this hillside, where he could have stashed the briefcase."

"Looks like perfect gila monster territory," Rose whispered to me.

"All the little bushes, the crevices, and rock piles, we will need to be careful poking around," I said.

"How far away from the mine should we extend our search?" Charles asked.

"We'll start in the immediate area and go out fifty yards in all directions," Stillman said.

It made sense to me, but searching an area the size of a football field, even with the five of us, would be a lot more work than I anticipated.

"What I want us to do right now is to conduct a preliminary walk through. Kaiden you take the area that goes out from here to that large boulder and over to that group of trees and back here." Stillman continued on giving us each a portion of the ground to be searched. He kept the steep hillside that the mine had been dug into for himself. "We don't have any equipment, so for now, I want you to get a feel for the terrain and look for any spots that appear like they may have been tampered with by someone trying to hide a briefcase."

As we wondered off to our respective areas, Stillman's phone rang. He talked for a few minutes. After the call, I noticed he studied the skies around us. I wondered if he was looking for a drone or an approaching helicopter.

Nothing in my search zone appeared to have been tampered with by anyone in the recent past. Of course, that didn't mean much, since I didn't wonder into the areas of thick ground cactus. Most of what grew close to the ground had burs, thistles, or thorns. A few piles of rocks would also have to be taken apart, but I didn't feel like that was what we were supposed to be doing at the moment. Few plants grew in the immediate area of the mine's entrance, but further away I could see the scattered Cholla cactus, desert plums, and Russian thistle.

The wind picked up and started blowing the dust around. I looked around at the others. Only Kaiden appeared to be making a thorough effort of searching her area. Charles relieved my concern about being the first one to finish by shouting to Roger that without tools and work gloves we were wasting our time.

"Come on in everyone," Roger shouted to us all.

We gathered around him at the entrance of the mine.

"I knew it was a long shot that we might simply stumble upon the briefcase. This first walk around was to give us a feel for the area. My plan was to go back to the truck, retrieve our tools, and work until dark. Unfortunately, the call I received a few minutes ago was to tell me that we have a nasty line of thunderstorms bearing down on us." Roger looked at his watch. "Should be here in an hour."

"That's great," Charles said.

"We'll head back, and I don't know, but we may want to take the tents down and ride the storm out in the truck or the trailer," Roger said.

"That's a good idea, Roger," Kaiden said. "With the pickup's cover, everything will stay dry. It'll only take a few minutes to set them back up."

Charles nodded.

"Okay, let's do that; however, before we go, did any of you see anything that's worth noting at this time?"

"Not me," I said, and everyone echoed me.

The small, light green Kia blocked most of my view of the Mustang when we drove into the camp area.

"Damn," Roger said.

"Who the hell can that be?" Charles muttered.

Rose and I kept our thoughts to ourselves.

A lone man struggled to set up a small tent near his car. As we drove past, he looked up, and I recognized Victor Spann. I glanced at Rose, and she nodded to me.

"It's that reporter, Spann," Rose said.

"Who?" Kaiden asked.

"Victor Spann," Roger said. "He's a free lance reporter who showed up in Cloudcroft wanting info on what's going on. We don't have anything on him, but you know that means diddly."

"How did he know we were here?" Kaiden asked.

"While I was making sure no one was following Jim and Rose, he apparently followed me."

I had to give Roger credit for readily taking the blame.

"My guess is that he's very good at what he does. He's had a couple of pretty good exposes in the past. He may not be easy to shake," I said.

"Well, let's ignore him for right now," Roger said. "Maybe the storm will drive him away."

Charles parked adjacent to the two tents, and we all got involved in taking the tents down and securing everything in the bed of the pickup. I could see that Spann watched us with curiosity. The storm clouds could be seen in the distance, but overhead the sun still beat down on us.

Spann walked over to us as Charles was closing and securing the truck bed's cover.

"Don't tell me that I'm the reason for your departure," Spann said.

"What are you doing here, Spann?" Rose asked.

"I told you. There's a story here. I think it might be a big one, and I want it. I'm no threat to you."

"If we thought you were a threat," Roger said, "you'd be cuffed and stuffed in here with our tents."

"FBI? Right? I'm Victor Spann," he offered his hand.

"We know who you are. What we want to know is why you're here?" Roger asked. He ignored the extended hand.

"I just told you," Spann said. "I'm within my rights, and you know it."

"I would think that the shootout in Cloudcroft would be the story, not us," Rose said.

"Deputy Luna, that story was old news within hours of it occurring. The story is with Mr. West, here. Why were they after him, why is he out here, and why isn't he either arrested or in protective custody somewhere?" Spann looked at me.

"Maybe that's why they have me hidden out here," I said. "Now you want to tell everyone where I am."

"Bull. You're not here in Camp Hideout," Spann looked around. "I can't imagine why you all came out here, unless you came here to find something. Did you find it, and that's why you're leaving?"

"How about this, Spann? You leave now, and when we're done, I'll personally call you and let you in on what's going on," Roger said.

"No way. Heard that too many times before. From now on, you'll just have to get use to my being around."

"There's no way we can guarantee your protection," White added. "If you have any concept of what we're doing, you must know we're dealing with a very dangerous situation."

"I think that's my risk to take," Spann said.

"Well, we're leaving. You'll never get your tent packed up before we go," Roger said.

"I'll get it packed up as quickly as you can hook up your trailer," Spann said.

Roger's face turned red. His bluff had backfired. He shook his head, "I'm going to the trailer."

"Victor, what do you know?" I asked.

"What do you mean?"

"What do you know about why we're here, why those guys

back in Cloudcroft were after me, who they were, etc?"

He looked at me suspiciously. "You know more than I do," he said.

"Then why not let us know what you know?" Kaiden said.

He looked at her and then back at me. "The shootings got my attention along with the rumors that you have something the shooters wanted. The word on the wire is that the men were part of a drug cartel. The FBI gets involved, so it's big, not something local. Then there's you, West. You've been the common link in some pretty strange stories the last half dozen years. I don't quite get you. Anyway, I have a feeling this will be quite the scoop when it's over, and I want to be the one with the story."

"How'd you know to follow us out here?" I asked.

"I'm good at what I do."

"I believe you, but how did you know we were leaving?" I asked.

"I was watching you. You saw me. I thought you were going to get shot this morning," he said.

It seemed longer ago than this morning. "I almost was."

"Who was that guy?" he asked.

"They're trying to find that out right now," I said.

"Anyway, I made some calls immediately after that to try to find out what happened and was informed I had to get the information from the FBI. Specifically, Agent Stillman's name was given to me, but when I tried to reach him I was told he was out of touch and would be leaving this morning. From my vantage point it looked like he was sticking with you two, so I decided to stick with him."

"You did a good job," I said.

"I've probably followed more people that any of you have. Comes with the job."

"Then you must know why we're here," Charles said.

"Only in the broadest sense."

"What does that mean?" Kaiden asked.

"Whatever you're looking for must be out here somewhere," Spann said.

"What are we looking for?" I asked.

"That I don't know. I picked up something about a briefcase, but that came from bar chatter. Obviously, the container is not important. The contents are, and I can only guess that it's money or drugs. This much interest, though, has me second guessing that." He looked at us for some sort of confirmation.

No one gave him any confirmation.

"So does that mean I'm right?" he said.

A loud clap of thunder interrupted our conversation.

Spann turned around and saw the ominous clouds closing in on us. "Damn," he said and started running toward his tent.

"Let's head for the trailer," Charles said.

The wind began to swirl, and I sensed that the rain would reach us soon. More thunder rumbled in the distance. I followed everyone else into the trailer. Before I closed the door, I looked back at Spann and saw that he was hammering in a spike to further secure the small tent from the gusting wind.

"He's going to get soaked," I said.

"I wonder if he'll ride out the storm in his tent or the car," Kaiden said while looking out one of the trailer's windows.

"They told me it was going to be a nasty storm. That's why they called to warn us," Roger said.

The trailer shook as thunder reverberated around us.

"I think they got the weather right this time," Charles said.

Heavy rain pinged off the outside of the trailer before becoming a steady loud blast against the outside of the trailer. We all took positions around the few windows to watch the storm, but perhaps more so to see what was happening to Spann.

"He's in the tent," Kaiden said. "The extra weight will keep the tent from blowing away, but I'm betting he gets soaked."

The violent storm lasted for about thirty minutes. At one point, small hail fell intermittently with the heavy rain. The dirt clearing became a mud clearing with several rivulets running through it. By the end of the storm, one side of Spann's tent had collapsed. A light rain continued to fall.

We sat out the storm in relative comfort. I didn't hear anyone express any guilt for not warning Spann about the arriving storm. Despite it being obvious, Roger declared our work finished for the day, but warned us that we would start work at dawn.

"Once I can get back out to the truck, I'll get what I need to start dinner. I have spaghetti planned for us tonight. Sorry, but no red wine to go with it," Kaiden said.

"Sounds great," Rose said.

"There's no restaurant for thirty miles, so we have to do our own cooking," Kaiden said.

"What are we going to do about Spann?" Charles asked.

"I'm not sure," Roger said.

"You know, he'll follow us tomorrow," I said. "Maybe we ought to put him to work."

"We can't trust him," Roger said.

"You're right," Rose said, "but unless we call the area a crime scene and keep someone behind to prevent him from getting too close, I don't see what we can do to keep him away from us."

"The biggest threat is his leaking this and making our presence public knowledge. We don't need the cartel sending people here," Charles said. "It makes more sense to swear him to secrecy and let him do some of the digging for us."

"We're not going to get HQ approval to release anything to the press at this point," Roger said.

"We don't have to tell him a thing. We just keep him close by and try to get him not to publish anything before we give him the okay," Charles said.

Roger shook his head. "Let me think about it. I guess we can't simply shoot him and bury him somewhere out here in the middle of nowhere."

"Wish we could," Charles said.

The rest of us grinned at the suggestion, but we knew he wasn't serious.

We stayed in the trailer after the rain stopped. Thunder continued around us and lightning periodically lit up the sky. The storm clouds took the last of the sunlight with them as they blew by. Kaiden opened the door of the trailer and paused to look around before she went out to the truck. I stepped out of the trailer and breathed in the cool air. I had an urge to check on Spann, but the muddy ground kept me from going anywhere.

"Can't help but feel sorry for him," Rose said from behind me.

I turned and saw her in the doorway. "Yeah."

Rose stepped out to let Kaiden back in the trailer.

"Be careful of the mud out here," I said.

"I can see it. I wonder if he sent something out that compromises us, if the cartel would send more people or not."

"I think they would, but they might be more discreet this time. Plus, I've been thinking more and more that that last guy in Cloudcroft might have been sent by someone else."

"Could be," she said. "It's getting cold."

I took that as a suggestion. "Let's go back inside."

"What's Spann up to?" Charles asked, as we entered the trailer.

"Putting his tent back up," I said. "Even from the distance, he looked miserable. You all were smart to dismantle the tents."

"The girl scouts idea," Charles said. I could hear the admiration in his voice.

"By the time we finish eating, most of the water should have run off. We can put the tents back up, and hopefully we'll stay dry," Kaiden said.

I went outside with the three FBI agents after dinner to help them with the tents. Charles and Kaiden had one tent up before Roger and I had secured one side of ours.

"Step aside rookies," Charles said with a big grin.

We gladly did, and the two of them finished the second tent's assembly in no time at all. Headlights shot into the clearing as a vehicle approached. Charles and Kaiden instinctively moved behind the pickup to put it between themselves and the approaching vehicle. Roger took a couple steps toward the oncoming vehicle.

"Go back to the trailer," he said to me.

I did, but rather than go inside, I waited by the door as the vehicle, an old jeep, stopped next to Roger. I heard voices. A few seconds later, the jeep made a u-turn and headed out of the camp area.

"Just the owner of the general store checking on us. I told him you were okay, Spann," Roger shouted.

"Thanks," Spann called back. "Did you ask him to send out some dry clothes?"

We didn't answer.

CHAPTER 14

I heard the shower running when I returned to the trailer. We hadn't discussed the use of the shower, so I stepped back outside. "Who all wants to use the shower tonight?"

"I think I will," Kaiden said. "Should I come now?"

"Sure," I said. Neither of the other two said anything, so I went inside.

Rose stepped out of the bathroom wearing a knee length tee shirt that sported a large UTEP Miners graphic on the front.

"Your turn," she said.

"I think Kaiden is next."

A quick knock followed by the door opening proved my comment. Kaiden entered carrying a towel and a small bag. She glanced at Rose. "How's the shower?"

"Not bad."

"I'll be quick. There's not that much water in the tank," Kaiden said and entered the bathroom.

"How about the other two?" Rose asked.

"I offered, but they didn't respond. Maybe in the morning," I said.

"Their loss," Rose sat down on the couch. The nightshirt rode dangerously up her legs. "Eyes up here," she said. "I left all the cold water for you."

Rather than comment, I walked over to the window and looked toward Spann's tent. The portable lanterns next to the FBI tents provided the only light around. I had a hard time seeing anything around Spann's tent. I didn't see him.

"Anything going on out there?" Rose asked.

"No, not a thing. It's still warm in here from sitting in the sun all day, but I wonder how cold it'll be tonight."

"We should be okay," Rose said. "You want to help me with this couch? It converts somehow into a bed."

The two of us tugged and pulled until the bottom slid out a little.

"You think that's it?" I asked.

"I think it's just for a child, but it'll do for me."

Kaiden came out of the bathroom as we were trying to put the sheets on the bed. Unlike Rose, Kaiden had put her shorts back on and a clean tee shirt. "I see you figured that out. It's not much of a bed, is it?"

"It'll be fine," Rose said.

"Kaiden, are you sure you don't want to sleep in here tonight?" I asked.

"No, no, I love to camp out. The tent will be great. See you all in the morning." She started to walk out but stopped. "Rose, will you lock this after me?"

"Sure." Rose walked over and locked the door after Kaiden left. "So, what did you have in mind asking her to stay the night?"

"What do you mean?" I asked.

"Were you trying to upgrade by having her stay and me go out to the tent, or did you want both of us to stay in here with you all night?"

I knew she was only giving me a hard time. "Can't blame me for trying," I said.

We talked for a few minutes before I took my shower. When I came out of the bathroom, Rose was in bed playing with her phone.

"Not much room in that shower," I said.

"Never fit two people in there," she said without looking up.

I walked by her and stopped at the bedroom door. "Hey," I said.

She looked up at me.

"She wouldn't be an upgrade."

"Liar," she said, but I could see a faint smile on her lips.

I closed the bedroom door behind me and climbed into bed. My mind returned to trying to figure out what in the world possessed Stu to make a run with the briefcase. If the briefcase was full of money, he would have been smarter to have taken one stack of bills. It might not have been missed, and he could have come out thousands of dollars ahead.

Movement and soft conversation woke me up. Only a hint of daylight came through the small window. The room felt chilly, and I had to force myself to climb out of bed. I got dressed and joined Kaiden and Rose. Rose sat on the couch that had been pushed back together, and Kaiden leaned against the diminutive kitchen counter. Bacon started to sizzle in a skillet on the stove.

Kaiden wore similar clothes to what I had seen her in the day before, except now she also had on a black sweatshirt. Rose wore camouflaged slacks, black boots, and an olive green, pullover shirt with long sleeves.

"You two must have gotten up early," I said.

"A woman's work is never done," Rose said.

Kaiden smiled. "How are you this morning, Jim?"

"Might be too early to tell," I said.

"Coffee's made," Kaiden said.

I poured a cup. We talked about the trailer for a few minutes, and Kaiden had started to take the bacon out of the skillet when the door opened and Roger entered. He looked agitated.

"Another damn car has shown up," he said.

"What?" Kaiden said, and we all three went to look out the window.

"It just drove in," he said.

The vehicle, an older model Suburban, sat at the far corner of the clearing.

"See the driver?" I asked.

"Not really. Looked like a single person, a man, in the car as it went by, but the windows are tinted so I can't be sure."

"I wouldn't have thought this place did so much business," I said.

"The guy at the general store said we'd probably have this entire area to ourselves. Definitely gave me the impression they don't get many visitors," Roger said.

"We may have doubled the local population already," I said.

"Did you get a tag number?" Rose asked.

"Can't read it. It's got mud splattered all over it," he said.

"That would be suspicious except for all the mud out there," Kaiden said.

"I think it's still suspicious," Roger said.

The door opened and Charles entered.

"What do you all think?" he asked.

For the next twenty minutes we sat around eating breakfast and discussing our options. We decided to ignore the new arrival and head out to the mine immediately after breakfast.

"Did anyone see Spann this morning?" I asked.

"He was in his car," Roger said. "He either spent the entire night in that little car or moved into it sometime during the night."

"Must have been miserable," Kaiden said.

"Hope so," Charles said.

Roger grinned, and I tried not to. I noticed neither of the women approved our pleasure at someone else's suffering.

"If we're lucky, we'll get away while Spann is still sleeping," Roger said.

"What do you want to do if the other guy follows us out of here?" Rose asked.

"We'll have to stop and ask him what he wants without compromising who we are," Roger said.

As it turned out, the Suburban didn't follow us out of the area, but Spann did.

"We could call in the reinforcements and have them take Spann away for questioning or some other ruse," Charles said.

"We'd lose half the morning, if not longer, and he'd be right back. I'm afraid if we piss him off, he'll publish something," Roger said.

"Yeah, you're probably right," Charles said.

"Want him to work the area with me?" I asked.

"No, we better not. If he ended up being one of the bad guys and killed you, we'd all be assigned to Icebank, North Dakota," Roger said.

I doubted if there was such a place, but did notice his concern centered on their careers rather than my life.

"He can stay with me," Rose said.

Roger glanced at Charles and Kaiden. They didn't comment, so Roger agreed with Rose babysitting Spann.

"I don't even mind keeping him away from the search area. We could simply call it a crime scene," Rose said.

"No, he'll see us with the equipment and walking toward the mine. He knows we're looking for something. You might as well have him tag along and try to see if he'll do the heavy lifting for you," Roger said.

When we stopped, Rose got out and watched Spann park about ten yards away.

"Trying to make me jealous," I said.

"Maybe I'm upgrading," she said and walked toward Spann's car.

I joined the others and started to remove the equipment from the truck. Before we had gotten it all out, Spann and Rose joined us.

"What can I carry?" Spann said. He looked like a kid who had been given a birthday present to open.

Charles handed him a shovel and a pick ax.

As we began the short hike to the mine, I leaned close to Spann. "You know they're going to have you search the area where they saw the rattlesnake den yesterday, so be careful," I whispered.

I thought I'd get away with my harassment, but Kaiden laughed and looked back at us.

"Don't worry, there may be snakes out here, but we didn't see any yesterday," she said.

"So you're a comedian, too," Spann said with no hint that he appreciated my remark.

"He thinks he is," Rose said, but then she surprised me with a wink when Spann wasn't looking.

At the mine, we separated and started exploring our

designated areas in earnest. I used a shovel to turn over rocks, poke around bushes, and dig into areas of the ground that gave me the slightest hint that it might have been disturbed. The rain had softened the ground and made the digging a lot easier than it would otherwise be.

"Hey!" Charles shouted, "I've got something."

Everyone left their search areas and joined Charles. He had dug a hole about eight inches deep and a foot in diameter next to a large boulder.

"I don't know what it is, but it seems to be something wooden rather than a briefcase. I noticed this rock has a white paint spot on it, like someone had marked it."

I thought the paint had been placed there decades ago, not in the past few months. Charles' digging had exposed the top of a wooden crate.

"Doubt if that's it, but I guess he could have removed everything from the briefcase and transferred it to a wooden box," Roger said.

"Who?" Spann asked.

"Patience," Rose said.

Charles and Kaiden attacked the moist ground around the box with their shovels until they could get the end of a shovel underneath it. They could have smashed through the top. The wood looked worn, but they decided to get it out in one piece.

"Geez, it looks like a tiny coffin," Roger said.

Spann took a step backwards and wiped sweat off his forehead.

"It's nailed shut," Kaiden said. "We've got it loose. If we're going to open it, should we take it out of the ground?"

"Yes. Let's be sure. Let me get it," Roger said.

Charles and Kaiden moved aside. Roger knelt in and worked the wooden box back and forth until it slid out. He placed it on the ground next to the hole. Charles handed him a crowbar and without any hesitation, Roger popped the lid open. I thought the nails might hold and the wood break, but the lid and nails popped up without any damage to the rest of the box.

Roger recoiled briefly upon seeing the bones in the box.

"A dog," Rose said. "Someone buried their family dog here. Looks like it's been in the ground for a long, long time."

"I suppose that's not the prize you've been looking for?" Spann said with a touch of sarcasm in his voice.

"You're looking for it, too, Spann," I said.

He didn't respond. I felt like telling him he wasn't making any friends, but Rose grabbed his arm, and the two left to resume their own search.

Roger pressed the lid in place and put the coffin back in its shallow grave. Charles shoveled the loose dirt on top of it and pressed it in place by tapping it down with his feet. Kaiden tossed a small red wildflower on top of the grave.

"Let's hope we didn't just curse ourselves," she said.

CHAPTER 15

We saw the man while we sat around in a circle taking our lunch break. We were all sweating, and evidence of the mud left behind by the rain clung to our shoes and gloves. We munched on prepackaged sandwiches and chips that Kaiden and Charles had picked up on their drive down. Even Spann got a sandwich.

The man stood off in the distance and watched us. A cowboy hat covered his head, and he wore sunglasses that wrapped around his face.

"Is he wearing a jacket? He must be burning up," Rose said.

"He's not out here working," Roger said. "The air is cool. It's our working in the sun that's making it so hot for us."

"Still, it's not cold, and you can't help but wonder if he's wearing the jacket to cover up something," I said.

"That's true," Roger said and dug out his binoculars from the pack he had next to him. He looked at the man. "I don't recognize him, but you can't see much of his face. Here," he handed the binoculars to Rose.

She took them and looked at the man. "He's leaving," she said.

I thought the man realized he was being scrutinized by us, and for whatever reason, he had decided to leave.

"I didn't see enough of him to tell if he was someone I knew or not," she said and handed the binoculars back to Roger.

"Maybe he's a local. They must have some curiosity," Kaiden said.

"Yeah, you're probably right," Charles said. He looked at Roger. "Think one of us should follow him out of here and see if we can ID a car or something?"

"No, he'd be long gone before we'd get out there."

Roger's answer made sense, but if it were up to me, I'd be running down the trail in an attempt to identify the guy or his car.

By four o'clock, we were exhausted and hadn't found any evidence of the briefcase. Frustration had settled in among us.

"My back is going to be sore for a month," Charles said when he and I took a break. He sat down at the same spot he sat for lunch. I sat down next to him.

"I hope we're done for the day," I said.

"Me, too. I think I turned over every rock out there. I dug a dozen holes only to refill them. If it was here, I think someone may have already discovered it."

"Could be. Could also be in the mine. I didn't see Roger go into it yet," I said.

"I don't think he has."

"Hey, Jim, Charles, did you have as much fun as I had today?" Rose asked. She stretched her back to the left and then to the right before plopping down next to me.

Spann followed a few paces behind Rose and carried their tools. His face looked pale, and I wondered if he was about to pass out.

"You okay, Spann?" I asked.

"Just tired," he said and sat down a few yards away from the rest of us.

I grabbed a bottle of water out of the cooler and tossed it to him.

"Thanks," he grunted.

"Looks like we've got another fan," Rose said and pointed up a hillside nearly a half mile away.

I looked and saw a kid squatting on the side of the hill watching us. He looked to be about ten to twelve.

"No threat, I'd say," Charles said. "Wonder where he lives?"

"Looks like a Star Wars shirt that he's wearing," Rose said.

"Better eyes than mine," I said.

"You're a lot older than me," she said with a grin.

Charles motioned with his head towards Spann. Rose and I looked back at him. He was wiping sweat off his head and looked even worse than he had a moment earlier.

"Why don't you lay back, Victor," Rose said. She stood up and went over to him.

"I think I will, but I'm really fine."

Rose rolled the light weight jacket she had brought along but hadn't worn all day and placed it under his head.

"Really, I'm fine," he repeated.

"Did you drink some of the water?" Rose asked.

"Yes."

"Is he okay?" Kaiden asked as she approached us.

I saw Roger not far behind her.

"What's going on," Roger asked.

"Spann's worn out, but he says he's fine," Rose said.

"I doubt if he got much sleep last night. I'm surprised he lasted as long as he has," Kaiden said.

"Good point," I said.

"Better not be anything worse, we're a long way from any hospital out here," Roger said.

"I'm okay. Just got a little dizzy," Spann said.

"I should've warned you about Rose. She has that affect on men," I said.

"Only those with weak minds," Rose said.

"None like that around here," I said.

One of the few clouds that had been in the sky all day finally gave us some shade from the sun. The wind picked up a little bringing with it a little chill.

"That feels good," Charles said. "The wind has changed from this morning. It's coming out of the north."

"May mean we're in for a cold night. What are we up here, about five thousand feet?" Roger asked.

"Around that," Charles said.

I looked for the kid on the hillside, but he had disappeared. This would be a place full of adventure for a boy growing up. Hopefully, he had some other kids his age around with whom he could play and explore.

"You sure you don't want me to look around inside that mine for you?" Rose asked Roger. "I can get in and out a lot easier."

"I don't think it's very safe to be poking around in there, so like I said before, I don't want any of you in there. I'll do it in a few minutes," Roger said.

I had looked into the opening of the mine earlier in the day and didn't think there would be much danger until one went deeper into the mine. I even saw a candy wrapper on the ground about eight feet inside the barrier. At the time, I didn't think much about it, but now I wondered if the boy we had seen had been in there. A couple of two by fours and a danger sign wouldn't be sufficient to keep a curious kid out of anything.

Spann sat up and turned his attention to the mine entrance. "If I was going to hide something in there, I wouldn't hide it at the opening. I'd go a little deeper in the mine. Not too far, but where it starts getting dark."

I agreed with him. I didn't think Stu would make it too easy, but he would want me to find it. I had always thought the briefcase would be within ten yards of the outside of the mine or somewhere inside the mine.

"You may be right," Roger said.

Something in his voice made me feel that he wasn't looking forward to entering the mine. I wondered if he suffered from claustrophobia.

"Did any of you see anything that made you think the briefcase could have been hidden and later discovered at any point out there during your search," Roger asked.

"Not me," Charles said, leading off a round of negative responses from everyone else.

"Okay," Roger said as he stood up and began his slow march toward the mine.

"He's making it rather melodramatic," Rose whispered to me.

I nodded. We all stood and followed Roger to the entrance. Even Spann came along. His face still looked a little pale.

"Will a couple of you shine your flashlights into the cave," Roger asked.

"I wonder why they simply didn't board up the entrance, so nobody could get in?" Rose asked.

"Good question," I said. "Maybe further into the mine it is boarded up."

Everyone except Spann lit up the interior of the mine with

their flashlights, and Roger crawled between the boards that made up the lower X. Wherever he went, we aimed our flashlights to help him in his search. Three additional wooden frames supported the walls of the mine before the walls suddenly closed in and a narrow tunnel continued into the darkness.

Roger scrutinized every section of the mine's walls and the ground. He moved loose rocks and poked into a few shallow depressions.

"Nothing here," he finally said.

"What's down the tunnel?" Kaiden asked.

"Nothing at all. Like someone said, it's boarded up a little ways in there. I guess they wanted to keep the front of this mine open for some reason."

"Is there space enough for the briefcase?" Kaiden asked.

Roger focused his flashlight into the tunnel. The lights from our flashlights did little to help him; his body blocked most of the tunnel entrance. He leaned into the tunnel but didn't enter it. For the next two to three minutes, he stood like that, bent over and still.

"It's not in there," he said when he finally backed away. "I think we definitely need to regroup."

"Damn, what a waste of time," Charles said.

"It has to either still be here or someone has already found it," I said. "The numbers on the page matched exactly."

"We're not blaming you," Kaiden said.

"I know."

"Why don't we stop for the day? We've put in a lot of work, and I need to contact the field office. Maybe we'll come back tomorrow and give it one more effort. We can change up who gets what sections." Roger didn't sound very enthusiastic.

We trudged back to the pickup carrying our tools and supplies. No one said anything until we reached the vehicles.

"For what it's worth, I thank you all for letting me join you today," Spann said.

"Mum's still the word," Kaiden said.

"Don't worry, I'm keeping this quiet until we either find the briefcase or you give me the okay."

"Even if we find the briefcase, you need to keep a lid on this until we give you the okay," Roger said.

"That's what I mean," Spann said.

I thought he meant it, too.

"There's that kid again," Rose said and pointed out the window.

I didn't see him. The pickup made a u-turn and my visibility was blocked.

"See him?" Rose asked.

"No," I said.

"I did," Kaiden said. "I do hope he has a friend somewhere. It could be lonely out here."

"How much water did you women leave us in the shower?" Charles asked.

"Not much. We should get some more water for the tank," Kaiden said.

Since Rose and Kaiden had showers the night before, they insisted on going for the water while the men showered. The two said they would shower later in the evening.

"What the hell!" Roger exclaimed as soon as we parked next to the tents.

"Someone's been through our stuff," Charles said.

Both tent flaps that covered the screen mesh entrances to the tents had been folded back and the zippers closing the mesh openings were unzipped.

"They broke into the trailer, too," I said.

Charles let loose with a volley of expletives that reflected how we all felt. I noticed Rose had removed her pistol from her pack.

"I doubt if he's still there," I said.

The others drew their weapons and all converged on the trailer. I saw Spann watching from across the clearing. I took a few steps away from the trailer. As I expected, no one responded to their shouts to come out of the trailer, and their subsequent search yielded nothing.

"You want to help us with the water?" Rose asked after they all came out of the trailer.

"Yeah, I was going to offer," I said.

"Did anyone leave anything significant behind today when we went out to the search site? Roger asked.

"The bacon," Charles said.

That brought a few chuckles.

"It was still there," Kaiden said.

Everyone agreed that none of us had anything important with us other than the handful of items like our phones, weapons, a couple laptops, and wallets that we took with us.

I went over and checked my car. I hadn't left anything at all in the Mustang's interior. I didn't see any signs of tampering. I opened the trunk, and the few things I had in there appeared to be untouched. Swann inspected his car while I did mine.

"You took your car out with us," I said. "It should be fine."

"It sat out of sight all day, but it looks okay," he said.

"Think it was the guy in the old SUV that came in here this morning?"

"Could be. He's gone now, and fortunately nothing appears to be missing," I said.

"Jim! Ready?" Rose called.

"Yes."

"Where you going?" Spann asked.

"We're going to get more water for the shower."

"You got a shower?" he asked.

"Yep," I said and left him to join the two women at the truck.

"We've got a ten gallon thermos we can put the water in," Kaiden said to me as she drove us out of the camp area.

After a very short drive, Kaiden steered the pickup into a rest area situated in the center of Chloride. I noticed the area had both water and electricity. I also noticed a man standing not too far away wearing a hip holster that looked like it held a large revolver. He also wore a wide brimmed cowboy hat. He started walking in our direction.

"We're going to have company," I said.

"Oh, yeah, that's the guy that runs the store and the museum," Kaiden said. "He's a nice guy." She started walking toward the man. Rose and I fell in behind her. Kaiden greeted the man and called him by name, but I didn't catch what it was.

Underneath his hat he wore a big grin and welcoming eyes. "Howdy young lady, I was glad that you all weren't washed away by the storm. You're welcome to camp here in the rest area. Less prone to flooding. Of course, it may not rain here again for a long time."

"We're fine. Just came in to get some water for the shower

in the trailer. Will that be ok?"

"Sure, I'll give you a hand." He looked at Rose and me. "If you haven't visited the museum, please do. We're pretty proud of it. A lot of the interior is exactly like it was a hundred and twenty years ago. The place was a general store that was shut up and abandoned for years. Family finally came back to see what was there, and we were able to buy it as is from them and convert it into a museum."

"We'd love to," Rose said.

Twenty minutes later the three of us explored the small museum.

"This town had a short but exciting history," I said after reading one of the placards.

"A boom town for a few decades and then a bust," Kaiden said.

"You know, I've always understood the rush to these places by the miners and their families, but I've never understood the women who flocked to these places to work the saloons," Rose said.

"You mean the working girls?" Kaiden asked.

"Yes. I understand life has always been hard for many women, and often they didn't have many choices, but a hundred and thirty years ago, one didn't jump into a car and drive a few hundred miles like they can today. There wasn't even a convenient train that came here. This had to be a hard trek. So what motivated these women to make such a hard journey just to come out here and work the saloons and dance halls?"

"Maybe they were forced into it," Kaiden said.

"A few and many may have started out that way elsewhere,

but why come here?" Rose asked.

"I don't know, but if I were to guess I'd say that most of the women who came out here for that reason didn't think of doing it on their own. I imagine the men and women who were building the saloons here in Chloride reached out to places like El Paso and Santa Fe and negotiated with the owners of the larger operations in those cities. Might have procured them the same way they bought their horses or mules," I said.

"That's kind of crass," Rose said.

"May be right though," Kaiden said. "It's not like today's pimps don't do similar things. Let's talk about something else."

Ten minutes later we were driving back to our camp. In addition to the water we were bringing back, Rose carried a bag with six Snickers and six Butterfingers. She and Kaiden insisted we bring the extra two back for Spann. They even discussed if they should invite him to dinner. I didn't feel any sympathy for him. He wanted to be here. I didn't.

Chapter 16

D inner was a mix of tasty and healthy. Hot dogs, mine came
with a lot of mustard and ketchup, filled the tasty square.
Canned peas and canned corn covered the other.

"You guys know how to pack for a campout," I said.

"I didn't pick the hot dogs," Kaiden said.

Charles grinned. His lower lip sported a nice dollop of
mustard.

Kaiden touched her lip and motioned with her head in that
universal language that means "wipe off your lip." Charles
kept his grin, but cleaned his face.

"Thanks for having me over," Spann said.

We sat in a big circle next to the tents. Kaiden and Rose had
again insisted on doing the cooking and had done so in the
trailer. With the addition of Spann to our group, we decided to
eat outside. Roger had built a small campfire, remarking that it
would keep some of the cold away. The calm, cool air felt good
to me.

"Have another one, Victor," Kaiden said and offered him the
last hot dog.

"Are you sure," he said.

"They've all had two," she said.

I looked at Charles. He had the same look of disbelief as I
felt. I had already wondered if I should grab the last hot dog
and run or offer to share it with him. So what if we each had
had two. At first, I thought that maybe both Rose and Kaiden
would only eat one hot dog. That would leave an extra one for

both Charles and me. Roger didn't quite finish his second and already stopped eating. Rose, however, had ruined that idea by eating a second dog.

"Thanks, Kaiden," Spann said and took the last one.

I looked back at Charles who watched Spann, and whether he knew it or not, he was shaking his head. Charles looked at me and rolled his eyes back in frustration. His head still moved slightly from side to side.

Rose nudged my foot. I looked at her only to receive a stern look in return. I looked back at Charles, but he had already looked away and fiddled with the lone pea on his paper plate like he had no part in our nonverbal conversation.

"And the best part," Kaiden said and reached into the bag next to her, "Who wants a Butterfinger and who wants a Snickers?"

She displayed six of the twelve she had purchased, and somehow our selections came out to an even three and three. I chose a Butterfinger.

We spent a few minutes trying to figure out how we could turn the candy bars into s'mores without Graham Crackers or a good substitute. A purely theoretical discussion as the candy bars disappeared before we came to any conclusions.

"Anyone else sore?" I asked.

"I think we all are," Kaiden said. She rubbed her left shoulder. "Did you bring your Alleve or Advil?" she asked Charles.

"A large bottle."

A rustling in the bushes not far from us got our attention. Roger pointed a flashlight in the direction of the noise, and Charles stood up. The clear, dark, moonless sky didn't provide any light, and the flashlight's beam seemed to be swallowed by the darkness on the other side of the nearest bushes.

"Just an animal," Roger said.

"Hopefully not a chupacabra," I said.

"What's that?" Charles asked.

"They're not real," Rose said.

"I hope not," Kaiden said.

Charles looked like he was going to ask another question about a chupacabra, but changed the topic instead. "So what's the plan for tomorrow, Roger?"

"We'll take one more look around. As I said, we'll swap search zones. After that, we start interviewing people."

"That won't take long," Charles said. "There's no one out here."

"Unless we uncover something, we should be finished by tomorrow night," Roger said.

"Thank goodness," Charles said. "This sleeping on the ground sucks."

I wondered if that was my cue to offer him the trailer. I didn't take it; we had been down that road before.

"Jim and I can move out, and you and Roger can have the trailer tonight," Rose said without making any eye contact with me.

"No, no, we'll survive one more night," Roger said.

"You know you snore," Charles said.

Kaiden laughed. "You both do. When you both got going it was loud."

It seemed late when we finally broke up and headed to bed, but the clock on my phone claimed it was only eight forty five. Charles and Roger had already showered. Kaiden offered the use of the shower to Spann, but he declined.

"I have a hotel room for the night, but I'll be back bright and early tomorrow," he said.

"Wait a minute," Roger said. "We have a deal."

"And I'll honor that deal. Nothing goes out until I get your okay," Spann said.

"Driving all the way back to Truth or Consequences?" I asked.

"It's not far, and it's still early. You want to come?" he asked.

"No, just asking." I could tell that no one was happy with his decision to leave for the night, but they didn't say anything more to dissuade him.

Rose and I offered to clean the few items that needed cleaning from dinner and returned to the trailer. Kaiden came in and took a shower while Rose and I finished up in the kitchen.

"You didn't stay in there long enough to get wet," I said. "We have plenty of water for the three of us."

"I'm fine," she said as she walked to the door. "Tomorrow night I might spend an hour in a shower. Good night."

Rose sat down on her make shift bed, and I sat in one of the small folding chairs that we had taken outside earlier for dinner.

"You know, I can't blame Spann for heading to a hotel tonight. His stuff in the tent may still be damp," I said.

"He didn't sleep well last night. That's for sure, but I know his leaving concerns our FBI friends."

"His story won't be any good unless we discover the briefcase," I said. "It wouldn't make sense for him to publish anything now."

"What if he's not really after the story? What if he is working with the cartel?"

"Don't say that. We've discussed that possibility before, and it won't do us any good to start thinking that again."

"I know," she said.

"It's that other guy I'm worried about."

"You mean the man who came out to our search site and watched us from a distance?"

I nodded. "Think he was the same guy who drove in this morning?"

"I think he's the one who went through our stuff today, too. I keep thinking about him. There was something about him that bugs me. I keep thinking he's someone I've seen before," she said.

"His size? He looked kind of chunky. Maybe my height?"

"It'll come to me," she said.

"If he was with the cartel, it means they know we're here."

"They'd never hit five of us, or six of us if they thought Spann was also with the FBI," Rose said.

"I don't know. It's pretty desolate out here," I said.

"Still, they'd have to think there were more of us around. I think they'd rather count on you somehow getting the briefcase away from us and getting it to them."

"Or maybe simply destroying any list of names, if that's what their main concern is. You know what I've been thinking?"

"No, should I?"

"That boy, the one who's been watching us," I said.

"The one we saw today."

I nodded. "If he's out there a lot, he may have seen Stu. I'm thinking it's more likely he watched Stu stash the briefcase, and then after Stu left, the kid checked it out."

"And if he opened it? My guess is that he would have run off with it," Rose said.

"Without a doubt, but would he take it home or hide it somewhere else for himself? I think we should find out who the kid is and talk to him and his parents."

"Have you noticed the few cars in this place are brand new?"

I thought about that for a minute. "You think maybe the entire town is in on it?"

"That would only be about seven or eight people," she said. "It's not like it would be a very big conspiracy."

"And it would be abandoned property. It's not like anyone stole anything. It'd be the same thought process that Stu went through."

"I think you've got something there. Not bad for a civilian." She smiled and kicked my foot with hers.

She didn't kick hard, but the contact caused a definite increase in my pulse rate.

"Why don't you take the first shower? I'll take mine after you're done," I said.

"No, you go first," she said. "I want to make a couple of calls."

I was in bed when I heard her come out of the bathroom. I didn't expect her to say anything else to me, so she surprised me when she tapped on the door and opened it. She had on the same long, pullover night shirt she had on the night before.

"I'm going to suggest to Roger in the morning that you and I skip the search and find the boy instead," she said.

"Good. Sounds like a plan."

"Good night," she said and closed the door.

My brief shower had helped with some of my aches from the day's work, and I was half asleep when Rose had knocked on the door. Her fifteen second presence at the door had brought me back to being wide awake. She hadn't annoyed me. She had brought up other emotions. I lay there wondering about her, the search for the briefcase, and how I had gotten into another situation that had more control over me than I had over it. More often than not, my mind went back to her.

I hadn't yet resolved anything in my mind before I heard the door open again. This time she didn't say anything, and I didn't either. She slipped into bed next to me. Only then did she say anything.

"Let's keep this between the two of us."

She didn't get an argument from me.

CHAPTER 17

"Is that Kaiden at the door?" I asked.

Not quite awake, it took Rose a couple of seconds to comprehend my comment. She untangled herself from me and sprang up.

"Damn," she mumbled and hurried out of the room. Her step seemed a little awkward as though she was not fully awake. She closed the door behind her.

I heard the door to the trailer open and the two women talking, but couldn't quite make out what they were saying. I reached for my phone and saw that it was almost seven in the morning. That gave me another thirty minutes before I needed to get up, but I decided to get dressed and join the women. Despite the passion and energy she displayed during the night, I knew Rose wanted me to act like nothing happened when I was around the others.

I walked out of the bedroom, and Kaiden looked at me and smiled. "Good morning," she said. Her eyes stared at me like she was trying to read my mind.

At least that's what I felt. On one hand, I got the feeling her eyes were shouting "I know your secret." On the other, it seemed like she might be trying to read my reaction to the events of the last eight hours. I looked at Rose. Her expression confirmed my guess that Kaiden had somehow figured it all out.

"Don't worry, your secret is safe with me," Kaiden said. "I mentioned to Rose that it would've helped if she messed up her bed a little."

I looked over at the pull out bed and saw that it was still neatly made from the day before.

"It's no big deal, guys," Kaiden said. "Rose, get dressed while Jim and I start the bacon."

Rose grabbed some of her things and went into the tiny bathroom.

"We don't have much bacon left," she said.

"We don't have much of anything left," I said.

"Coffee's ready," she said.

I poured a cup of coffee and started to offer her one when I noticed a full cup next to the stove top.

"Have you thought about what you want to do if we can't find the briefcase? It's a fifty-fifty guess whether or not they'll actually send more people after you."

"I've been hoping we'd find it, and that might take me off the hook."

"I'm not sure that would do you much good," she said.

"Do you know anything more about the lone gunman that came after me in the lodge's parking lot?" I asked.

"We think he's a fixer, and an effective one, who works for some very wealthy individuals. We've had our eye on him for a long time. They're being creative to hold him as long they can, but my guess is that they give him back to the locals today or tomorrow, if they haven't done so already. I don't think you'll ever see him again. There are other resources out there, and this guy has been very elusive."

Nothing new, I thought.

"You know we have a fairly decent witness protection plan. You wouldn't exactly qualify, but we've bent the rules before."

She transferred the last of the bacon onto a stack of paper towels covering a paper plate.

"Thanks, but whether or not we find the briefcase, I can't help but think that this will run its course over the next few months. Maybe I could take one of those long cruises I've heard about."

"Too bad Rose has a job. She'd be a good travel companion and bodyguard," Kaiden said. "Hey, how about you help me push that bed back into a couch before the guys show up."

Rose came out of the bathroom looking refreshed. "Thanks," she said when she saw the couch.

"Instant pancakes," Kaiden said, holding up what could have passed for a milk carton. "Want to help?"

"Sure," Rose said and walked by me without making eye contact.

An hour later, we had all eaten.

"Let's clean everything and get packed up before we head back to the mine," Roger said. "Find it or not, we won't be staying out here another night."

"Are they giving up on us?" Charles asked.

"Only the ruse and the search. Later today and tomorrow we interview everyone we can find around here. We'll spend the night in T or C, and the other guys will join us in interviewing managers of restaurants, gas stations, and hotels in the area. Any thoughts or questions?" Roger scanned all of us, but didn't get any feedback.

The three FBI special agents left the trailer, and Rose and I stashed our few items into whatever we had for luggage. She surprised me when she came into the bedroom and kissed me.

"I'm not going to lie. I enjoyed last night, but it was a

mistake. Don't plan on it happening again, at least not any time soon. This is no place or time to get emotionally entangled with you. Am I making any sense?" she asked.

"Sounds like a fancy way to say a 'it's not you, it's me' breakup," I grinned.

She smiled back. "There's nothing to breakup. Perhaps I just needed a one night stand and lowered my standards." She punched me on my chest, turned, and walked away.

We didn't wait for Spann. Although Roger didn't say anything on the drive to the mine, I felt that Spann's absence bothered him. Kaiden must have sensed Roger's feelings, too.

"Victor was tired, and Truth or Consequences isn't right around the corner. I'm betting we'll see him around ten," she said.

Charles grunted his agreement.

"If it was me," I said, "you wouldn't see me until noon. Except I wouldn't want to miss one of Kaiden's breakfasts."

"Hey, if I didn't get into the FBI, I would've given some serious thought to becoming a chef," Kaiden said.

"Too much work and you don't get to carry a gun," Charles said.

We arrived at our parking spot near the mine, and after discussing whether or not to lug out all the equipment again, we decided that each person take a shovel or a pick, and anything else we needed we'd come back to the pickup and get. I think our optimism that we'd find something had hit rock bottom.

This time we spread out to form a search line and walked as a group going back and forth until we had covered the entire area. We moved some rocks around, and we dug and refilled a few holes but discovered nothing. After we finished, Kaiden convinced Roger that she should check the inside of the mine. She spent five minutes studying the same solid rock walls that Roger had earlier chipped and poked. As expected, she didn't discover anything that Roger had missed.

We sat in a circle as we had the day before, and Kaiden passed out the last of the sandwiches.

"Where the hell is Spann?" Roger finally asked.

I had to give him credit for waiting as long as he had. Before anyone could answer, my phone rang. I looked at the phone and saw that it only identified the caller as "out of area." I looked at Rose before I answered.

"Where's my briefcase, West?" the voice at the other end of the call asked.

I pushed the speaker button before I answered, and raised my hand to indicate silence.

"I haven't found it yet."

"I know. I also know you are working with Agent Stillman and the FBI. I know where you are, and I also know you have a cute little daughter at home. She and that dog of yours could go missing if you don't get me the briefcase and soon. You understand?"

"If you know all that, you must know I'm looking for it," I said.

"Should I give you more of an incentive?"

"No, and let me save you some trouble. I don't have a daughter. The girl you saw with my dog must belong to the dog walking service I use. I don't know her, so she means nothing to me. Leave her alone. Do your homework, and you'll see I'm not lying. I have no son, no daughter, and no wife. No one seems to care about me but you."

Silence. I looked around at the others but they offered nothing. Charles studied the area around us.

"You still there?" I asked into the phone. No answer came back. I pushed the end button. "Wonder how he got your name?"

"I've got no idea," Roger said.

"I don't see anyone out there," Charles said and sat down.

"Spann?" Rose asked.

"It better not be," Roger said.

"I don't think it is," Kaiden said. "He really needed this story."

"Then where is he?" Roger said.

"Let me see if I can reach him," Rose said and dialed his number. She shook her head. "Went straight into voice mail."

"Something's not right," Kaiden said.

Roger stood up and walked off a few paces. He called someone and started giving instructions for the hotels in Truth or Consequences to be checked for any record of Spann. It sounded like he said to follow up with the police and the hospitals if the hotels didn't turn up anything, but a side conversation distracted me.

"Think something could have happened to him?" Kaiden asked Rose.

"Very possible."

"He could also just be ignoring your calls," Charles said.

"That doesn't make sense to me," Kaiden said. "There are other places they could've gotten the info."

"Let's head into Chloride and do some interviewing. There's not much more we can do out here," Roger said.

Charles dropped Rose and me off at the clearing near my Mustang. We planned to meet up with the rest of the team at the museum.

"We have a visitor," Rose announced.

I looked in the direction her eyes took me. The young boy stared at us from the edge of the clearing. He looked frightened, and I thought he might bolt if we made any move toward him.

"Stay here," Rose whispered.

She took a few steps toward the kid. He wore blue jeans and tee shirt that could have been a gray or a faded olive green.

"Can I talk to you, please? I'm a police woman. I think maybe you can help us in an investigation we're running." The kid didn't run off, but he didn't say anything either. "Here's my badge." Rose held her badge up in the air. She continued walking, and to my surprise the boy walked toward her.

I stayed where I was until Rose gave me a signal to approach them.

"Jim, this is Manny, short for Manuel. He wants us to follow him. He has something to show us."

"Hi, Manny," I said. He looked at me briefly before turning his attention back to Rose. My thoughts went immediately to the briefcase. In a flash it made sense to me. The kid must have seen Stu hide the briefcase. I wanted to start questioning the kid, but Rose gave me a look that shut me up.

"He says we need to walk there, and that we need to hurry. Lead the way, Manny."

The boy didn't need any additional encouragement. He turned and started jogging. We followed him.

"Let's walk for a while," I shouted after about a half mile run through the uneven terrain. I looked back to get a fix on where we started. Thirty yards ahead of us, the boy started walking.

"This is almost laughable," Rose gasped, perspiration rolled down her forehead.

"You okay?" I asked.

"Me? You should see yourself."

"What did he say he saw?" I whispered.

"Something that scared him. In case you didn't notice, his face was flushed and his hands shaking."

"So he's not taking us to the briefcase?"

"No, but to answer your question, he didn't say what it was he wanted to show us. He said he didn't do anything. I tried to ask him to explain, but he insisted on showing us. I'm going to try to get him to talk to me some more. Stay back here." Rose jogged ahead and called to Manny.

He slowed until she caught up with him. They continued walking together and I followed. I tried to listen to them, but they were too far ahead. Suddenly, they started jogging again.

"Damn," I muttered to myself and started running. At least we were not going uphill at the moment.

I figured we had run another half mile when the duo ahead of me stopped abruptly. The kid pointed to somewhere ahead of them.

"Jim, hurry!" she shouted and ran off leaving the boy.

I ran past him and followed Rose. It took me a few seconds to see what had her attention. A body lay on the ground about thirty yards ahead of me. I knew immediately it was Spann.

CHAPTER 18

Something on the ground scurried away from the body as Rose approached. She stopped a few feet away from the body, and I stopped next to her.

"Spann," she said without emotion.

We didn't have to check the body for signs of life. The large slice in his neck had stopped bleeding hours ago, and one of his eyes appeared to be missing. I looked around and scoured the area for anyone who might be watching us. Manny had already disappeared. He could've been out there watching us from some hiding spot, but I didn't see him. I didn't see anyone else either, but I did see Spann's car about a quarter mile away.

"Rose," I said.

She raised her hand indicating for me to wait, and I saw that she had her phone up to her ear.

"Roger, we've found Spann.....Yes........I'm not sure how to tell you to get here...."

I tapped her on the arm, and when I had her attention, I reached for her phone. She looked at me quizzically but gave me the phone.

"Roger, take the road out of Chloride like your heading back the way we came in. I can see the road and will call you when you come into view. It's not far........Okay."

I returned the phone. "They're coming right now. Over there is Spann's car." I pointed to it, but Rose couldn't see it. I realized the extra nine or ten inches I had on her gave me an advantage. "Just beyond it is the road. I can see a small section of it."

"Do you see enough of it to not miss them?" I knew she referred to the FBI team.

"I think so, but why don't you stay here, and I'll walk back up a little higher. It'll give me a better view of the road."

She agreed, and I hurried to a spot about forty yards away from Spann. It put me about five or six feet higher and gave me a better view of the road. We didn't see Spann's car during our approach to Spann's body because by that time we were focused on the body. His car sat a distance off to our right. I noticed the car had been driven off the road to a secluded spot that might keep it hidden from anyone driving down the road.

My wait lasted only a few minutes. The large pickup sped into view.

"You're here! You need to stop," I spoke louder than I probably needed.

The pickup squealed to a stop.

"Look out the driver's side windows. At your ten o'clock position, you should see me, maybe a half of a mile."

"Got you," Roger said. "Are you sure he's dead?"

"Yes. You've got another car coming up on your rear," I said.

"I know. It's okay."

I watched the pickup maneuver off road to a spot a little closer to Spann's car. The jeep that had followed the FBI stopped on the road. Two men got out of the jeep and walked up to the FBI team that waited for them by the pickup. I walked down to Rose who knelt down near the body. I squatted next to her.

"I don't see any evidence that someone dragged him out here. No trail of blood and no drag marks. Whoever did this had him walk out here, and then they killed him," she said.

I thought it might be possible that they carried him, but kept the thought to myself.

Rose' phone rang. "No. My guess is that his killer had him walk up here…..Jim, stand up so they can see you and wave at them. They don't want to walk straight up here."

I stood and waved my arms again. Kaiden pointed at me, and the five started walking a diagonal direction slightly away from me. I realized they didn't want to do anything to the most likely path Spann and his killer or killers took.

Rose stood up next to me, no longer on the phone. "Poor Spann. What do you think happened?"

"I think this is how they got Roger's name," I said.

"I think so, too. Did you see his fingers?"

I looked back at his hands. Two fingers in his left hand looked bent out of shape and discolored. I wasn't an expert on death, so I wasn't sure about the discoloration of the fingers, but they were definitely broken. I looked at his other hand but the fingers looked normal. Then I noticed the wrists.

"Look at his wrists," I said.

"I noticed that. His wrists might have been bound. The lab should be able to tell us with what."

"The way his hands are laying at his sides looks like whoever did this undid his wrists after he fell and dropped the arms to his sides. Have you ever seen marks like he has on his wrists before?"

Her eyes suddenly shot at mine. "Handcuffs?"

"Yes."

"That's not normal," Rose said.

"Not at all," I said.

"Doesn't mean a cop did this."

"I know. A person can buy his own set of handcuffs."

"How the hell did you find him?" Charles asked as the group approached.

"Manny, the young boy, brought us here," Rose said.

"Young boy? Where is he?" Roger asked.

"Ran off," I said. "Can't blame him."

"Did you say Manny, Manny Aranjo?" asked one of the men who followed Roger and the others out. I didn't recognize him.

"Don't know his last name, but how many eleven, twelve year old boys run around out here?" Rose asked.

"It's him. He's a good kid. Lives with his grandmother not far from here."

"We can talk to him later. What do you think happened?" Roger asked.

Rose briefed the FBI trio on what we believed happened. They seemed to accept our theory and agreed with us that the bruising to the wrists appeared to have come from handcuffs or something similar to a set of handcuffs.

"The sheriff has been notified, so we should back away and let them take over the crime scene when they get here. In the meantime, Kaiden, get as many pictures as you can of all this," Roger moved with his hand in a circle indicating the body and the area around it. He also pointed toward Spann's car.

Rose and I backed away. She looked in the direction that we last saw Manny.

"Think he's out there somewhere?" I asked.

"Yes. I'm hoping he'll show himself. He didn't explain how he discovered Spann, or if he saw what happened to him."

"I hope he didn't witness the murder."

"It would be good if he could give a description of the killer," she said.

"Yeah, but witnessing someone have their throat sliced open isn't something a young kid needs to see."

Rose nodded. She walked over to Roger and talked to him briefly. The two then walked over to the two men from Chloride and the four huddled for a few minutes. When the four broke up, she walked back to her spot next to me.

"You made me think of something," she said.

I looked at her and waited for her to continue.

"We talked about our need to talk to Manny, but we also stressed the need to keep his involvement in all this confidential. If word gets out that the kid may have seen something, both his and his grandmother's lives may be in danger."

A stream of flashing lights appeared in the distance coming from the direction of Truth or Consequences. The two locals started walking toward the road. I was impressed that the two retraced their trail coming to the crime scene rather than taking the direct path.

After an hour, I started feeling trapped at the scene. Not that I didn't find it all interesting, and I was impressed how well the sheriff and his deputies accepted the involvement of the FBI and Rose, but no one wanted my help. Rose had twice come up to me to ask how I was doing. She sensed how I felt, and while I didn't need the sympathy, I did appreciate her concern. The two locals had left the area about twenty minutes after the sheriff arrived.

As if we didn't have enough people working the crime scene, the FBI reinforcements who had been in Truth or

Consequences showed up. Roger went and met the two near the road.

What followed surprised me and pissed me off. However, I think I handled it better than Rose did.

CHAPTER 19

"Deputy Luna, Mr. West, I'm Special Agent Ferguson. This is Agent Miller." Neither agent extended a hand. "We need you both to hand over your phones."

"What?" Rose said. She didn't use her happy voice. "What the hell is going on, Roger?" She looked at Roger who was busy talking to the sheriff.

At first, I thought he was going to pretend not to hear her, but since everyone else there now stared at her, he answered her. "It's routine elimination, Rose. Please bear with it. They'll be checking our phones, too."

I doubted that last part, but I didn't see we had much of a choice. I handed him my phone. Rose said something in Spanish that made me happy Manny wasn't within hearing distance, but she did hand her phone to Ferguson.

"Thanks, Deputy. If we really thought you had been in contact with the other side, we'd also be taking your service weapon."

Rose bristled but didn't say anything.

"I hope Stillman told you that you'd find a few suspicious calls on my phone." I figured we should be all official now, no more pretending we were all buddies.

"Follow Miller down. I'll catch up with you in a second," Ferguson said.

We started for the cars, and Ferguson went over and talked to Stillman.

"Good thing you mentioned that, or these asnos would have

you in cuffs and sitting in a cell before dinner," Rose said.

Agent Miller didn't seem very pleased at her attitude. Her reference to them as jackasses in Spanish didn't help.

"Miller, before you get too angry at my partner in crime here, please understand that we've been a team with the FBI crew up there for the last few days. We're only here at the FBI's request, and I for one thought we'd been cooperating like good citizens." I wanted to keep talking, but I knew if I did I would likely say something that would ruin my pretend conciliatory mood.

"I bet you were a kiss ass in the military, too," Rose whispered.

All three of us laughed at that. Miller's hearing was better than Rose had given him credit.

"Look," Miller said. "The reason Agent Stillman wanted the two of us to do this is because we haven't spent the last couple days with you. He thought we could be more objective. It's a step we have to do. You know if we find the murder weapon, we'll have to compare any prints we find with yours."

It made sense. I imagined the fingerprints of the agents at the scene would also be compared against those found on the weapon. The technology had improved since I left the Air Force Office of Special Investigations. I believed the system was more comprehensive. In addition to comparing suspect's fingerprints with those found at the crime scene, the computers today compared those found at the scene against all fingerprints in a national database. My mind was reworking this idea when my thoughts were interrupted by Rose elbowing me on my arm.

I looked at her and saw her eyes turn toward a ridge line about a half mile away. I followed her gaze, and after a few seconds saw what she had.   Manny crouched along the ridgeline partially hidden by a bush and watched us. I didn't have to wonder why she didn't say anything. The last thing we needed was a bunch of grownups chasing the kid and scaring him.

A thought struck me. Manny might not be the only person watching us right now. I looked around but didn't see anyone else.

Our interviews took place leaning against Ferguson and Miller's government sedan. The fact that they didn't separate us set a better tone and calmed Rose down. My phone came back first. Of course, my phone history could be compared to that of a hermit.

"Not much for texting are you?" Miller said when he returned my phone.

They spent a little longer on Rose' phone copying contacts, messages, calls, and for all I knew email contacts.

"Glad to see you're a little more normal than he is," Miller said when he returned her phone.

"Couldn't you all have done this remotely since we've given you permission to monitor our calls?" I asked.

"Takes a lot more time, and we only got that permission from you," Miller said.

Ferguson took over from there and for the next twenty five minutes we explained what had happened since we left Cloudcroft, and what we thought happened to Spann. This latter part was easy, since neither of us had anything substantive to tell.

"You know Spann's wallet and phone are missing," Ferguson said.

"We heard," Rose said. "Whoever killed him didn't want anyone to find him for a while and then didn't want identification to be easy. If the boy hadn't brought us to him, the killer or killers would have succeeded."

"Why do you think they left his car out here? That would defeat the purpose of concealing his identity," Ferguson said.

"They moved it off the road quite a distance. I haven't driven this stretch to see if we can see it from the road, but maybe they planned to come back tonight and move it to a different location," I said.

"If one person killed him, they couldn't drive off in both cars at the same time. He or she would have to get help and come back for it later," Rose said.

"My thoughts exactly," Ferguson said.

Sure, I thought, after Rose walks you through it.

"We've been brainstorming ideas and theories with Agent Stillman and his team for the last couple of days," I said. "I imagine they will get a pass from the locals from being interviewed. I don't know if Rose and I will be offered the same courtesy, and I'm not asking for you to run any interference, but we need you to find out from Roger how much of what we were doing out here he wants me to tell them."

"I'll do that, and I'll go one step further. I'll recommend they not waste their time interviewing either of you," Ferguson said.

The way my luck had been ever since Stu's letter landed in my mailbox, I should've expected what would happen next. The sheriff agreed to one of his deputies getting a brief verbal statement from Rose at the scene, but they wanted me to follow one of his deputies back to his offices in Truth or Consequences.

I didn't like leaving Rose, but both the FBI and the sheriff said they would give her a ride.

I had hoped the word coming back from Roger would be for me to only talk about discovering the body, but they had already decided no more veil of secrecy. Rehashing the entire series of events since receiving the letter from Stu took a couple of hours. If they hadn't asked so many questions and debated things among themselves, I could've talked them through it in a lot less. However, when I got to the shootout in Cloudcroft, my interviewers went from one to three, and my interview started over.

Although I occasionally felt like one or more of the deputies thought I was holding back something from them, a natural feeling for most law enforcement types since it's usually true, they treated me okay. They treated me to a cup of lukewarm, bitter coffee that even included a few grounds of coffee that had somehow made it into the pot. By the time they let me leave, the sun had set.

I dialed Rose on my phone when I stepped out of the building. I didn't need to since she was sitting on the hood of the Mustang. I slid my phone back into my pocket on the first ring.

"It's me," I said when she reached for her phone.

"You okay?" she asked.

"Yeah, just tired and hungry. I told them most everything, but I didn't tell them about Kay. She needs to stay out of this."

Rose nodded. "Nothing personal, but you could use a shower and some clean clothes, too."

"I don't know if I have any clean clothes left. Do you know where we're staying tonight?"

"A local hotel, not a chain, but they do have a place you can do your laundry," she said.

"Everyone else there, too?"

"Afraid so. Charles is still out at the crime scene, but the rest of us got back about thirty minutes ago. Come on, I'll show you where it is."

She directed me into the heart of the small city to La Plaza Hotel.

"Looks as old as the city," I said.

"It's not bad," she tossed me a room key after we got out of the Mustang. "You're across the hall from me. FBI is treating. Kaiden talked Roger into it," Rose grinned as she said this last bit.

"Can't blame him for wanting to get rid of us," I said.

"But when he does, it means they're giving up on the briefcase."

"I'm ready to give up on it."

"Hang in there," she gave my arm a squeeze. "The more I think of it, the more I feel Manny has that briefcase."

"I think you're right. Has anyone found him yet?"

"Not when we left. One of the deputies has met the grandmother in the past. He said he would try to get in touch with them this evening."

"One deputy by himself?"

"Are you starting to see bad cops everywhere?" she asked.

"Paranoid, sorry."

"Here you are," she said and pointed to my hotel room. "Take a shower and put on something halfway clean. Then I'll buy you supper."

"I won't feel safe in there by myself."

"Take your weapon with you into the shower." She must have sensed I had a childish comeback. "Don't say anything."

Kaiden joined us for supper, and for nearly the whole meal, we avoided discussing the investigation. Moments after we asked the waiter for our bill, Kaiden received a call from Roger.

"That's interesting," she said after the call. "No one answered at Manny's home. No reason they couldn't have gone somewhere this evening, but still it's not very comforting. Also, Spann had a broken finger and a couple broken ribs."

"It almost had to be the same person that watched us from a distance at the mine," I said.

"Or the person who drove into our camp grounds yesterday. Was that only yesterday morning?" Rose said.

"Yes, time flies when you're having fun," Kaiden said.

"Some fun," Rose said.

"Whoever killed Spann got our names and the results of our search from him first. That's how they had Roger's name when they called me today," I said.

"I wonder if he had family somewhere?" Rose asked.

"I don't know," Kaiden answered.

CHAPTER 20

I slept better than I thought I would that night. My fatigue took over, and I fell asleep within seconds of putting my head on the pillow. I don't think I dreamed. The rumble of a truck woke me a little after six in the morning. I dressed and went out for a walk.

Last night, I had hoped that Rose might have wanted to share a bed again, but the last thing she said before we parted ways was for me not to get any ideas. She said all that she could remember happening our last night in the trailer was that she had a bad dream. Neither her tone nor the twinkle in her eyes led me to believe she was serious, but she still closed the door in my face.

My mind returned to the mysterious man who showed up at our search site a couple days earlier. I started thinking again that I had seen him somewhere. As I walked, I tried to match what little I saw of his face with all the people I had met over the past week. I gave up, but something about him gnawed at me.

At dinner the night before, the three of us had come up with possible ways Spann's killer could have gotten him to stop on that stretch of road. The killer could have been standing next to his car pretending that it had broken down, he could've been hitchhiking, but the one that struck me as the most effective way was for him to pretend he was a cop. If he had flashers and signaled Spann to stop, Spann would've. That led to a further discussion on whether or not the killer was a cop. Kaiden and

Rose said no, and while I tended to agree with them, we had so many leaks in this investigation I couldn't rule out a cop being involved.

When I finished my walk, I showered and after making a cup of coffee in the room, I took the coffee and my laundry down to the coin operated machines in the basement. I peeked into the small café as I went by, but didn't see any of our group. I called Rose from the laundry room, but my call went directly into voice mail.

I didn't see any of them in the cafe when I returned to my room, and Rose didn't respond when I knocked on her door. Becoming a little concerned, I decided to treat myself to a big breakfast. Nothing helps denial like a large stack of pancakes.

My breakfast had just arrived when all four of our team walked into the hotel's small café. Rose joined me at my table and the other three grabbed an adjacent table.

"Did you meet a Sergeant Tremble in Fabens when you talked to Detective Kent?" Rose asked.

"The name doesn't ring a bell," I said.

"He might have been at the desk that day."

"The policeman eating," I said. "You don't think he's the guy we saw?"

"I think he was. He's been on sick leave the last couple of days. I don't know why it took me so long to think of him," Rose said.

"It's not like we ever got a good look at him."

"I know, but his build, his size, his round face. It came to me last night?"

"You mean you weren't thinking of me?"

"Thankfully not. Seriously, though, I think he's our guy,"

she said.

"You think he killed Swann?"

"I don't want to go that far, but it's possible. Anything's possible."

"Are they trying to find him?" I asked.

"Yes, but very discreetly. They're putting a big net around him to hopefully identify who he's in contact with."

"That's great, Rose. Let's hope it pans out."

"I think it will. I feel like everything's going to come to a head soon."

The waitress interrupted our conversation.

"Let me have what he's having," Rose said.

For the rest of the morning we sat around and did very little. The instructions Roger received from above told us to stay put. The sheriff's department made another unsuccessful attempt to contact Manny's grandmother at noon. At two in the afternoon, with nothing else to do, Rose and I decided to head back out to Chloride.

"So what's our plan," I asked Rose when we drove out of town. She had been a little evasive about why she suggested our return to Chloride.

"I didn't want the others to come this time. I want us to try something."

I glanced over at her while I waited for her explanation.

"If Manny sees us out there, and I think he sees just about everything, I think we might be able to get him to talk to us."

"So, instead of trying to find him, we let him find us."

"Yes," she said. "I didn't want to press our luck by having someone else come with us. We're a little out of our jurisdiction doing this, so it's just as good for everyone to think we encountered Manny by chance."

"If we encounter him at all," I said.

"That's right. If we see him at all."

We drove straight out to the small clearing where we had camped, and I parked the Mustang in the spot I had used before. Except for the emptiness of the place, everything looked the same. A dry, cool breeze came in from the north bringing with it a scent I didn't recognize.

"It's really nice out here," I said. "I don't think we really got to appreciate it with all the work we did."

"Our work isn't finished quite yet. I suggest we take a walk out to some of the higher points around us. Try to make ourselves obvious to any small eyes studying the area."

"Lead the way," I said.

"It doesn't have to be that official," Rose said and grabbed my hand.

"This is more like it," I said.

Our romantic stroll didn't last very long. The terrain didn't allow much walking side by side. After no more than fifty yards, we let go of each other and focused more on not stepping into some thorn bush or tripping over a rock. Without any intent, after thirty minutes, we came to a high point where we could look down and see what was left of the crime scene. The body and car had been removed, but a lone deputy sat in a collapsible chair next to an area that still had police tape around it.

"If it wasn't for the deputy and the police tape, I doubt if I would have even recognized that's where we found the body," I said.

"Same here. Do you see Manny anywhere?"

I searched the surrounding area but didn't see him. Rose looked, too.

"Some antelope over there," I pointed across the road.

"Think we can walk in this direction without getting lost?" Rose pointed in a direction taking us away from the crime scene and the road and at a right angle from the direction we had come.

"I never get lost," I said.

"If we do, you're in trouble then."

"We should have set our phones' GPS settings at our parking spot," I said.

"Should have and could have, what did my mom tell me about those words?" Rose said.

We started off, and it didn't take long before everything started to look the same. Despite the cool air, I felt myself start to perspire. Hiking along this route turned out tougher than it had been during our first stretch away from the clearing.

"I hate to say this, Rose, but I think those two buzzards up there are following us."

"You know where we are, right?"

"Nope, but that doesn't mean we're lost." I grinned and held out my hand.

"Look," she said and nodded her head toward a series of large boulders about thirty yards away.

Manny sat on top of one of the mid-sized ones. Rather than approach him, Rose waved at him and smiled.

"Let's stay here for a minute," she said. "I'm glad he showed up. I was worried that something may have happened to him and his grandmother."

"Me, too. I still wonder why they weren't able to make

contact since they knew where Manny lives."

"Why are the police bothering my grandmother?" Manny called out to us.

We started walking over to him. "The police want to talk to you, not your grandmother," Rose said.

"Me?" Manny asked. He stood up when he spoke, and I thought he might sprint away.

Rose must have sensed what I did, because she stopped walking when I did, giving Manny plenty of space.

"It's nothing bad, Manny. They only want to know if you saw what happened to the man you took us to."

"I didn't see anything. I came to get you right after I found the man. I ran all the way. I didn't see anything. Is he dead?"

"Yes, he was dead. You did a good thing taking us there. Now the police have a good chance to catch who did this to him," Rose said.

"Who killed him?" Manny asked.

"We don't know yet?" Rose said.

Manny seemed to think about this for a minute. We started walking toward him again. He didn't seem to be bothered by our approach.

"How did the man kill him?" Manny asked.

"We think he may have stabbed him with a knife," Rose said.

"I didn't see anybody else. You think it was that other man?"

"What other man?" Rose asked.

"The man that came after you did. He watched you while you were hunting for something by the mine. And then he went back to your campsite and went into your tents and the trailer. I think he was a bad man."

"You saw him go through our tents?" Rose asked.

"Yes. I can run there as fast as you can drive. The road goes in a big circle."

"If I showed you a picture of the man would you be able to recognize him?" Rose asked.

"Why?"

"In case he was the same man, it would be good to know who he was. Don't you think it would be good to know?"

"I guess so. Do you have a picture of him?" Manny asked.

"I think I might," she said. "It'll take a second."

We reached the boulders. Manny must have decided that we were okay, because he made no effort to get away.

"If you know the police wanted to talk to you and your grandmother, why didn't one of you talk to them when they came to your house?" I asked while Rose fiddled with her phone.

Manny grinned. "We weren't there. We were building my fort up on the hill in the backyard and saw them. My gran' said if it was important they would come back."

"Did they come back?"

"I don't think so," Manny said.

"Here, look at these four pictures and see if the man you saw was one of these," Rose said holding her phone up for Manny to look at the screen.

"That's him," he said after seeing the second picture.

Rose looked at the picture. "Not one of these others?" She showed him the last two pictures.

"No. It was the one I said."

"Good. Thank you very, very much!" Rose said.

"Is your house very far from here?" I asked.

"No. My gran doesn't know about the man."

"Then we won't talk to her about him," I said. "Does she know about the briefcase?"

"No." His response slipped out. He looked down at the ground. "I think I better go."

I knew my question spooked him.

Rose looked up from her phone. She looked at me, and I felt like she thought I had rushed it. "Manny, no one is mad at you for taking the briefcase. I would have done the same thing."

He didn't look like he believed a word she said.

"That's what we were looking for," she said.

"I know," he said. "Is that why someone killed that man?" He kept his eyes focused on the ground.

"Yes. Some bad men are looking for that briefcase," Rose said. "Manny, look at me. Please."

He finally raised his head. "Are they going to kill me?"

"No," we both said in unison. Without taking her eyes off the boy, her left hand gave my right arm a gentle tug. I had been married long enough to realize the tug was her gentle way of telling me to shut up.

"No one else knows you have the briefcase, and we will never tell anyone else. Jim and I know this is your land. Nothing happens out here without you finding out about it. The others don't know you like we do." She paused to let Manny speak, but he said nothing. "Manny, it's very, very important that we get that briefcase from you and give it to the FBI. You know about the FBI, don't you?"

"Yes. What if I lost it?"

"What do you mean?" Rose asked.

"Lost it, you know, but then I found it again. If something is missing, it doesn't mean I took it."

"Of course, besides no one will even know you had it. That will be our secret," she said.

"Promise?"

"Yes," Rose said. "We'll tell everyone that we found it on our own. We won't mention your name."

Manny looked at me.

"I promise, too."

"Okay. You can have it." He jumped off the boulder and started walking away.

We followed staying about ten yards behind him. We didn't do so to give him some space. He walked faster than we did, and we had a hard time just keeping that close to him. I sensed the excitement in Rose and felt the same. I also realized that I was entering the most dangerous phase of this strange situation.

"What did you get me into, Stu," I mumbled to myself.

"What?" Rose asked.

I didn't know what to say to her, so I simply shook my head.

CHAPTER 21

Manny led us to a small cluster of mesquite trees. He reached behind a thick bush that sported thorns the size of sewing needles. Between the bush and a tree, he pulled out the briefcase.

"It wasn't locked, and there's no name on it. I've been watching for the man to come back looking for it. I would've returned it to him." He gave the briefcase to Rose without any prompting. "There's a bunch of money in it. I thought Gran and me could use it."

"Everyone will be a lot safer now. Once the bad guys learn the FBI has the briefcase, they'll stop looking for it," Rose said.

"I'd better get home now," Manny said.

"Before you go, Manny, what direction do we take to get back to where we had the tents and trailer?" I asked.

"That way. It's just below that hill," Manny pointed.

"Thanks, Manny. Remember, this is our secret. We won't tell anyone about your involvement," Rose said.

"Okay," he said and started jogging away.

"I think we should open it," I said.

She knelt over, and after placing the briefcase on the ground, she opened it. Leaving the briefcase on the ground, Rose stood and backed up a step or two. She whispered something in Spanish.

I knelt down to get a better look. The briefcase was crammed with packets of one hundred dollar bills. A wide rubber band held together each stack. One stack had no rubber band and while most of the bills had stayed in place, a few bills had spread around loose in the briefcase.

"Think maybe Stu used some from that stack," I said.

"Hopefully, Manny took some, too. I feel like taking four or five and giving them to him," Rose said.

"Me, too, but it would be a lot safer for everyone if we didn't right now. We're both going to be answering a lot of questions, and it might be better if we were to keep our number of lies to a minimum."

"I know," she knelt down next to me and I saw that she had put on crime scene gloves. She removed one stack of hundreds. Another stack sat below it. She replaced the stack. She then unzipped the pocket on the inside of the top of the briefcase. "Nothing here," she said as she leaned over to get a better view. "Oh, wait a minute." She reached into the pocket, and after straining for a few seconds with her finger trying to grip something, she pulled out a small flash drive.

"What do you bet that's what all the fuss is about? I said.

"You call it fuss?" she asked. "I'd use a stronger word."

I stood up and looked around. "Suddenly, I don't feel so safe out here."

She closed the briefcase and stood next to me. "See anything?"

"No, but I suggest we hurry back to the car and get that thing to the FBI as quickly as we can." We started walking.

"So, you don't want to split the contents and say we didn't find anything?"

"I wish. What would you do with all that money?" I asked. I knew from the tone of her voice she was kidding, but the thought of keeping all that money had a pull to it.

"I'd buy a new house, a new car, and I might adopt my nephew. How about you? Would you spend it all right away, or are you a saver?"

"I don't really need anything."

"Liar," she said and shifted the briefcase from one hand to the other.

"If you give me one of those gloves, I'll carry the briefcase. Promise I won't run off." I stopped walking.

She hesitated for a second before setting the briefcase on the ground and giving me the glove she had on her right hand. I took the glove, and after putting it on, I picked up the briefcase. We continued our trek.

"This briefcase is heavy with the money in it, but I imagine I could still outrun you," I said grinning and not believing a word of it anyway. Speedy has never been a word used in my resume.

"Why do you think I gave you this glove," Rose said holding up her right hand. "This is my shooting hand."

A movement off to our right had us both stopping.

"Just some deer. Maybe we should walk a little faster," I said.

We would have missed the campsite if we hadn't caught sight of the Mustang a couple hundred yards off to our left.

"There it is. See, never a doubt. I never get lost."

"We almost walked right by it," Rose said. "Who's that?"

I saw him, too, a man walking away from the Mustang. He crossed the clearing to a Jeep partially hidden from our view by a couple of Cholla cacti a dozen or so yards in front of us. He stopped at the Jeep and leaned against it.

"I think it's the man from Chloride. I don't believe he poses a threat, but I don't want him to see the briefcase," Rose said.

"What do you want to do?"

"We're not letting go of the briefcase. Let me go down and distract him. Once his back is turned, you come and get the briefcase in the car as fast as you can." She walked off in the direction of the man and my Mustang.

I let her get a good lead before following her. I did my best to keep myself behind whatever cover was available in case the man looked in our direction. Fortunately, he was on his cell phone with his back toward us. I did wonder who he had called. When she reached the clearing, I found a thick bush to squat behind. She called to him, and he looked up smiling and putting a finger up to indicate he'd be with her in a minute. Rose walked on by him and picked up something off the ground.

I stayed where I was until the man got off his phone, and Rose approached him. When she extended a hand to shake, I walked as fast as I could without making a lot of noise toward the car. I could see Rose displaying her badge and then showing him something on her phone. The man nodded acknowledging something she must have said. I reached the Mustang, and keeping the car between us, I opened the driver door and tossed in the briefcase. When I looked back up the man was looking at me. Behind him, I could see Rose smiling. Mission accomplished. I waved at the man, and he waved back. Rose said something else to the man before hurrying over to join me at the car.

"Let's go," she said. "He came out to see if we needed anything. Someone saw us drive through Chloride and called him. For a town that supposed to be a ghost town, there sure are a lot of busy bodies."

"Did you show him the picture?" I asked.

"Yes. He confirmed it. Tremble was here. He said he only saw Tremble that one day. The same day we did. He hadn't seen him or anyone else in the area since then."

"Do you think he saw the briefcase?"

"No. I couldn't believe how slow you were getting to your car," she laughed. "Didn't they have any physical fitness programs in the military?"

"That was a few years ago. Are you going to call Roger?"

"Yes," she said. "He might be upset with us for moving the briefcase."

"Tell him we had no cell reception where we were, that there were no landmarks, and that we felt like sitting ducks. Someone could have been watching us from a distance, so we needed to get the hell out of there."

"Why were we out there alone?"

"Tell him the truth. We went out to see if we could find Manny, but say that we found the briefcase instead," I said.

"Why would the briefcase be in the middle of nowhere and not by the mine?" she asked.

"Okay, say we found it just outside our search area. We could say that if we searched another fifty yards away from the mine we would've found it."

"Except we had phone reception there," she said.

"Well, we do need to keep Manny out of this," I said.

"I know what I can say." She dialed Roger. The conversation didn't last long. I heard her say that we didn't want to sit out in the open, and for the moment, Roger accepted that excuse. She gave me a thumbs-up after the call. "To say he's excited might be understating it."

"Think he bought our excuse for not calling them out when we discovered it?" I asked.

"For the moment, and just to keep our story straight, if they press us, I'm going to tell them I found the briefcase in that rock pile not too far from where we searched. Do you remember it? It was outside the section I had to search. I did think at the time on the last day that I should check it out, but by the time I finished the area we had, it had slipped my mind."

"Sounds good. You know, they may find Manny's fingerprints all over the case and the money, but I imagine it's a safe bet that he's not in any database yet."

"In ten, fifteen years, if some future computer program links him to the briefcase, it won't be important to anyone," Rose said.

I knew she was right. I figured most of the fallout would take place in the next couple of years. For me the window could be measured in days.

"You know, in addition to keeping Manny out of this, I think we need to convince Roger to keep my name out of the discovery," I said.

"You mean only out of any press release, right?"

"Yeah. I wouldn't like for my anonymous phone caller to know I had my hands on the briefcase and didn't call him. It'll sound much better saying that you guys found it without my being there."

"Makes sense," she said.

I slowed down and pulled over to the side of the road. "Let's go the rest of the way in style," I said and lowered the top of the convertible.

"Too bad you didn't bring a bottle of champagne."

I turned the radio on to a jazz station, and we drove off. We hadn't gone a mile and Rose rested her hand on my thigh. For the moment, things couldn't have gotten much better. We had less than three miles to Truth or Consequences when we spotted a car about a half mile in front of us with what looked like official police flashers turned on.

"Looks like a detective's vehicle. Think someone is out here to escort us in?" Rose asked.

All I could think of was Spann. I wondered if this was how he met his end. I slowed, but as we neared it, I didn't see anyone around the car. Rose sat up straight, and I sensed her body tense. About thirty yards from the car, I floored the accelerator and the Mustang flew past the sedan. We had barely made it back in our lane when a spark flew off the frame of my car above the rear view mirror. Simultaneously, a chunk of rubber vaporized, and I heard a sound that I knew was a round ripping through the car's frame at the top of my windshield.

"Down!" I shouted, but Rose had already reacted by ducking. I couldn't tell if our assailant fired another round at us or not, but we made it around a bend and out of view. I stopped the car. "Now it's our turn."

I counted on our assailant thinking that we raced all the way to Truth or Consequences. I knew he could drive away in the opposite direction, but he didn't. Without any comment, Rose sprinted across the road and back in the direction we had come. She stopped behind a four foot high pile of rock and other debris that had been dumped there some time ago. I had the Mustang to use for cover. The sedan raced around the bend before slowing to a crawl. It continued toward me in no particular hurry. I stepped out into the road blocking his lane.

We couldn't have planned the way things unfolded any better than they did. The car started to accelerate, but then the driver stopped the car adjacent to Rose. I don't think he saw her with his attention most likely focused on me. She stepped out from behind the rock pile and shouted at the driver to get out of the car. She had a clear view of him.

"Out of the car, Tremble! Now!" Rose ordered. She aimed her service pistol at him and took a step into the road.

I had my pistol out and displayed it in front of me to make sure Tremble knew I was armed, too. He only had two choices. He could either surrender on the spot or try to drive away. Of course, that's always when things go to hell.

CHAPTER 22

I saw what looked like Tremble displaying both hands in the air. No weapon. My relief that he decided to get out of the car without choosing option two and trying to drive over me was short lived. The driver's door opened and the explosion of gunfire ripped through the air. I involuntarily took a step back before I saw Rose collapse to the ground.

Adrenalin overtook logic and safety, and I sprinted at Tremble's car firing my pistol repeatedly in that twenty yard dash. I wasted my ammo. I stopped adjacent to the front, driver's side wheel and looked down at Tremble. He had one foot out of the car on the ground. The rest of him slumped in a wad half in the car and half looking like his body was about to slide out of the car onto the ground. His head pressed into the open door and had taken an odd angle facing downward.

Despite indicating to us that he didn't have a weapon, he must have had one concealed and fired at Rose as soon as the door opened wide enough. With her down, he could have used the door for cover while he fired at me. His plan didn't work. She shot him at the same time he fired at her.

I didn't see his weapon. He didn't look alive, and I needed to tend to Rose, but I had to make sure he posed no further danger. I grabbed his shirt behind his neck and yanked him out of the car. He collapsed to the ground and a large revolver fell next to him. A gasp escaped his throat when he hit the ground, but he didn't look like he was about to move again. She had hit him in the center of the chest. I kicked his gun away from him and turned my attention to Rose.

She had a head wound. I could see the blood spreading around her head, but she had fallen face down, and the way her head settled prevented me from getting a clear view of the wound. I didn't feel comfortable picking her head up or rolling her over.

"Rose, Rose," I said, but she didn't answer. I dialed 911 and cursed myself for not dialing it when Tremble's car appeared. The 911 operator told me someone would be at my location in less than five minutes. I could hear the sirens before we disconnected. Someone in the responding ambulance would be calling me in a minute.

Rose' cell phone stuck part way out of her back pocket. I grabbed it and hit redial. Roger answered instantly.

"Do those sirens have anything to do with you?" he asked before I had a chance to say anything.

"Yes. Tremble attacked us. Rose has been shot and is down. I need you all out here now."

"We're already rolling. We saw the ambulance and cops head that way, so we decided to follow. How far away are you?" Roger asked.

"Only a couple miles from town."

"Okay, we'll be there soon."

"Thanks," I said.

The call from the ambulance came at the same time I could see its flashers in the distance. I described Rose' condition the best I could and asked what I should do. She responded by saying they could see us and would arrive in less than a minute. She told me to keep talking to Rose. They would do the rest.

I sat down on the road next to Rose. I kept my eye on

Tremble while I talked to Rose. Neither of the two moved. I slid my hand under her hand and held it. "Hang in there, Rose. We're safe now, and the ambulance is here."

An ambulance and a sheriff's vehicle pulled up at the same time. More flashers appeared in the distance. I didn't get much of an explanation out to the first responders before one of the deputies escorted me away from the scene. My day didn't get any better.

Roger and the others arrived three minutes later, but by then, I had already been handcuffed and placed in the back of one of the sheriff's sedans. My 9mm had been taken as evidence. I didn't help my cause by telling the deputy that I needed the FBI team to arrive before I provided a more comprehensive explanation. I knew I was being paranoid, but after all that had happened, I didn't want anyone else to get their hands on the briefcase.

The FBI group split up on arrival. Kaiden went over to Rose. Charles and one of the agents from the back up team, who had interviewed Rose and me after we had found Spann, joined the deputies around Tremble and his car. Roger came over to me.

A deputy came with him and let me out of the car. He refused to remove my cuffs, and Roger didn't push the issue. It didn't take an expert at body language to tell Roger wasn't very happy at the moment.

"Where's the briefcase?" he asked.

"In the trunk of the Mustang. I didn't mention it to them."

"The keys?"

"In my front right pocket."

He gave me a look like he'd rather do anything than put his hand in my pocket, but he did and removed the keys.

"Stay put," he said and walked over to the Mustang.

Fortunately, while the locals had looked into the passenger compartment, no one had asked me to open the trunk. It donned on me then that no key was even required as the car had a button next to the steering wheel that would open it. I saw Roger open the trunk and lean over. The trunk lid blocked my view, but a moment later the trunk closed, and Roger walked back to me with the briefcase.

"Just money in here? No sheet of paper?" he asked.

"There's a flash drive in the pocket. It's still there."

"Ok. We can discuss this later. What happened here?"

"We were driving back from Chloride, and as you can see, almost reached town when we saw that car with its flashers blocking our lane. I slowed, but when we got close, I couldn't see a cop anywhere. It made me think of Spann, so I floored it, and we drove by. As we did, a round took out a piece of the Mustang. I think we both knew then that it was Tremble. I rounded that bend and came to a stop."

"That was stupid," he said.

"Yes, it was. I wished I had kept driving, but I didn't. I stopped. Rose ran back to that rock pile, and I stood in the road next to my car. He drove around the bend and stopped right there." I nodded to where the car sat in the road. "Rose came out from the side and told him to get out. I saw him raise both hands signaling he wasn't armed. Obviously, we both knew he had a gun in there somewhere with him. When he opened the door, he shot Rose, and she must have fired at the same time. I only heard one sound, but it lasted longer than one shot should've. When Rose went down, I went a little crazy and charged the car firing all the way. I didn't know it, but he was already slumped down from Rose' shot. I don't think any of my rounds struck him."

"Hey!" Roger called to a nearby deputy. "You can put him back in the car now."

"Come on, Roger." I said, but he walked away.

A second ambulance arrived, along with a fire truck and two state police vehicles. A van showed up, and a couple who were with the press got out. At first, no one appeared interested in me, so I had plenty of time to curse myself over and over again for not driving all the way into Truth or Consequences once we got by Tremble.

The sound of a helicopter interrupted my thoughts. It landed on the road, a little past Tremble's car. I watched as two medics rushed a stretcher carrying Rose to the helicopter and helped lift her into it. I knew her injury was life threatening, and while the helicopter would make sure she got to a hospital that could best handle her wound, its presence also reminded me how close to death she was.

The helicopter had barely lifted off the ground when I sensed someone outside the window. I turned to see a young man with a large camera pointed at me. I turned my face away from him in a futile attempt to stay out of whatever story they planned to run. Besides, handcuffed and sitting in the back of a police cruiser is never a good time to have your picture taken.

Two deputies began to inspect my Mustang. I watched them, more interested in whether they would notice the damage caused by the bullet that Tremble had meant for me than their discovery of anything in my car. One of them opened the trunk, and after they inspected that, the same man opened the front hood. When they closed the hood, one of the deputies finally noticed the damage to my car. They both leaned in close to study it before calling over a third deputy who took pictures of the damage.

When they finished, the deputy who took the pictures walked over and opened the door next to me. "How did this occur?" Using his camera, he showed me one of the pictures he took.

I explained how Tremble ambushed us.

"You're lucky he was a bad shot. If he only got off one round here at this scene, and if his weapon was loaded when you first encountered him, then he fired three times at you when you drove by him."

"Did you see any other damage to my car?" I asked.

"Nothing else was pointed out to me."

"Good, I hope that's the only damage. I didn't get a chance to inspect it."

"I'll take a look at the rest of your car," he said and walked away. He surprised me by leaving the door open. The fresh air felt good.

I saw them take more pictures and a variety of measurements. They left Tremble on the ground while they worked. That confirmed my suspicions that Tremble had died. Too bad in a way, since it would've been good to have had him answer a bunch of questions, but he deserved to die.

"No other damage to your car. With the top down, no way to tell how close the other rounds came to either of you," the deputy with the camera said.

"Thanks," I said.

"Come on out of the car," he said.

I did.

"We're going to leave the handcuffs on for now," he said.

"Oh, come on."

"Patience," he said. "Show me your movements after you stopped the Mustang." He started walking toward my car, and I followed him.

For the second or third time that day, I described where I stood in the road and watched Tremble drive around the bend and then stop. I told him how Rose had sprinted to the pile of rocks. When I reached the point in my story where I ran toward Tremble and started shooting, he had me walk toward Tremble's car. He took a series of pictures while we moved up the road away from the Mustang.

"Thanks. You shot the hell out of that car, never hit the dead man. The pictures will help tell the story." He turned and took one last picture in the direction of my car.

"In my defense, when I started running at him, I think he hadn't yet slumped over."

"Hey, believe me, you're in a lot better position not having anything to do with his death. You know, the whole issue of who shot first, etc. The fact that two of your shots went into the driver's seat pretty well establishes the fact that you fired after he had already been hit."

"He killed Spann and had just shot Rose. I wouldn't have had any regrets," I said.

"I understand," he said, and I think he did.

Another deputy approached us and removed the handcuffs from my wrists. Kaiden joined us.

"How are you doing?" she asked.

"Not good. How's Rose?"

"Bad, real bad," she said.

CHAPTER 23

K aiden drove with me to the law enforcement complex. To her credit she didn't question my decisions for that day. She didn't even press me on how Rose and I got our hands on the briefcase. Maybe she knew she didn't need to; I would spend the rest of my day answering questions.

They had me wait in an interview room for about a half hour before anyone showed up to talk to me. Kaiden stayed only for my first few minutes in the room.

"Hang in there. I'll make sure they don't give away your room at the hotel," she said before she left.

I gave her a half-hearted smile, and she left. I didn't really care what they did with the hotel room. The picture of Rose on the pavement with the growing circle of blood around her head wouldn't go away. Knowing I caused it didn't help.

Sheriff "Nip" Harding started the interview with a young female deputy taking notes off to the side. I couldn't read her name tag and nobody introduced us. He had me go through my story for the umpteenth time. Other than reinforcing the fact that I was an idiot for stopping to confront Tremble, this first stage of the interview was what I expected.

When FBI Special Agent Sisk joined the interview things got nasty. I hadn't met Sisk and didn't anticipate the new track the interview would take.

"Why did you and Deputy Luna go back to Chloride without telling any members of the team?" Sisk asked.

"We were bored and thought another hike around the area

looking for the case would be a better use of our time."

"Of course only you and the Deputy can substantiate that, if she survives that is," Sisk said.

Maybe I should have stopped the interview and asked for a lawyer at that point, or maybe I should have said something about what he could do to himself, but I let him continue. The hairs on the back of my neck shouted at me to be careful, and for once, I heeded them.

"I hope she survives, Agent Sisk," I stared at him and tried to give him a look that implied if she didn't I might take it out on him. Stupid, I know, but it's what we guys do sometimes when we're trying to be macho and can't do anything else.

"What's the real reason you two went out there?" Sheriff Harding asked.

"I told you," I said and then paused. I had been focused on keeping Manny out of this. They didn't know about Manny, so they had something else in mind.

"We know what you told us. I'm just concerned the two of you have been playing us for fools. How long have you or the deputy been in contact with Tremble?" Sisk asked.

"We hadn't."

"We know you had contact with him in Fabens, and we know she has had multiple contacts with him in the past. It makes a lot more sense to me that you three were working this together, than for us to think he was here by himself or had been turned by some cartel," Sisk said.

"I met him once and didn't even know his name. I'd stake my life that Rose wasn't working with him."

"You sure you haven't gotten too close to her. Maybe you simply didn't want to see what was going on," Sisk said.

"You're full of crap," I said.

"You're only going to get this one shot. Tell us about the deputy and Tremble, and we can make it a lot easier for you. Don't be an idiot, you know how this works. You aren't the first man to be tricked by a woman. She played you, didn't she?" Sisk looked smug when he stopped talking.

Could I have been played? It's not like I've been a genius in my dealings with women throughout my life. I couldn't believe it, though.

"She showed up at the very beginning of all this, didn't she?" Sisk asked. When I didn't answer, he continued. "She also came to Cloudcroft without any prompting, right?"

"So?"

"So?" Sisk mimicked. "Not too many coincidences yet for you? How about the nurse getting assaulted the same day you tell her about the letter you received?"

"She had nothing to do with that. Tremble could have been responsible for that, and we know he was involved."

"Come clean with us. Was it the money, or did you just fall for her?"

"You're wasting your time. Neither Rose nor I were involved with anyone other than the FBI. I can't speak for Tremble's motivation--"

"Hell, I can!" Sisk shouted. "Maybe he felt double crossed! Maybe he expected that you'd hand over the money to him."

"You're crazy," I said.

"You think I'm crazy? Explain to me again how the two of you managed to waltz out there and just find the briefcase?"

"I told you. There was a rock pile Rose noticed that was outside our search zone but she thought might have been an obvious spot to hide something close by. It bothered her last night, so she suggested we drive out there. We had absolutely no contact with Tremble until he tried to kill us."

"Then how in the hell did he know you were driving back to town with the briefcase?" Sisk asked.

That had bothered me, too. "I don't know."

Back and forth we went for another thirty minutes. Finally there was a knock at the door and the three of them left. They let me sit there stewing there for another ten minutes. As I waited, I wondered what had caused them to come at me like they had. They had access to my phone calls, and I'd been with them for the last few days. Rose might have called someone who sparked their suspicions, but I still couldn't believe she had done anything wrong.

The door opened and a deputy I hadn't seen before told me I could go. He backed away from the interview room door but kept an eye on me as he led me out of the building. I didn't see anyone I knew until I got to my car. Charles leaned against it.

"You doing okay?" he asked.

"How's Rose?" I asked rather than telling him I was pissed.

"She's in Las Cruces, still alive. She's a fighter Jim. There's a chance she'll pull through."

"I'm heading down there."

"Not tonight, Jim. She's in a coma that the doctors induced. The bullet took a piece of her head off." He touched the top of his own head above the right eye. "No one is going to be able to talk to her for a while."

"Does her family know?"

"I'm sure they have been contacted, but come on back to the hotel with me and I'll confirm that. Roger also wants to talk to you."

"You've got to be kidding me. Why didn't he just listen in to the interrogation you all just put me through? You guys can't really have any evidence against Rose, do you?"

"None of this was our doing, but come on back and talk to Roger," Charles said.

I would have driven off right then to Las Cruces, if it wasn't for my curiosity about Rose. Charles rode back with me to the hotel in my Mustang.

"How'd you get stuck with coming to get me?" I asked.

"Roger wanted someone to listen to the interview. He didn't want to and neither did Kaiden. That left me."

He didn't elaborate, and we arrived at the hotel too quickly for me to follow up, but I found his answer interesting.

"Where's Roger?" I asked when we entered the lobby.

"His room."

We went straight there and found Kaiden waiting in the room with Roger. Kaiden tossed me a cold Bud Light when I walked in. I wasn't about to be bought off by a bottle of beer, but I did feel like I needed it at the moment.

"Sit down and join the celebration," Roger said.

Nobody looked happy.

"What you just went through wasn't our idea. In fact, we argued against it. Keep this conversation between the four of us, but there's no evidence that Rose did anything to compromise our investigation. A couple senior people in D.C. wanted to play a long shot. They thought it was too much of a coincidence that you two found the briefcase and killed Tremble all in the same hour," Roger said.

"If we didn't know you two as well as we do, we might have

had similar doubts," Kaiden said.

"So, drink up, that's not all the bad news," Roger said.

"Rose?" I asked.

"No. Thankfully they got her to the clinic in time for the doctors to stabilize her. All we can do now is wait," Roger said.

"She's tough," I said more to reassure myself than anyone else in the room.

"She is," Kaiden said.

"They took the briefcase, and it's already on the way to our field office," Roger said. "They want to be very careful with the flash drive. You know, worried about some software deleting all the information if it's opened incorrectly. Our efforts have been shut down, and we're all to go home tomorrow."

"The flash drive will most likely be in D.C. tomorrow. It won't stay at our field office. Too important, they'll say," Kaiden said.

I didn't have much sympathy for any of them. They were stewing over being dropped from the case now that the briefcase was discovered. They should have been used to it. The old need to know excuse that allows those at headquarters to seize the prize once the worker bees in the field have found it. I had little doubt that the possibility that the drive held the names of important US government officials led to the need to control access to the information.

Depending on the importance or sensitivity of the information on the flash drive, I thought the three of them may never know the entire contents of the drive. The irony of it to me was that the three would probably receive commendations, while Rose, Kay, Manny, and I were the key contributors to the briefcase's discovery. I didn't want a pat on the back, but I didn't feel sorry for them. It's how the world works.

"Did you really expect anything different?" I asked.

"No, but it still bugs us," Charles said.

"To Rose," I said and lifted my beer in the air.

"To Rose," they said in unison.

"Any of you have the number to the hospital?" I asked.

Kaiden got up, went over to her purse, and retrieved a small piece of paper. She looked at it before handing it over to me. "Write it down when you get a chance and let me have it back."

"While our job is over, Jim, what do you want to do? The guys that were after you may or may not go away when they discover we have the briefcase," Roger said.

"I don't know. Maybe I'll get my dog and live on the road for a few weeks. Give you guys time to clean things up. I know a lodge up by Santa Fe where I could stay."

"That's a good idea," Roger said. "My guess is that the cartel won't carry out their threat anyway. They wanted the briefcase. Once they know it's in our hands, they'll go into damage control."

"Has word gotten out in the press about what happened today?" I asked.

"Locally, but I haven't seen anything on the larger networks, and no mention of the briefcase," Roger said.

"Wonder how long it will take them to find out that we have it?" I said.

"For sure when we start questioning people. That is if there are names listed in the drive. I guess we really don't even know that yet," Charles said. "Damn, wouldn't that be the pits if it was just a blank flash drive."

"Good question, Jim. They may not know that we have it for

a while. That puts us and you in a different dilemma," Roger said.

"Might give me a head start," I said.

"This whole thing isn't right, Jim," Kaiden said. "Rose gets shot, you're still a target, and we get to drive off with the prize."

"How does that old saying go? Life's a bitch, and then you die," I said.

"I'm serious," Kaiden said. "Roger, can't we do something more."

"I'll talk to the boss in the morning. Despite what they had you go through today, most of us know you're on our side," Roger said.

I finished my beer and turned down an offer for a second. Fatigue had overcome anger and frustration, and all I wanted to do was shower and go to bed.

CHAPTER 24

I slept for about two hours, and despite feeling tired I couldn't fall back asleep. After tossing and turning for about twenty minutes, I finally got up. I called the hospital in Las Cruces and checked on Rose. All they would tell me was that her situation hadn't changed. I knew it might be days before she came out of it, or before we would know that she would never come out of the coma.

The television didn't offer anything appealing, so I found the weather channel and stared at the television while I dozed on and off for thirty minutes. My phone buzzed.

"Turn on your television to channel five," Kaiden said.

"Okay," I said and hit the remote. "Damn, I was hoping that shot wouldn't be used."

The television screen displayed a picture of me in the back seat of the sheriff's vehicle, while the commentator droned on about what he referred to as a shooting west of town. The news commentator stated they only had partial information regarding the cause of the incident, but that it had drawn the attention of the FBI and the state police. One individual had died and another individual was believed to be in critical condition. No names had yet been released. The screen changed to a video scan of all the people at the scene. The video didn't display anything of significance other than a good shot of Roger standing off to the side talking to Charles. In the picture, one could easily see the briefcase in Roger's hand.

"See that?" I asked.

"Yes," Kaiden replied.

The report on the news about our shootout with Tremble moved to an interview of the sheriff conducted while he was still at the scene. Roger could be seen standing next to the sheriff. The reporter identified Roger as an FBI agent, but again gave no explanation for his presence at a local crime. The news transitioned to a story about a fire at a house on the north side of town, and I turned off the television.

"Guess that's it," Kaiden said.

"Not too bad," I said and immediately wondered why I said it. I heard Roger's voice through the phone but couldn't catch what he had said.

"I'm not going to tell him that," Kaiden said.

"What did he say?" I asked.

"He made a dumb comment about the television shot of you. He said you shouldn't mind it because out here chicks dig the outlaws or something dumb like that."

"What does he think about the shot of him with the briefcase?"

"We don't like it, but there's nothing we can do about it. It's a long shot that anyone will pay it any attention."

"Yeah," I said. "Thanks for the heads up. I'm going to sleep now."

I turned the television off and tried to go to sleep. Rather than sense any relief at everything coming to a head today or thinking that life should slowly return to normal, I felt full of dread. I kept waiting for my phone to ring. If the man from the cartel called again, I could lie and say I did my best but got arrested for my effort. I could refer him to the newscast to the scene with me handcuffed in the back of the sheriff's vehicle. I didn't think he would buy it, but there was a chance he would realize how little influence I had over the situation and that it was useless to hound me anymore.

While I knew it was too soon to get a call about Rose's condition, my mind couldn't stop worrying that if the phone rang it could be someone telling me Rose had passed away. That would be worse than another call from the cartel. I checked my phone to make sure I hadn't missed anything. I hadn't.

Despite my mind racing around like a mouse in a maze, I somehow dozed off around midnight. When I heard the gunfire and screams, I first thought I was dreaming. After a few seconds, I jumped out of bed and grabbed for the Sig before I remembered that the locals had kept the weapon to compare it with Rose' and Tremble's to verify which one fired the rounds into Rose and Tremble. I didn't think they had recovered the round that struck Rose, but I knew they still had to go through the process.

I cracked the door to my room and peeked into the hallway. Whatever was happening wasn't occurring on my floor. I heard another series of three or four shots being fired. I closed my door and put my jeans and shoes on. The screams had turned into crying and loud talking. The gunfire had stopped. I could hear the sirens from emergency response vehicles. I opened my door again and saw a dozen people now sticking their heads out the doors to their own hotel rooms.

"Anyone see anything?" I asked and entered the hall.

Most simply looked at me suspiciously, and two room doors shut without any response to my question.

"No," one person said. Three others echoed the response.

"Stay in your rooms," I said. I went to the stairs. I didn't want to use the elevators. I knew I was doing something foolish, but I had a strong hunch I knew where the shots had originated.

The lack of any additional gunfire encouraged me to continue. I listened for a second before I hurried down the stairs the two flights to the floor where the FBI team had their rooms. The chaotic sounds from the people reacting to the initial gunfire became louder. Someone barked instructions and the screaming subsided. I didn't hear any sound that might indicate that someone might be using the stairs.

I cracked the door and peered into the hallway. I saw Charles sitting on the floor with his back against the wall. He pressed both hands against his stomach. His white tee shirt had a large red stain that spread out from his hands. His service weapon rested on the floor next to him.

Pushing the door open, I saw two men I didn't recognize on the floor outside the door to Roger's room. One moved his fingers in a motion that looked like he was tightening and loosening his fist. He lay on his back, and I didn't see any other signs of life from him. The other man on the floor lay in such an unnatural position that I thought he must be dead.

As I stepped through the door, Charles turned his head to look at me. I couldn't tell at first if he recognized me, but then he gave me a slight nod of his head. I hurried over to him. The bullet wound looked too low to have hit anything vital, but what did I know?

"Hang in there, Charles. The medics should be here any minute."

Charles looked at me without expression. He looked like he

was in shock. I noticed his eyes were looking past me. I turned my head and saw a third man sprawled on the ground a few feet passed the door I had come through. I instinctively reached for Charles' pistol before realizing that the man didn't pose a threat to anyone.

"Jim," Kaiden called me from Roger's door. She must have been in his room. She looked pale and held her service weapon in a tight, two handed grip with the barrel pointed down in front of her. Blood covered her hands and a drop fell to the floor.

I looked at her. I had an urge to ask a hundred questions, but I waited for her to talk.

"Go downstairs and get the medics up here right away."

"Okay. Are you alright?" I asked.

"Yes. Go, please."

I turned and took the stairs down the last flight to the lobby. Not surprising, no one was in the room. The flashing lights from an ambulance or a police car indicated a vehicle had arrived out front. At first, I wondered if I had missed them, but the front doors opened, and two policemen and two medics came rushing in together.

"They need you on the second floor," I shouted at the medics. "I think all the shooting is over," addressing this comment to the cops. "This way," I led them to the stairs.

I was happy no one argued with me, but one of the police did tell me to slow down and tell him what had happened while we walked. I told him that a team of FBI agents had been attacked by some armed men, but the FBI now had control of the situation. A number of people had been shot. The way he looked at me didn't give me any confidence that he believed me. The two cops had their weapons drawn and the medics stayed behind them as we climbed the stairs.

When I reached the door to the second floor, one of the cops grabbed my shoulder and held me back. He cracked the door open and slowly entered.

"Police entering the hallway! Any weapons need to be put away or placed on the floor!" he shouted.

We entered the hall and the medics immediately started checking the status of the injured and dead. Charles had slumped over, and I felt a knot develop in the pit of my stomach.

"Kaiden!" I called.

One of the police officers glared at me.

"In here," Kaiden shouted.

One of the police officers walked cautiously into Roger's room. The other officer stood in the hallway looking back and forth. I thought I saw a look of desperation in his eyes.

"Is backup coming?" I asked as calmly as I could.

"Yes. What the hell happened here?"

"I'm not sure. My room is on the fourth floor."

One of the medics started talking into his radio in an attempt to describe the scene and number of injured. He repeated second floor to someone and then said keep them coming.

"In here!" the officer who had entered Roger's room shouted, repeating Kaiden's request.

One of the medics and the second police officer ran to the room. I had been avoiding going into the room. I figured Roger had been shot. An irrational thought that my running into Roger's room would be tantamount to ignoring Charles' injury kept me in the hall.

The police officer who had been in the hall with me returned from Roger's room. He looked paler than before.

"Hey," I shouted to the medic hunched over one of the men on the floor who I didn't know. "This guy is an FBI agent. All those guys are the bad guys. I know what your oath says, but how about getting over here now."

To my surprise, he didn't hesitate but rushed over to check Charles.

"Thanks," I said.

He didn't answer me but began studying Charles. "Help me lay him down on his back," he said after his initial inspection.

"One nasty bullet wound in the gut. Can you hear me?" he asked Charles.

"Charles, Charles, can you hear us?" I asked.

His eyes flickered. They didn't seem to focus, but his mouth opened and shut.

"That's good enough," the medic told Charles. "You relax. We'll have you at the hospital in a few minutes. You're going to be okay."

The door to the stairs opened and more emergency responders entered the hallway. I noticed that a number of the hotel guests had come out of their rooms and stood by their doors watching the proceedings. Everything seemed quiet despite the additional crowd in the hall.

I backed away from Charles to let one of the new responders lean in and receive instructions. The elevator doors opened and two gurneys were pushed out into the hall. One gurney went into Roger's room and the second was pushed next to Charles. I stepped away as they lifted Charles onto it.

Charles gasped and his eyes opened. He saw me. "Jim," he

croaked.

"It's all over. You're going to be alright."

He lifted his head a little and asked in a voice I could barely hear. "How's Kaiden?"

"She's fine," I said.

I saw a slight smile form on his lips. He nodded once before laying his head back down. His eyes closed as they wheeled him away.

The hall had become crowded with law enforcement and medical personnel. One of the deputies I recognized from earlier in the day, or maybe now it was yesterday, came up to me.

"What happened?" he asked.

"I don't know." I looked over and saw Kaiden come out of Roger's room. She looked years older than she had a few hours earlier. "She can tell you."

He looked over at Kaiden and then went to her. I followed him.

"What the hell happened here?" he asked in a growl.

She didn't seem to notice his tone, but I did.

"Take it easy," I said. "She didn't cause any of this."

"What happened?" he asked again without emotion.

"They busted into Special Agent Stillman's room looking for the briefcase."

"What briefcase?" the deputy asked.

Kaiden didn't respond right away. I had a feeling she was still attempting to get all the events of the night organized and under control in her mind.

"It's a long story, Deputy, but we believe the briefcase might have some information that these guys and their masters didn't want the FBI to have," I said.

"So important that they busted into a public hotel and shot up the place?" he asked.

"Seems like it," I said. I tried not to sound sarcastic.

"Damn," he said.

A second deputy came and pulled him away.

"How's Roger?" I asked Kaiden when we were alone.

"Bad, real bad. Shot twice in the chest. I tried to stop the bleeding," she shook her head. "I felt bad about leaving Charles, but Roger was dying. Charles told me to do what I could for him."

"Charles should be fine. The EMT guy thought so, too. It's an ugly wound but it didn't look like anything vital was struck," I said with as much conviction as I could. "How do you know they came for the briefcase?"

"Roger was conscious for a while. They kicked in his door and charged him. He was asleep but the noise of the door being kicked open woke him. He had his gun next to him. He got one of them, but took two shots to the chest. They wanted to know where the briefcase was."

"They asked him?"

"Yes. They were looking around the room for it and shouting at him. He said he laughed at them and told them it was already gone. One of them hit him across the face with something, maybe his gun. When they left the room they ran into Charles. If I wasn't so slow, maybe I could've at least saved Charles from being shot."

"None of this is your fault."

"Charles had put one of them down, and I think he wounded another. I came out of my room to find one of them leaning against the wall opposite Charles and one at the door to the stairs. I took them both out."

She didn't say it with any pride. In fact, her voice seemed devoid of emotion.

"Well the home team is here now. You can relax. The docs will take care of Roger and Charles."

"I think it's too late for Roger," she said.

"Do you need to call anyone?" I asked.

"Yes. I better," she said and looked around.

A handful of medical personnel surrounded a gurney being rushed out of Roger's room and down to the elevator.

"Come on," I said and walked her to Roger's room. For the moment it was almost empty. A dead man took up space on the floor in one of the corners of the room. "Why don't you sit over here and make your call. You might have a minute or two of privacy."

"I better use my room," she said. I walked her the couple doors down to her room. Her door stood open. I looked in and saw the room was empty. She moved to the chair and made her call. I left the room. Sheriff Harding had arrived and was in an earnest conversation with the deputy who had started to interview Kaiden and me. A man in city police attire stood close to him. They looked around like they were surveying the scene. When the sheriff saw me, I could see his eyes narrow. Someone to blame, I thought, and for once I didn't blame him. We had turned his peaceful county into a war zone.

I saw one of the EMTs talking to a small boy in the doorway of a hotel room down the hall. The knot in my stomach tightened up again. Had an errant round struck a guest in the hotel? I walked down to the room.

"Is everything okay?" I asked.

The EMT looked up at me. He looked about twenty years old and very nervous.

"Yes, sir," he said standing up.

"I don't mean to interrupt. Is everyone okay down here?"

"This young guy was just shaken up. His mother wanted someone to reassure him that the gunfire was over."

I glanced into the room and saw a young woman in a bathrobe huddled in a chair. She had her arms wrapped around her legs that were drawn up to her. She looked more frightened than the boy. The boy looked at me.

"Everything is okay now," I said.

He looked back at the young EMT who nodded his concurrence to what I had said. I took a couple steps away to give them their space and looked up and down the hallway. A number of half-dressed people stood in the hall. I had a feeling some of them had come from other floors in the hotel. Although sunrise was hours away, I knew many of the hotel's guests would not be able to get back to sleep tonight. I knew I wouldn't.

Kaiden came out of her room. The sheriff made a bee line for her. The man in city police attire stayed close behind him. The three went into her room. I knew it wasn't my place, but I also entered her room. I figured Kaiden might need some support.

They weren't yelling at each other, but all three voices sounded on edge as I entered the room. I went straight to the bed and sat down next to Kaiden. The two men had moved chairs next to the bed. They gave me an unwelcome look, but didn't say anything.

"We had no idea whatsoever that this was going to happen," Kaiden said. "We'd been instructed to pack up and go home tomorrow."

"We have three dead bodies and three more who may not make it through the night. These guys hit a hotel in my county and went after FBI agents. This wasn't some drive-by shooting. This had to be something very big, and you're telling me that they caught you by surprise?" the sheriff asked.

"You know we were looking for a briefcase that we thought might have something very important in it. You also know we found it earlier today, or yesterday. The briefcase was immediately taken out of town by the other agents who have been here the last few days. One reason they took it away was to prevent anything like this from happening here," Kaiden said.

"Well, they obviously thought the briefcase was still here," the policeman said. I noticed a name tag that read Chief Hardy.

"If you would have told us how important the briefcase was, we could have had a unit here watching the hotel," the sheriff said.

"It may be a good idea to leave one here for a while now anyway," I said.

"If I want to hear from you, I'll ask you a question," the sheriff said.

"He's right," Kaiden said. "They took this much effort to retrieve the briefcase and failed. They may make a second effort since they may still think it's here."

"You saw the hallway. We'll have people here for the next forty eight hours, probably longer. The hotel will be surrounded by police cars, because we'll have people here working around the clock." The sheriff's sarcasm couldn't have been less subtle.

A couple of angry shouts came from outside the door. I didn't know what caused them, but the sheriff shook his head in frustration. "Damn people and their cell phones. Chief would you mind making sure anyone trying to take pictures out there have their phones confiscated for evidence?"

The chief grunted a response and hustled out of the room.

"What instructions do you have from your headquarters?" the sheriff asked Kaiden.

"To cooperate with you and give you any support you need."

"You know I need you both to stick around a few days," he said.

We nodded.

"What exactly was in the briefcase?" he asked.

"Money, but there was also a flash drive that we have reason to believe may list people in the U.S. who cooperated with a Mexican drug cartel," Kaiden said. "We only verified the existence of the flash drive today. We don't know what's on it."

"Must be very important to do this. They also tried to take you out in Cloudcroft, too," he said to me.

"I think at that point they were only going to break a few bones, but basically you're correct."

"Lost four there and four here. Means they either will never stop going after you, or they'll figure you're not worth the cost," he said.

"They have had the misconception that I can get the briefcase and turn it over to them. Hopefully, by now they understand that I can't and will leave me alone."

"Makes sense to me," the sheriff said. "If I were you, though, I'd disappear for a few weeks. Just don't disappear until I tell you that you can. We'll keep an eye on you while you're here.

Even if no one comes looking for you, it might keep you from causing more problems for us."

I didn't know what he meant, but I didn't want to say anything that might discourage the added protection. Kaiden glanced at her blood stained hands, got up and went into her bathroom.

"She's handling it pretty well," the sheriff said.

"Got to be tough on her. I don't think she's shot anyone before, and her two friends might not make it through the night," I said.

"We have your weapon, don't we?" he asked.

I figured he had been wondering why I wasn't any help in taking out the bad guys and had finally figured it out.

"It didn't matter. My room is two flights up. By the time I got down here, it was all over. I wouldn't have been any help."

He nodded. Kaiden came out of the bathroom. She had washed her face and hands and had brushed her hair. She had a determined look to her, like she had given herself a pep talk in the mirror. For some reason, she also looked a lot younger.

"If you two don't mind, let me get dressed now. That way, Sheriff Harding, I can do whatever you need me to do for the rest of the morning. No way that I'm going back to bed," she said.

"None of us are," he said. The sheriff and I left her room.

Once we were out in the hall, a deputy walked up to the sheriff. "We've secured room 213 for a command post. The medical examiner and her staff are here along with a doctor they called in to help. Between us and the city we've got fourteen investigators here at the scene or outside controlling the area. Hell, even the fire chief showed up to help," the deputy grinned like it was some inside joke.

"We getting a lot of pictures?" the sheriff asked.

"Yes, but everything has been moved or walked over. The scene's a mess. Luckily, we have a million eye witnesses and no civilians got hurt."

"Good, I was worried about that," the sheriff said.

"A few stray shots went into guest rooms, and they're making a stink about that, but ideally we'll be able to blame those guys for them." The deputy motioned with his head at the two remaining bodies in the hall. As if he could read my thoughts, the deputy said, "The one that was only wounded is at the hospital. We have Anderson with him, but even if he makes it, he isn't going to be a threat to anyone for a while."

"Any of these guys have any ID on them?" the sheriff asked.

"No, but we may have found their car outside. If it's theirs, I bet we find their wallets in it. We'll ID them." The deputy looked at me. "Sorry about your fellow agents."

"Thanks, but I'm not FBI."

He glanced at the sheriff, and I saw an embarrassed expression on the deputy's face.

"That's alright. He's been in the heart of this whole mess before it even came to our sleepy little county," the sheriff said.

"Any word on Special Agent Stillman?" I asked.

"Not that I've heard," the deputy said.

"Are we doing any interviews yet?" the sheriff asked.

"Just preliminary ones."

The sheriff looked at me. "How about going with Deputy Canton here and be our first? You can give them the big picture along with what you discovered when you first got to this floor."

"Sure," I said. What else could I say?

CHAPTER 25

In some ways every law enforcement agency, big or small, is a bureaucracy in which all the parts don't like being told by outsiders that they don't need to hear something that you may have already told the other fifty percent. In other words, I had to suffer through Deputy Canton saying, "Hey do me a favor and start at the beginning." He didn't mean at the beginning of the night either.

With the interview being recorded, I told him and the city police officer who joined us the abbreviated version. When I got to the shooting west of the city earlier that day the deputy stopped me.

"Was that you they had in the interview room today?" he asked.

"I was there. Not sure I'm the one you're thinking of." I knew I was, and I guessed he was trying to figure out how I was on the wrong side of the table this afternoon and was back on the team tonight. "If you're confused, how do you think I feel?"

"Okay, maybe we ought to focus on tonight," Deputy Canton finally said.

I smiled. "Thanks."

In ten minutes, I summarized what I had observed from the point when I heard the gunshots to the arrival of the first police officers. It took a couple of eye to eye denials before the deputy seem to accept the fact that I did not know any of the men who attacked Special Agent Stillman. As we finished, Kaiden stepped into the room.

"What's going on?" She didn't sound happy. She stared straight at Deputy Canton, and I sensed she was about to say something more.

"It's okay, Agent Small. We were just talking." I turned back to the two locals. "Anything else you two need?"

"Later today, we'll likely need you to put in writing just the very last part of what you've told us," Deputy Canton said. The police officer nodded in agreement.

"Not a problem," I said.

Kaiden and I walked out of the room.

"I'm sorry, Jim."

"Don't be. I'm fine."

"You've gone through hell and have been treated awful by everyone. We ought to be thanking you, not constantly treating you like the scum these guys are."

The scum she referred to were being bagged when we went back out into the hallway. The place had started smelling like a gym locker. Not from death, it was too early for that. I did think I could smell the coppery odor of blood, but that could've been my imagination. However, the odor from the sweat of fifteen to twenty nervous and hustling first responders didn't require any imagination.

For the first time since the shootings, the hotel seemed quiet. Police tape had cordoned off both ends of the hallway and all the doors to the rooms on this floor stood open.

"Did they move the guests into other rooms in the hotel?" I asked.

"Yes," Kaiden said. "They moved the last of them out when I came looking for you. I heard there were only seven other rooms occupied on this floor."

"Makes sense," I said. "I guess someone could have been hiding in one of the rooms."

"There wasn't. I'm going to the hospital. No one here knows anything about Charles or Roger, and they only give me lip service on the phone. Want to come?" she asked.

"Of course." I looked around. "Can we just leave?"

"Why not? We're just in the way now."

No one said anything to us as we left by the stairs. On the first floor, two men and a woman stood behind the reception desk. A police officer leaned against the counter. They stopped their conversation and stared at us when we entered the lobby.

"Just us," Kaiden said and displayed her badge.

"Morning," I said to the group.

They just nodded back at us.

A police car with lights still flashing sat in front of the hotel. An ambulance had been pulled up diagonally behind it and had one wheel up on the sidewalk. We walked over to the parking lot.

"I hope you're driving," I said. I remembered that I didn't have my keys or wallet with me.

"I got it," she said. "I think Charles will be okay, but I'm really worried about Roger."

I knew she was rehashing out loud what we had both been thinking and had already talked about.

"The SAC will be here in the morning," she said, referring to her boss. "I think that's good."

"I'd like a chance to talk to him." I didn't care if I saw him or not, but thought I should say something in response to her remark. I knew that SAC meant Special Agent in Charge, but I didn't know who he or she was. "It may not be necessary, but I want to insure none of this falls back on any of you."

She either wasn't listening or chose not to follow up on my comment. When she stopped the car in front of the hospital, she didn't immediately open her door. I had mine open but stayed seated.

"How'd they get here so fast? How'd they know where Roger's room was? And what could possibly drive them to make an all out assault like that?"

"Let's go check on the guys. We can spend the rest of the night talking about that. Come on," I said.

The hospital lights seemed too bright at first, and despite the hour, the hospital buzzed like the middle of a busy day. After getting directions, we hurried to check on Roger and Charles and encountered a crowd gathered in the hall. A doctor who looked to me like he may have come out of surgery addressed the group. Someone interrupted him with a question.

"That's right. Now let's all get back to work," the doctor said.

The crowd began splitting up. I noticed a deputy, whom I recognized from the day before, sitting on a couch off to one side and reading a magazine. Kaiden made a beeline toward the doctor. She identified herself, and I could tell instantly the news wasn't going to be good.

"I'm sorry, but Agent Stillman didn't make it," he said. "We did everything we could."

"How about Agent White?" she asked.

She asked the question so softly, I almost couldn't hear her.

"He's going to be fine. They're finishing up with him now, but it'll be a while before he's out and able to talk to anyone."

"Thank you. I know you did everything you could," she

said.

"You want to sit down," I asked Kaiden.

We started to walk away from the doctor.

"Do you want to know about the third man?" he asked.

I wanted to say no, that we didn't care about him, but the doctor didn't wait for a response. He may have suspected how we felt.

"He didn't make it either."

I nodded and Kaiden didn't respond. We joined the deputy on the couch. He only took his eyes away from the magazine article when we sat down.

"Oh," he said and started to stand. "Morning."

"Don't get up. We're going to join you here for a few minutes," I said.

Despite my comment, the deputy stood up. "No, I've been sitting too long. Ma'am, I'm sorry about Special Agent Stillman." He walked away from us.

Kaiden took her phone out and pressed a couple buttons. When the person at the other end answered, Kaiden told the person that Special Agent Roger Stillman had passed away. After a moment, she passed along the name of the hospital and ended the call.

"You going to be okay?" I asked.

"Yes, it's just hard. Roger had a family. He had two kids," she shook her head. She studied her fingers, and I remained silent. "He didn't ask about Charles." She looked at me for some answer.

"He already knew Charles had been shot. Right?"

"Yes," she said.

"Then maybe he thought no news was good news."

She nodded her head but didn't say anything. "I wonder if anyone can give us anything more specific on Charles?" She stood up without waiting for me to respond and headed for a nurse who was standing behind a counter a little further down the hall.

I didn't think she would be able to get much out of the nurse, and the couch felt comfortable. Fatigue had caught up with me as the last of the adrenalin rush I had been on the last couple hours dissipated. It took quite an effort to push myself up and follow her.

By the time I reached her, the nurse was already describing the situation. "Doctor Franklin has joined the team operating on him right now. He's our most experienced surgeon. The last word I received was that they had every reason to believe he would pull through. Nothing vital was hit, but they need to do a lot of patching him up inside. It'll be a while."

"Thanks," Kaiden said. She looked at me. "What do you want to do?"

I looked at my phone and saw that it was a few minutes past five. "I suggest we find a place to get some coffee, maybe check to see what's going on at the hotel, and then we can come back here and wait."

"Okay. You ever feel like you're in the middle of a bad dream?" she asked as we left the hospital.

"Yes, more often than I like."

"How'd we escape the carnage? Rose, Roger, Charles." She shook her head and looked down.

We stopped at a Denny's a block from the hotel and had some coffee. We talked about the possible damage the bullet wound could have done to Charles gut, and what the doctors had to do to fix him up. When we were about to leave, Kaiden brought up another topic that was bothering her.

"Those were the first people I've ever shot. I've never even had to draw my weapon before."

"You may never have to use your weapon again. It's not uncommon to go through a whole career without having to shoot someone," I said.

"I know, but the thing is …. it doesn't bother me. I don't feel a thing for the two men I shot. No guilt, no nothing. I would think it would've bothered me more."

"It's too soon, Kaiden, but you just did your job. You had no choice. Remember that and try not to let it bother you down the road. You couldn't have created a more righteous scenario for having to shoot someone."

Her phone rang. Her side of the conversation consisted of a few "yes sirs" and not much else.

"The boss," she said when she hung up. "He'll be here in an hour. Wants to use my room as his CP unless I can get him one next to mine."

"Won't be hard. All the rooms should be available." I said.

"That's right. I'll be glad when he gets here. He can make all the decisions. Let's head back there."

I stayed with Kaiden until we confirmed the use of the room next to hers could serve as the FBI's command post for the day. I didn't know how long they would need it and didn't really think they did, but I figured it was likely that having one checked off one of the blocks on the contingency operations standard planning chart. I wondered how many agents would be traveling with the Special Agent in Charge.

"If their timing is right, they should be here in fifteen or so minutes," I said. "I'm going to go freshen up and will be back before then."

"Go take a nap. Don't worry about them," Kaiden said.

"No. I want to be here when he arrives."

"Ok, and thanks, Jim."

I needed a quick shower and a real shirt. I thought I could use another cup of coffee, too. With that last thought in mind, my reaction should have been better when I smelled coffee upon entering my hotel room.

CHAPTER 26

"Shut the door," he said. The man sat in a chair in my room drinking coffee and holding a pistol pointed at me.

"If that's the coffee from the room, you'll have to go get another packet for me. They only leave us one."

"The door," he repeated.

I closed it. I had already stepped into the room and didn't have another choice.

"Where's the briefcase?" he asked.

"You're kind of late, aren't you?"

"You better hope I'm not."

"They told me you were too good to come back after your first attempt didn't work," I said.

Jim Jamison, the man who had tried to kill me in the parking lot of the lodge in Cloudcroft, stared back at me.

"This is different, and you might want to listen up. They paid me to kill you there. Now I'm on my own, and no one is paying me to kill you. I just want the briefcase. I get it, I go. I don't, and you die. Understand?" he said.

His voice and facial expression didn't tell me anything. Stone cold, he'd be good in a poker game, and he obviously had this assassin gig down pat. Yet, I knew he was lying. I'd be dead as soon as he decided he didn't need me.

"You expect me to waltz into the local police station and retrieve the briefcase for you?" I asked while doing my best to only show a little fear. That wasn't easy since terrified would better describe me, but I hoped he would read my look as an attempt at hiding my fear rather than the fact that I was lying to him about the location of the briefcase. It had never been at the police station, and for all I knew, the briefcase was already in D.C.

"That's exactly what I want you to do, but you won't be going in alone. I'll be going in with you." He displayed a badge.

"That can't be real," I said.

"The badge and credentials are real. My picture is the only thing that shouldn't be there."

I imagined the name on the credentials belonged to the original owner and wasn't Jamison's either. His plan became apparent to me. "You expect us to simply walk out of there with the briefcase and all that money?"

"Not exactly," he smiled. "We'll only ask to look at the briefcase for a minute. We won't try to walk out with the money or the briefcase."

"Then why go through all this? Why did you come back?"

"Good question. It's my family. We're, uh, what is the word? Dysfunctional? Yeah that's it, but the one I do care for is my little sister. You could say I'm doing this for her."

"That doesn't make sense. Why weren't you with the storm troopers who attacked the FBI agents tonight?" I asked. I wanted to keep him talking, to stall.

He looked at me like I had picked my nose in public. "Those guys are idiots. Did they all die?"

"Yes."

"Good. Did they really believe that an experienced FBI agent would keep all that money in his room?"

"I guess they did," I said.

"Jerks. I work alone. Why did you come back to your room?"

"To shower and change shirts."

"Forget the shower, but you can get a new shirt." He motioned towards the closet with his gun. "Don't be stupid and try something. You still have a chance to walk away from all this."

I doubted that he would want to leave any witnesses around no matter how well I behaved. I grabbed a shirt and put it on.

"I did a little checking up on you. Seems like you have a history of sticking your nose into places you shouldn't," he said.

"It's definitely a curse."

He finally smiled. "I think I like you," he said. His smile didn't make him look any friendlier. He looked like one of those old time gangsters you saw in the movies. Not very big, thin, a sharp nose that almost gave him a mousy look, but not in a funny way. His eyes were like ice. He'd probably never shed a tear.

"Are you driving, or am I?" I asked.

"You are." He stood up and pointed at the door.

"What does your sister have to do with all this?" I asked.

"It's complicated and none of your business," he said but then continued. "She's married to a bastard who dragged her into this mess. Used her to cover his tracks, and they've got two kids. Can you believe it? I should've killed him long ago."

"I'm not following you," I said, but I had. He believed that either her name or her husband's name was on that flash drive. If her husband had used her as a go between or a courier, then she would be pulled into the investigation and possibly face prosecution. This was why he was taking an extra risk. He needed to destroy the flash drive to protect his sister. It made sense to me, but it wouldn't make me less dead in the end.

"Move," he said. He stayed behind me and to my left while we walked down the hall. We took the elevator to the lobby. When the doors opened, I don't know who was more surprised, me or the gunman next to me. In the lobby, not far from the elevators, Kaiden stood with three men in suits, the FBI contingent. Next to the FBI agents stood the sheriff and two deputies. Our arrival caught their interest, and everyone turned and looked at us.

"Jim," Kaiden said, and then I saw recognition in her eyes.

I motioned as subtly as I could for her to stay calm. "Just going out to the car for a second," I said and stepped out of the elevator. My shadow stayed with me. Although I couldn't see him, I doubted that he had even broken into a sweat. I stopped when we were in the open in the lobby. Turning my head to the gunman, I whispered, "Two things: first the briefcase is already on its way to D.C., it's not here. Second, they already recognize you. I don't want to die, how about you?"

He looked uncertain for a second.

"There are seven of them, and you haven't really done anything yet," I said.

"Okay," he said.

"Show them your hands."

He took his right hand out of his pocket. As he did, all seven in the room went for their weapons.

"It's okay," I said. "We were just going to talk." I didn't plan on sticking to this story, but at the moment, I wanted to keep everyone calm.

Kaiden shouted at him, "Arms further out." She realized I

was in danger and had drawn her weapon first.

He obliged.

In seconds, two deputies joined Kaiden, and the three had Jamison handcuffed and patted down. One of the deputies studied the pistol with the silencer and walked it over to the sheriff.

"Look at this," he said.

One of the FBI agents joined the sheriff to look at the pistol. They seemed impressed with the weapon. Of course, they had a different view of it than I had a few minutes earlier. I hadn't been impressed. I had been frightened. For some odd reason my mind thought of that old saying: weapons don't kill people, people do.

They pushed Jamison into a chair. The one deputy stood next to him while Kaiden had his driver's license and the bogus credentials in her hands. She took a picture of them with her cell phone. She then pushed some buttons that made me think she was sending the picture somewhere. Keeping the items, she walked back to the two FBI agents who hadn't moved. She motioned for me to join them.

"Are you okay?" she asked.

"Yes, seems like we're asking each other that a lot today," I said.

She introduced me to her SAC and the second agent. They were cordial, but neither appeared interested in saying much around me.

"You know, that's the same man who tried to kill me in Cloudcroft."

"I do know," Kaiden said. "Maybe we can hold him a little longer this time."

I turned to the man Kaiden had identified as her boss. "For what it's worth, I've been around a lot of Bureau agents in my life, and I'd rate Special Agent Small right up there among the most professional that I've met. She was the real hero tonight. She saved Agent White and a lot of innocent civilians in this hotel. If you want me to put that in writing for you, I'll be glad to."

"You're not telling me anything I don't already know, and we will be getting back to you," the SAC said.

I took the hint and walked over to the sheriff. He looked up from the pistol and saw me approach. He handed the pistol back to his deputy and took a step away from the others. "What the hell was that all about?" he asked.

I looked over at the prisoner. "He wanted me to help him get access to the briefcase."

"That damn briefcase. I never even got to look at it and everyone's killing everyone for it. How were you supposed to get it? I understand it's not here anymore."

"It's not, but I told him it was at the police station. He was going to kill me when I wasn't any use to him anymore. I was stalling, and I appreciate everyone being here to help me."

"Hell. I came down here to meet the FBI bigwig. I didn't expect you. Besides, I've been wondering, does anyone really know which side you're on?"

I couldn't blame him for asking the question. After all, I had been handcuffed in the back of one of his cars earlier that day and then interrogated in his building by the FBI like I was Public Enemy Number One.

"I'm on your side, Sheriff, always have been."

He grunted.

"Your prisoner was arrested just a couple of days ago on a weapons charge, maybe more. My guess is that he might be out on bond," I said.

"Where'd this happen?"

"Cloudcroft."

He looked at me for a second. I imagined the shootout registered in his mind, rather than the guy almost killing me in the parking lot, but that didn't matter.

"I hope you aren't staying in my county much longer," he said and walked over to the FBI group.

"My sentiments exactly," I said to no one in particular.

The prisoner sat upright in the chair. He wasn't the type to slump or to look defeated. A defiant one, I thought, a professional.

I walked over to him and pulled over a second chair. The deputy started to say something to me. I waved a hand at the deputy without looking at him as though I had some authority in this room. My bluff worked.

"I'm not going to lie for you," I said.

He looked at me with eyes that had all the emotion of a rock.

"But," I said in almost a whisper, "I won't mention your sister. Okay?"

He nodded. The movement was so slight I almost didn't see it, but I did. I stood up and walked away. Luck had been with me twice with this guy, but I didn't think I could count on it again. He scared me, and I hoped my concession to him about not mentioning his sister might keep him away from me in the future.

I took the stairs back to my room where I immediately went to the shower. I stayed in there with the hot water beating against my body until I figured the low level warning lights were flashing at the nearby Elephant Butte Reservoir.

After the shower and despite all the excitement of the past twenty four hours, I crawled into bed and slept. I could've slept a long time, but ninety minutes later my phone rang. The deputy who had taken my statement earlier that night asked me to come to the station and provide a second statement. This one would be the basis for filing assault, attempted kidnapping, and whatever other charges they could throw at Jamison.

I asked him to give me twenty minutes. I packed my things and left. I would've checked out, but I had never checked in. The FBI had rented the room. I provided the statement and told them I would testify if needed. When they let me leave, I did. I didn't stop driving until I arrived at the hospital in Las Cruces.

CHAPTER 27

I sat in the room with Rose for the next two days. I knew they had her on drugs and in somewhat of a controlled state of unconsciousness, but their official prognosis seemed to be that she'd either come out of the coma or she wouldn't. So much for modern medicine. I talked a lot to Rose, and for whatever reason, I ended up telling her most of my life's story. Maybe I thought it would bore her to the point that she would wake up and tell me to shut up.

Her parents, some cousins, and a sister came to visit her. We talked a little, but they eyed me with suspicion. When they visited, I left them alone with her. One of the cousins, however, found me in the hall on the second day and couldn't resist the urge to curse "that bastard" Tremble. While the cousin simply wanted to vent her anger with Tremble to anyone who wanted to listen, I did coax a few interesting items about Tremble out of her. A friend in Tremble's extended family, whom Rose's cousin had known for a long time, had contacted her after hearing that Tremble had shot Rose. This friend had said that Tremble had always been someone "who would sell his own children for a buck." Although she didn't know who, Rose's cousin said that someone from Mexico had apparently offered Tremble a lot of money to help them find the briefcase. I didn't know how factual her account of what motivated Tremble was, but it seemed plausible.

Kaiden and I stayed in touch. Charles' recovery was going well. Their boss and the rest of the FBI contingent left the same day they had arrived. Kaiden would stay on a couple days to help close out the local investigation and to visit with Charles while he recovered. I didn't think there'd be much of an investigation as all four of the bad guys had died.

One of the now dead attackers had clobbered the lone hotel receptionist over the head and left him in a heap behind the counter. The receptionist required a few stitches and had likely suffered a concussion, but he would recover. No other civilians had been injured.

The tags on the car believed to be the one used by the assailants had been stolen from a similar car parked in long term parking at the El Paso International Airport. It would be a while before anything much would be learned about the car. Unlike the local law enforcement's interest in cleanly closing its investigation on the attack, the FBI was determined to ferret out everyone behind the death of one of its agents.

The morning of my third day at the hospital, Kaiden called.

"You might be interested to know that the flash drive contained some very interesting information," she said.

"Good, like what?"

"No one has told me. Can you believe that the only way I learned anything at all was through a Bureau-wide message that announced that the FBI had seized a data storage unit from an international drug cartel that would allow the U.S. to make great strides against the proliferation of illegal drugs in America."

"Sounds significant. They are referring to the flash drive, aren't they?" I asked.

"Yes. It's not unusual for HQ to spread the word to the field prior to making some even more cryptic release to the national press or maybe congress. They're playing hard ball with Jamison. They booked him as an accomplice in Roger's murder."

"That'll shake him up. Not that I care, but you know he had nothing to do with those guys."

"I think most everyone agrees with you there, but he's slippery, and nobody thinks the gun charge would get much. The kidnapping charge is a loser. Maybe it's a game of bluff versus counterbluff, but at the least we can hold him and sweat him. They're taking this into the federal system, and the state is fine with that."

"I think it's a good plan. How's Charles?" I asked.

"He's doing a lot better. There's a good chance we can both go home tomorrow. More importantly, how's Rose?"

I turned to look at her. To my surprise, I saw her looking at me. "I think she's going to be fine."

The hospital staff chased me out of the room and for the next forty minutes I paced the halls. I felt a huge sense of relief. She had regained consciousness and had appeared to recognize me. She even tried to say something, but her voice just cracked. I did wonder what permanent damage the bullet may have caused, but she had taken the most critical step by regaining consciousness, so I tried to focus on that.

I finally received permission to return to her room. I asked one of the nurses if they had notified her family, and he said they had.

"Hi, Jim," Rose said in a voice I could barely hear.

"Hey, Rose. Glad to see you're back with us. How do you feel?"

"Sleepy, dizzy, thirsty, hungry."

"Sounds like you're back to normal," I said.

She grinned. "Is everything over?" she asked, and her expression became more serious.

"Yes. The briefcase is in DC and everyone has headed home." I didn't feel like telling her about Roger. That could come later.

"My memory is a little messed up. They tell me I was shot in the head, but I don't remember that. I can remember driving in your car with the top down. We had the briefcase with us, right?"

"Yes."

"I don't remember how we got the briefcase or being shot. I remember our searching for it with the FBI team."

"Do you remember coming to Cloudcroft?" I asked.

She looked at me puzzled for a few seconds. "Yes. Yes, I do."

"I'm no expert, but I think the few memories you lost will return. Did the doctors tell you anything about what to expect?"

"The swelling in my brain has subsided and that I have an excellent chance for a full recovery. They said I've been here for four days. Have I really?" she asked.

"I think so. I've been here the last couple."

She smiled. "You're sweet. I think I remember you talking to me. And my family, are they here?"

"They're on the way right now. They've been in and out each day."

"How bad do I look?" Her question surprised me.

"You look beautiful."

"Ha! Liar. I know a chunk of my forehead and scalp is missing. I got that much out of the doctors."

"Nothing that a little cosmetic surgery can't fix," I said.

"I remember something else. Something I think you said while I was out. Something about taking me on a cruise."

"What? Were you faking all this time?" I smiled. I did remember asking her while she was unconscious if she had ever been on a cruise and telling her she should get better so we could go on one together.

"No, but I think that comment was what brought me back. I wanted to tell you yes. I'd like to go on a cruise with you. Did you think I wasn't listening?"

"I was hoping you were listening. You get better, and we'll go on one. I promise."

I only stayed a few more minutes with Rose. She needed to recover, and I had been away from home more than twice as long as I had planned.

I left Las Cruces and stopped by the Lodge at Cloudcroft. After locating Kay, I told her everything. She had already heard about the shootout in Truth or Consequences, most of the nation had by then. I reassured her that Rose was going to be fine and thanked her for all her help.

The drive home would take about five hours, and it would be late at night before I got there, but I was determined to spend the night in my own bed. Besides, I had to sort out my emotions and convince myself that my life could settle back to normal. I knew I couldn't simply compartmentalize all the violence that I had been through and put it in some remote part of the mind to be forgotten. But at least, I could try.

Despite all that had happened in the past week, the dilemma that shot to the front of my mind on the drive home was my promise to Rose to take her on a cruise. I had no doubt that I really liked Rose, but going on a cruise with her would be the biggest step in a relationship that I would have made with a woman since my divorce. Neither of us were "spring chickens," but I couldn't see myself saying, "Hey, that was fun. We should get together again sometime," then shaking hands and simply walking away from her after a week together in the same cabin.

On the long drive home I never did resolve my concerns about taking such a significant step in a relationship, but I did know that I planned to keep my promise with Rose.

Acknowledgement

"I couldn't have done this alone. Some of you also deserve the blame.

Thanks."

Title: *Dead Men Can Kill*™
- Author: Bob Doerr
- Publisher: TotalRecall Publications, Inc.
- Hard Cover: ISBN: 978-1-59095-758-5
- Paper Back: ISBN: 978-1-59095-759-2
- Book: ISBN: 978-1-59095-761-5
- Number of pages: 320
- Publication: December 8, 2009

When Jim West, a former Air Force Special Agent with the Office of Special Investigations, moves back to New Mexico, his goal is simple: start an easy going second career as a professional lecturer on investigative techniques to colleges and civic organizations. He never envisioned that his practical demonstration of forensic hypnosis on stage with a state university student would stir up memories of an 18-year old murder mystery. When the student is murdered three days later, West finds himself ensnared in a web of intrigue that pits him and the small town's authorities against a ruthless, psychotic killer.

An aggressive reporter for the town newspaper seeks out West for help with the story, but after one of her co-workers is murdered, she quickly aligns her efforts with West and the Sheriff. As West works closely with her, he begins to wonder if this could be the first real relationship for him since his devastating divorce a few years earlier.

The killer, though, has other plans for the reporter and the story takes fascinating twists and turns, leading to an inevitable, riveting confrontation.

Look out for a new hero on the mystery/thriller landscape! Jim West, retired military investigator, is resourceful, intuitive, pragmatic and always competent. All of West's abilities are tested when he matches wits with psychopathic serial killer William White, a man whose appreciation for murder is surpassed only by his delight in domination. Bob Doerr has crafted a must-read addition to the genre in Dead Men Can Kill, which evolves from absorbing story to absolute page-turner as West closes in on a killer who is supposedly dead. Highly recommended!

--Dallin Malmgren, author of...
The Whole Nine Yards The Ninth Issue Is This for a Grade?

A Jim West™ Mystery/Thriller

Title: *Cold Winter's Kill*™
- Author: Bob Doerr
- Publisher: TotalRecall Publications, Inc.
- Hard Cover: ISBN: 978-1-59095-762-2
- Paper Back: ISBN: 978-1-59095-763-9
- Book: ISBN: 978-1-59095-764-6
- Number of pages: 288
- Publication: Dec 8, 2009

Cold Winter's Kill is a fast paced thriller that takes place in the scenic mountains of Lincoln County, New Mexico and throws Jim West into a race against time to stop a psychopath who abducts and kills a young blonde every Christmas...

It was one of those phone calls former Air Force Special Agent Jim West never wanted to receive--an old friend calling to ask if he could drive down to Ruidoso, New Mexico to help locate his daughter who has disappeared while on a ski trip with friends. Jim found himself heading to Ruidoso even though he believed, much like the local authorities, that if she had gone missing in the mountains in December, her survival chances were slim. He didn't want to be there when they found her, but still he drove on.

Once in Ruidoso, Jim discovers a sinister coincidence that changes everything. It appears that someone is abducting and killing one young blond every year around Christmas. The race is on--can Jim locate his friend's daughter in time? But why is this happening and who's doing it?

Jim can't wait for the local authorities to raise the priority of their search, or for the pending blizzard to pass. In his haste he puts himself in the killer's sights. Will he, too, suffer from a cold winter's kill?

"**GREAT SUSPENSE!** In *Cold Winter's Kill* Bob Doerr grabs your attention from the beginning and holds it until the last sentence. Hard to put down!"
> --*Shelba Nicholson*
> former Women's Editor, *Texarkana Gazette*

A Jim West™ Mystery/Thriller

Title: Loose Ends Kill™

- Author: Bob Doerr
- Publisher: TotalRecall Publications, Inc.
- Hard Cover: ISBN: 978-1-59095-717-2
- Paper Back: ISBN: 978-1-59095-718-9
- Book: ISBN: 978-1-59095-719-6
- Number of pages: 288
- Publication: Oct 27, 2010

LOOSE ENDS KILL **is a fast paced mystery/thriller** that takes place in the historic city of San Antonio, Texas, and throws Jim West into the middle of a police investigation of the murder of an old friend's wife. The police already believe they have the killer in custody – West's friend.

West is drawn into this mystery by a call from the old friend who requests his assistance. West agrees to help his friend and digs deep to try to find another suspect. In the process he soon discovers that he is being followed and targeted for harassment, but by whom?

West quickly discovers that he didn't know his old friend's wife as well as he thought. To his surprise, he learns that she has had a number of affairs dating back for more than a decade. In fact, while investigating the murder, he realizes that his friend and he may be the only two people unaware of her philandering behavior.

Theorizing that one of her lovers could have had just as much motive as her husband, West starts turning over the rocks identifying one lover after another. In doing so, West unintentionally ignites an outbreak of more death and mayhem. The police and his friend's lawyers want West to go back home. The police even threaten to arrest him.

Soon, West believes the real killer wants him gone or dead. Deciding the only way to resolve the case before the outside pressures force him to leave, he sets a trap for the killer using himself as bait. However, he soon learns he may have only outsmarted himself.

A Jim West™ Mystery/Thriller

Title: *Another Colorado Kill*™
- Author: Bob Doerr
- Publisher: TotalRecall Publications, Inc.
- Hard Cover: ISBN: 978-1-59095-784-4
- Paper Back: ISBN: 978-1-59095-785-1
- Book: ISBN: 978-1-59095-786-8
- Number of pages: 288
- Publication Date: September 06, 2011

It was supposed to be a short, fun golf outing, but when Jim West and his friend Edward "Perry" Mason stumble across a dead body in a restroom at a rest stop along I-25, things turn bad and then only get worse.

With the golf outing shot, West intends to stay in Colorado Springs only for a day or two. However, when two more murder victims turn up – one with West's name handwritten in her notebook - the heat on West skyrockets. The police instruct him to stick around, and soon he discovers that while the police may want to pin the crimes on him, the killer wants him out of the picture. Way out – like dead.

West's only ally is Lieutenant Michelle Prado, a tall red head with large green eyes that captivate West. Assigned to keep an eye on West, Lieutenant Prado decides the best way to do so is to keep him close. West and Prado do their own digging into the investigation. In the process, Jim wonders how close their relationship will evolve.

It seems to West that as the police focus less on him, the killer intensifies his focus on him. Barely surviving an initial confrontation, West realizes he must take the initiative. If he doesn't, or perhaps even if he does - he may end up as just another Colorado kill.

A Jim West™ Mystery/Thriller

Title: *No One Else To Kill*™

- Author: Bob Doerr
- Publisher: TotalRecall Publications, Inc.
- Hard Cover: ISBN: 978-1-59095-422-5
- Paper Back: ISBN: 978-1-59095-423-2
- eBook: ISBN: 978-1-59095-424-9
- Number of pages in the finished book: 352
- Publication Date: December 4, 2012

No One Else to Kill, **Bob Doerr, TotalRecall Publications** - In this newest book in the popular Jim West series, Mr. West finds himself stood up and out of town. Looking forward to some R & R he keeps his reservation at the remote hunting lodge. Located in the Pecos Wilderness area in New Mexico it's a hunter's haven. Expecting to do nothing other than relax, he has no idea what the rest of the weekend holds for him. When a murder takes place, the hotel guest are detained and no one is beyond suspicion. The sheriff is called in, and while the investigation is underway, a second murder takes place.

2013
Eric Hoffer Award
WINNER
Excellence in
Independent
Publishing

Both crimes are clearly related, but by whom and why? With time running out and unable to find a motive, the legal experts seek Jim's help.

2013
da Vinci Eye
FINALIST
Eric Hoffer Award
Excellence in
Independent Publishing

The cover for *No One Else To Kill* **is a 2013 finalist for the da Vinci Eye award.**

Bob's four previous novels in the series are titled *Dead Men Can Kill, Cold Winter's Kill, Loose Ends Kill,* and *Another Colorado Kill.* The latter two were selected as Eric Hoffer Award finalists for 2010 and 2011, respectively.

Bob Doerr's *No One Else To Kill* was awarded the Grand Prize in the "Books With Out Publishers" writing contest at www.AuthorsTalent.com

A Jim West™ Mystery/Thriller

Title: *Greed Can Kill*™
- Author: Bob Doerr
- Publisher: TotalRecall Publications, Inc.
- Hard Cover: ISBN: 978-1-59095-730-1
- Paper Back: ISBN: 978-1-59095-731-8
- eBook: ISBN: 978-1-59095-741-7
- Number of pages in the finished book: 280
- Publication Date: 2017

This adventure finds Jim traveling to Fabens, TX, in an effort to locate an old acquaintance who had written Jim a cryptic letter asking for his help in finding a briefcase. In Fabens, he discovers that someone has murdered his friend. Jim provides a copy of the letter to the local police explaining that he has no idea where the briefcase is or how to decipher the sets of numbers provided in the letter. Figuring there is nothing more he can do, Jim starts his trek back home. He plans to spend a night or two relaxing at the Lodge in Cloudcroft, NM, on his way only to find that he is being followed. An ominous, unidentified phone caller gives Jim an ultimatum - find the briefcase and turn it over to him within a week.

A violent confrontation in Cloudcroft verifies Jim's worst suspicion, a Mexican drug cartel wants the briefcase. The confrontation also brings the FBI into the picture. They also want Jim to continue his search. The search takes Jim to the New Mexican ghost town of Chloride where the final confrontation takes place and Jim finds out who the bad guys really are.

Author Bob Doerr Uses his special knowledge to provide authentic details in his novels about how law enforcement agencies do their work.

www.bobdoerr.com

A Jim West™ Mystery/Thriller

Title: *The Enchanted Coin*™
- Author: Bob Doerr
- Publisher: TotalRecall Publications, Inc.
- Hard Cover: ISBN: 978-1-59095-083-8
- Paper Back: ISBN: 978-1-59095-084-5
- eBook: ISBN: 978-1-59095-085-2
- Audiobook ISBN: 978-1-59095-278-8
- Number of pages in the finished book: 130
- Publication Date: September 17, 2013

We have all heard of tales of UFO's, ghosts, people who say they can talk to the spirits, ancient curses, and magical talismans. Most of us automatically dismiss them as false, figments of people's imagination, and understandably so. However, might not just a few of them be true? I don't know, but I heard this story from a young man the other day who swore the fascinating tale I have set forth in this book really did really occur, because it happened to him. You be the judge.

Title: *The Rescue of Vincent*™
- Author: Bob Doerr
- Publisher: TotalRecall Publications, Inc.
- Paperback: ISBN: 978-1-59095-279-5
- eBook: ISBN: 978-1-59095-280-1
- Audiobook ISBN: 978-1-59095-281-8
- Number of pages in the finished book: 160
- Publication Date: October 28, 2014

The Rescue of Vincent: Book 2 in The Enchanted Coin Series is a 31,000 word fantasy adventure targeted at Middle Grade readers. Imagine being a fourteen year old again and finding a coin that seems to give off a light of its own. The coin has your name on it, and instructs you to toss it into a fountain next to the Tree of Life. That's what happens in The Rescue of Vincent, and what starts my protagonist off on a magical adventure that many young boys and girls would love to have. This book is "G" rated.

Title: *The Magic of Vex*™
- Author: Bob Doerr
- Publisher: TotalRecall Publications, Inc.
- Paper Back: ISBN: 978-1-59095-309-9
- eBook: ISBN: 978-1-59095-310-5
- Audiobook ISBN: 978-1-59095-311-2
- Number of pages in the finished book: 140
- Publication Date: August 4, 2015

Samantha Gillespie's discovery of a magic coin results in her transportation to the strange world of Vex where magic is real and where she has to overcome a number of challenges if she ever hopes to return home.

What happened to Samantha was totally unexpected and quite frightening. It led her to an adventure that many might think impossible to believe, but it did.

You be the judge.

For a complete list of books by Bob Doerr, a previews of upcoming titles and more visit his website www.bobdoerr.com or find him on Facebook.

Title: The Attack™
- Author: Bob Doerr
- Publisher: TotalRecall Publications, Inc.
- Hard Cover ISBN: 978-1-59095-145-3
- Paper Back: ISBN: 978-1-59095-146-0
- eBook: ISBN: 978-1-59095-147-7
- Number of pages in the finished book: 288
- Publication Date: 2017

A terrorist team has just set off four explosive devices in an international airport close to New York City. The leader of the terrorists, Ahmad Khalin, survives the attack and plans to attack a second U.S. airport within the month. As Khalin makes his escape from the New York area he is involved in a shooting in Connecticut. Clint Smith, a U.S. government agent assigned to an ultra-secret agency, is at a restaurant across the street when the shooting occurs. He responds to the scene to see if he can help, but Khalin is gone. On a hunch, Teresa Deer, Smith's boss, sends Smith after Khalin. Smith's pursuit takes him to Bar Harbor, Maine; Wiesbaden, Germany; the Costa Brava, Spain; Northern Scotland; Lake of the Woods, Ontario, Canada; and finally into Saskatchewan, Canada, where the final confrontation takes place. Throughout the pursuit, a number of interesting characters add to the subplots and try to survive their involvement in the chase.

A Clint Smith Thriller™

Title: *The Group*
- Author: Bob Doerr
- Publisher: TotalRecall Publications, Inc.
- Hard Cover ISBN: 978-1-59095-568-0
- Paper Back: ISBN: 978-1-59095-569-7
- eBook: ISBN: 978-1-59095-570-3
- Number of pages in the finished book: 288
- Publication Date: 2016

Someone is killing off the world's rich and famous. The murders are sophisticated, requiring precision and skill. The international community is in an uproar but has no leads in its attempt to find the assassins. The victims were members of the Bilderberg Group, an international, loose knit group of the uber rich that meet annually. While the attacks have not had a direct impact on the U.S., Theresa Deer, Director of the Special Section, a small unit whose existence is known by only a handful in the U.S. government, sees this new age League of Assassins as a national threat. She sends her hunters out. Clint Smith finds their trail Switzerland where his discovery almost leads to his own death. The hunt leads him to Mallorca, Spain, where he witnesses a helicopter attack on a villa where a number of attendees from the Bilderberg conference were holding a follow-on meeting of their own. Smith picks up the trail a couple weeks later in Las Vegas, NV, and in his hunt finds out that he is no longer the hunter. He has become the prey.

A Clint Smith Thriller™

Author Bob Doerr uses his practical investigating experience and knowledge to provide authentic, in-depth details in his novels, about how law enforcement agencies do their work.

www.bobdoerr.com

For a complete list of books by Bob Doerr, visit his website (BobDoerr.com) and preview his upcoming titles and events. Locate Bob on Facebook and let him know how you like his books.

Titles by Bob Doerr

Mystery Detective Suspense Thrillers

Dead Men Can Kill

Cold Winters Kill

Another Colorado Kill

Loose Ends Kill

No One Else To Kill

Caffeine Can Kill

Greed Can Kill

Action Adventure Thrillers

The Attack

The Group

Mouse Gate Series

The Enchanted Coin

The Rescue of Vincent

The Magic of Vex